# THE
# MAYFAIR
# DAGGER

# THE MAYFAIR DAGGER

## A NOVEL

Ava January

CROOKED
LANE

NEW YORK

Copyright © 2024 by January Elizabeth Gilchrist

Published in the United States by Crooked Lane Books, an imprint of The Quick Brown Fox & Company LLC.

Crooked Lane Books and its logo are trademarks of The Quick Brown Fox & Company LLC.

Library of Congress Catalog-in-Publication data available upon request.

ISBN (hardcover): 978-1-63910-751-3
ISBN (ebook): 978-1-63910-756-8

Cover design by Lynn Andreozzi

Printed in the United States.

www.crookedlanebooks.com

Crooked Lane Books
34 West 27th St., 10th Floor
New York, NY 10001

First Edition: May 2024

10 9 8 7 6 5 4 3 2 1

*For H & D. Again.*

# CHAPTER 1

L ud, men were strange creatures.

Albertine held the glass jar to the light and gawked at it. She grimaced as the murky liquid in the vessel cleared, and the unblinking eye of what appeared to be a pickled octopus stared back at her. Why on earth would one wish to keep such a hideous thing in plain view? And in a position that indicated you might actually want to look at it.

*More than once.*

The eye gazed at her with disapproval.

"Don't judge me," Albertine whispered at it. "Until you've been in such dire straits, you can keep your judgmental looks to yourself."

Although, to be fair, spending eternity in a jar on a dusty shelf in a lord's study could be the very definition of dire straits.

Replacing the jar back in its position on the ledge, Albertine turned her attention to the mammoth oak desk. She gazed at it for a moment before turning to the jar and spinning the supercilious gaze of the octopus toward the wall.

She couldn't work with an audience.

Drawing a deep breath, she sank to her knees in front of the bank of drawers attached to the desk. A quick tug at the handles confirmed they were locked, as she had expected. A shiver of anticipation set her fingers aflame, and she shook them in the air before sliding the two long pins from their hiding place in her ridiculous and wholly inauthentic headdress.

Really, there were too few opportunities for a lady to put her lock-picking skills into action. An image of her brother showing her his new tools sprang to mind, promptly followed by the hot flash of anguish that always accompanied thoughts of Algernon. She shook her head. She had a task to do and didn't have time to wallow in the past.

It was that past that had gotten her in such a pickle.

Sweeping a palm along the bottom of the lowest of the three drawers, she checked for hidden levers or knobs. There was nothing but the smooth rub of bare wood.

Pushing her hook into the lock, Albertine pressed her finger against the pin until it sat flush against the circle of metal. Sliding the second pick into the latch, she raked it toward her twice. A soft, dull click sounded as the bolt released and she smiled.

Really, one should keep precious items under stricter conditions—but who was she to complain?

The cloying scent of women's perfume wafted from the drawer. It emanated from the thick pile of envelopes that lay at the bottom, tied together neatly with a red ribbon.

Albertine inhaled a deep, satisfied breath. If things continued this way, this would prove to be the easiest job she'd ever taken on.

The fact this was her first big job notwithstanding.

When her client—one of London's wealthiest and most influential ladies—had revealed to Albertine that she was being blackmailed with letters of a distinctly personal nature, by one of London's most powerful lords, Albertine had almost despaired. But she was never one to back down from a challenge. That (and a lack of other clients) made her determined to make the most of this job.

There had been too many nights of absolute despair, but here she was, making jam out of soft berries, as Papa used to say. A wave of pride washed over her, and she sat back on her heels surveying the scene before her. This was it, she could feel it. Her client would be thrilled and remunerate her generously, and whisper her name to the other wealthy ladies of society. Why, it wouldn't be long until she needed to employ other women to assist with the volume of detective work that was sure to be coming her way.

The heavy thud of feet moving along the hall reverberated through the floor, and Albertine froze, looking about the room. There was nowhere to hide.

The footsteps neared. Rather stupidly, now it seemed at least, she'd given scant consideration to the size of twenty letters and their corresponding envelopes. She couldn't just carry them out in her hand, and her costume left very little to the imagination.

The handle of the study door rattled. *Had she locked it?*

The knob turned, and Albertine ground her back teeth.

She hadn't locked it.

Shoving the packets into the bodice of her dress, she forced them down until they lay across the lower portion of her bust. Her eyebrows raised. The bulk of paper gave her a very pleasing shape. She would be sure to mention this effect to her modiste next time she visited.

The door swung open, and Albertine tugged at her neckline, ensuring her newly enhanced curves were on display. Her stomach twisted as the colossal figure of Lord Grendel stumbled through the doorway.

He released a belch, wiping at his ruddy face with his jacket sleeve. Their gazes caught and his foxy eyes narrowed.

"I say, what the devil is Cleopatra doing in my study?"

Albertine swallowed hard and moved out from behind the desk, kicking at the still-open drawer with her foot as she did so. She held the lord's watery gaze and undulated her hips, moving with a languid slowness until she came to rest against the curved edge of the table.

"I've been waiting for you." She paused. *Was his name Taylor or Jack?* For the life of her, she couldn't remember. "Your lordship."

He belched again, and she worked to keep her expression eager. The man really was a pig.

"Have you just?"

Albertine arched her back, thrusting her now-ample bust upward. "I was hoping to get a moment alone with you."

She closed her eyes, threw a hand against her forehead, and risked a glance at him under lowered lids. Surely, he would not fall for this codswallop?

His blurry gaze lingered coarsely on her chest.

"Is that so? Come here then, wench." He advanced toward her.

"Wait!" Albertine winced at the pitch of her voice, high enough to shatter glass. She inhaled deeply and forced herself to speak, slow and sensual. "That is to say, do you like games, my lord?"

He paused behind an overstuffed chair. "I like a saucy wench."

"Well, my lord." She ran her tongue along her bottom lip. "I am the mostest sauciest. I mean the most sauciest."

His face contorted, a lip lifted in confusion, and Albertine pressed on, fearing she'd lost him. "Saucy beyond your wildest dreams."

She purred like a cat and made a little scratching motion in the air.

Lord Grendel chortled loudly. "Oh, I say, that's more like it."

He moved around the chair and lowered himself into it with a grunt, releasing a straining button from his waistcoat. His stomach slumped out from between the jacket folds. "All right, kitten, show me your claws."

Albertine stared at him blankly for a moment, unsure of how to continue. She purred and clawed the air again, this time louder. The movement seemed to whip the fellow into a frenzy. *Oh, my.*

He gripped the arms of the chair, panting heavily. "Oh yes. Show papa some sugar."

Albertine blinked rapidly, trying not to grimace.

"Wait," he cried. With surprising speed for a man of his size, he leaped from the armchair and closed the door, turning the latch with a clank that echoed through the silent room. Albertine's heart clenched as he tugged the long iron key from the lock and placed it in the inner pocket of his jacket.

He met her gaze and gave her a lecherous wink. "Nothing like a bit of privacy, eh?"

Albertine's lip wobbled, and she forced her chin up. "Er . . . quite."

They gazed at each other in silence. Lord Grendel bobbed his head toward her. "Go on then. You were giving me your sauce." The pink tip of his tongue slid along his bottom lip, leaving a slick trail of saliva. Albertine shivered.

She now wished she had come dressed as a shepherdess. She could have beaten him about the head with her crook and made a run for it. When Albertine learned the ball was to be a costume party, she'd chosen Cleopatra because the oversized headdress was a great hiding place for her lockpicks. Not to mention Egypt's queen was a popular choice at fancy dress balls. She'd encountered four others while queuing for the water closet, making it easier to blend in should anyone see her somewhere she shouldn't be. Like here.

"Oh yes, indeed. First, perhaps a drink?"

"No drink," he said stoutly. "I don't have all night. Let's get to it, gel."

Albertine pouted. "I want a drink."

She batted her lashes at him. His face remained stern. She pulled at her bodice and leaned toward him, running a hand along her artificially enlarged bosom.

His eyes and mouth widened into large O's. "I say. One won't hurt."

"You stay there, let me be mother." He flinched at the word. It was a commonly used phrase, but even a new-to-towner like her had heard stories of his mother—the ferocious dowager Lady Grendel was notorious.

Albertine moved to the drinks trolley behind the desk, clutching the edge for a moment. Her knuckles whitened, and she sucked in a deep breath. Papa had always said there was no problem a calm and steady mind couldn't fix. He possibly hadn't been encouraging his only daughter to pick locks and drug a man when caught stealing letters from his desk, but here she was, and she would just have to make do. Although if one didn't want their daughter to behave in such a manner, one shouldn't have taught her how to concoct a sleeping draught in the first place. The hairs on the back of her neck prickled, and she darted a quick glance over her shoulder at Lord Grendel, breathing a sigh of relief when she saw he was still seated.

Albertine filled two glasses with a foul-smelling brown liquid from an elaborate crystal decanter and deftly unscrewed a bead from the bangle at her wrist. She discharged the contents of it into one glass and dipped her finger into it, circling it around to disperse the powder. She slung another look over her shoulder to where Lord Grendel was now sprawled in the chair. The buttons of his shirt strained at his stomach as he worked at the opening of his trousers. She narrowed an eye as she considered him. He was a big fellow. She unscrewed a second bead and emptied it into the glass.

She picked up both glasses and spun around with a bright smile on her face. Emphasizing the sway of her hips, she moved toward the sweaty man. His hand reached out for a glass and she paused, just out of his grasp. *Which one had she put the powder in?* The liquid in the glasses sloshed over the rims as her hands trembled. She ran through her movements; she had taken up the one intended for him with her left. It had been the left, hadn't it? He shook his hand impatiently. Albertine pressed the glass from her left hand into his and watched intently as he took a deep draught. He smacked his lips when he finished.

"Drink," he ordered, nodding toward the cup in her hand.

The bangles on her wrist jangled as she sniffed at the remaining drink. The very worst thing that could happen now was if she had put the powder in the glass on the right. Why hadn't she paid more attention?

*Here goes nothing.*

She raised the glass to her lips and swigged it down as if it were medicine. Almost immediately, her face heated and tears seeped from her eyes. The foul liquid burned a river from her throat to her belly, and she coughed violently. She braced her hands on her knees to steady herself as the burning in her chest slowly died to a smolder.

*Wonders!*

She felt as if someone had hit her on the back of a head with a mallet. No surprise half of London's ton behaved like buffoons. Albertine could feel her brain cells dying an agonizingly slow death.

"Decent drop," Lord Grendel was saying. "It's a three-wood single malt. Made up in the highlands of Scotland." He lifted his glass and peered at it through a squinted eye. "Peaty, smoky, and almost medicinal, eh?" He swigged at the drink and followed it with an enormous belch.

Albertine forced herself upright and wiped at her eyes. "It's definitely medicinal."

Lord Grendel slammed his glass on the small table beside his chair. "Right, where were we?"

Albertine eyed him warily. He seemed as hearty as ever. A hot flush lingered on her chest—was this from the awful scotch or her from special concoction? If she had accidentally taken the sleeping draught she'd escape from the attentions of the lord—but she'd be caught with the letters upon her.

"Oh yes," she breathed, shuffling backwards away from his grasp. "I was telling you how fascinating you are, my lord."

He grunted and shifted in his seat.

Was that tingle in her hands normal? She clenched and unclenched her fists.

"Oh, yes, your hair is very . . ." She gazed at the shiny bald plate of his head. "Tenacious."

She gulped for air, her tongue feeling thick and coated. Her hand came to her throat. Was it closing? Albertine blinked, fighting to keep Lord Grendel in focus.

He grunted again, his eyes drifting toward his nose slowly. He shook his head and thumped at his chest with a meaty fist. His eyelids fluttered closed and his mouth dropped open. Albertine leaned close to his face, ducking away quickly as he belched. A loud snore rumbled through him.

A wave of relief washed through Albertine, bringing with it a surge of energy. She leaned over the armchair, sliding her hand into the damp heat of Lord Grendel's jacket, feeling for the hard shape of the door key.

"Tell me your name, I'll wager it's something as sweet and delicious as you," he slurred.

Beads of sweat gathered around his hairline and his eyes traveled slowly toward each other as he worked to stay conscious.

Albertine waited until his eyelids fluttered closed before leaning in.

"My name . . ." she said, her breath hot and moist at his ear. ". . . is Dagger."

★   ★   ★

Albertine pulled the door closed quietly behind her and leaned against it, sucking in deep breaths. She pressed her knuckles against her lips to still the burst of utterly inappropriate laughter that threatened.

*Wonders!* That had been a close call. But she had done it. She had actually done it. Although she had promised her client she could, to be perfectly honest, she'd been working from blind faith and desperation rather than any skill or experience.

She ran a hand along the lump in her bodice. She had the letters, and once she returned them to the rightful owner, she would have enough money to get her detective agency off the ground.

Albertine had run an ad in the paper for the last month, but aside from outing a card cheat, locating missing first loves, and lost property, there had really been little opportunity for any gritty detective work. Or money.

Until Lady Roche had arrived one morning at Albertine's rented townhouse.

She'd been foolish, she had said, the admission clearly sitting uncomfortably. Foolish and blind, and she had behaved indiscreetly. The letters she had written to the object of her infatuation had been stolen and were now being used to blackmail her, and she needed help in retrieving them. Although Lady Roche was one of the most influential ladies in London society, even she would not have been able to weather the storm that the release of her private correspondence would have brought.

An invitation to the ball was promptly arranged, along with a floor plan and directions to where Albertine could find the letters, all of which had made the job seem possible despite her lack of experience in such things.

Albertine raised her gaze and a finger to the ceiling. *I did it, Papa.*

That was the only thing Albertine had left—her determination.

Too loud, too proud, too brash and rash. Too full of dreams and fancies. Too female to take over running the family estate when Papa had died, according to the law. Too expensive to keep on, according to her cousin.

But none of that mattered now because here she was, making her way on her own terms.

Delight surged through her, igniting her like a candle, and she skipped along the long flagstone hallway back to the ballroom.

She burst through the double doors that led to the ball, and the heat and sound hit her like a wall. Five hundred of London's highest-reaching ton members were in a space designed for one hundred. It was officially a crush.

Albertine searched along the wall where the ladies-in-waiting sat in shadows, anticipating a gesture of need from their ladies. Her eyes met Joan's wide, worried green ones, and she winked. Joan half lurched from her chair, her gaze flying to the closed door behind Albertine and then back. Her eyes moved to Albertine's augmented bust and widened. Joan gestured with her head and a raised eyebrow to the back of the room. Joan was mouthing something to her, but she couldn't make it out. Whatever it was could wait while she thanked the hostess.

Albertine adjusted her headpiece and scanned the crowd for Lady Grendel. She was in an animated discussion with a tall, broad-shouldered man. His back was to her, so Albertine couldn't see if he was as enamored as their hostess was. Albertine pushed her way toward them, bemused to see Lady Grendel's eyelashes bat in such a manner.

"Lady Grendel." Albertine pushed between them, a hand outstretched to grasp the other woman. The bangle on Albertine's wrist jangled lightly.

*The beads.*

What had she done with the beads? Cool sweat broke out at her temples and her fingers began to tremble. How could she have been so foolish? She had allowed panic to cloud her sensibilities—most unlike her. Albertine inhaled a deep breath. It would be fine, she reassured herself. Should anyone find them, they wouldn't be able to make sense of what they were, surely. And as they were a one-of-a-kind item made for her by her brother, they would be nigh impossible to trace back to her. There was no need to worry, she told herself, however irritating it was to lose them and to realize she had made such a blunder.

"Forgive the interruption." She dipped a quick curtsy in the man's direction, not sparing him a glance. "What a truly splendid evening. I have had a wonderful time, but I am afraid I must depart. Thank you for your gracious hospitality. My husband, the count, sends his apologies. Dreadfully sorry he couldn't make it. He's in Corsica. On business."

Albertine was aware that she was speaking rather too fast and altogether too loud. She took a breath, willing her blood to slow. She turned to leave, and her eyes locked with the sharply amused gaze of the most handsome man she had ever laid eyes upon. In fact, she was willing to wager he was the most handsome man *anyone* had ever laid eyes on.

"Oh." Albertine was certain her mouth had dropped open in shock.

His skin was the warm bronze of a man who spent hours outside in a warmer climate than England. His cheekbones were high and sharp, his nose perfectly angled, and strong dark slashes of brow arched above eyes the exact color of the lake at her beloved childhood home.

He smiled, showing a row of straight, stunningly bright teeth, and a small sigh escaped her lips. No wonder Lady Grendel was in raptures.

"How do you do?" the man-god asked, his voice deep and low.

Albertine stood stock still, blinking into the light of the ballroom.

She swallowed hard. "Very well."

A strange feeling overcame her. Her senses clouded and the surrounding room fell away, but she was hyperaware of the rise and fall of this man's chest. Her fingers tingled with the urge to reach out and run themselves along his jaw.

A flash of movement over his shoulder caught her eye. Joan was jumping up and down and gesturing madly to her left. Albertine narrowed her eyes, trying to make out what Joan was mouthing.

Frolic? Colic? Bollocks?

Albertine's blood chilled as it hit her.

*Wallop.*

"Excuse me."

Her wild gaze landed back on the handsome stranger, who was watching her with an amused expression that told her he had asked her a question that she hadn't heard.

"Forgive me, I must dash. I've just seen someone who I . . ." *Definitely do not want to see me.*

Without waiting for a response, Albertine lifted her chin and pushed through the milling crowd. Resisting the urge to place her hand on the package in her bodice, she wove through the throng, her gaze darting around the crowd of revelers. She needed to get out of here before Wallop found her and Lord Grendel woke. He wasn't likely to wake for quite some time, but it was better for all if she were not here to point the finger at.

Joan was hovering in the hallway beyond the ballroom with Albertine's cape and reticule in her hands. She swung the cape around Albertine's shoulders, her eyes wide and searching. "Ready, miss?"

Delivering these letters to their rightful owner was more than just getting paid, although that would put her on her way to independence. Both financially and from her awful cousin, Franklin, who had been trying to force her hand into marriage with the neighboring farmer, and his fifteen children, since Papa's death.

These letters were about honoring her brother, living the life he had wanted to live for himself and wasn't able to. Like she had promised him she would.

Albertine sucked in a breath.

*Was she ready?*

Albertine smiled. "I have never been more ready for anything in my life."

# CHAPTER 2

Spencer Sweetman, Marquess of Reading, and recently titled Duke of Erleigh, looked up as the door to his office opened. The round, cheerful face of David Mitchell appeared around the edge.

"I say, ah . . . sir." Mitchell coughed into his hand, but not before Spencer caught the hint of his smile.

"We need your help in the interview room. Jenkins is having a . . . er, slight *problem* with a Baron Wallop."

Spencer's lip curled. Baron Wallop was a buffoon of the highest order. Although Jenkins was as sharp as a tack and straight as an arrow, he was an East End boy at heart. Jenkins had worked his way up through the beats of the police force to the senior offices of Scotland Yard.

It had taken Jenkins a month to gather the courage to even lift his eyes to Spencer as they passed each other in the hallway.

Wallop, with his title and grandiloquent way of speech, would intimidate the hell out of him.

"What's Wallop doing here?" Spencer asked, shifting his chair from the desk and standing wearily.

Mitchell's cheeks rounded as he smiled. "Says he has some pertinent information regarding Lord Grendel's death."

Spencer pulled his jacket from the coat rack and shrugged into it.

Grendel's death had caused quite the stir. It wasn't every day a lord was found murdered in his study during the season's most anticipated ball.

Even one as detestable as Grendel.

Spencer had interviewed potential witnesses into the early hours of the morning and then come straight to the office to read the written reports from the people he hadn't personally interviewed. A wave of weariness hit him as he noted with some surprise that the skies beyond the windows were dim, the afternoon light fading quickly.

"Sir?"

Mitchell's voice brought him back into the small, drab offices of Scotland Yard office that housed him Monday to Friday. When the unwanted honorifics—*marquess* and *duke*—had been thrust upon him, Spencer had made it known that his men were to continue to address him as usual during working hours, and all had been happy to comply, to Spencer's immense gratitude. It allowed him to keep the door tightly shut on the feelings those titles evoked in him.

"I was woolgathering. Room one you said?"

Mitchell nodded, and they walked together toward the interview room.

As they neared the room, the echoes of Wallop's strident tones reverberated throughout the hall. Poor Jenkins would be quaking in his boots.

Spencer rapped his knuckle on the door twice before opening it and fixing Wallop with a firm stare. His usually ruddy face was reddened further from the effort of yelling. He was a large, imposing man, and he towered over the diminutive

Jenkins. A spike of anger heated Spencer's chest. There was nothing he despised more than a bully.

Although Spencer could not be considered a small man by anyone's standards, the Baron stood inches above him. Where Spencer's body was lean muscle from a youth dedicated more to sporting arts than his grades at Eton, Wallop had the physique of a fellow who lived life to excess. His cheeks and nose were marred with the red lines of a heavy drinker, his face framed by the sagging jowls of a hearty eater.

"Wallop. Control yourself, man." Spencer gestured to the chair behind the baron's corpulent backside. "Seat yourself and be quiet. I will not have you making a mockery of Scotland Yard with your hollering."

Wallop gaped at Spencer a moment, his mouth moving like a fish on dry land. As a mere baron, and one whose family was rumored to have purchased the title, albeit one hundred years ago, Wallop was rungs below Spencer on society's convoluted ladder.

A fact both of them were fully aware of.

Though he was never one to pull rank, the assertion of power over a bully like Wallop gave Spencer a rush of pleasure.

"This little—"

Spencer held up a quelling hand. "I will not tell you again. Sit."

Jenkins gazed up at Spencer with an open mouth, appearing awed by Spencer's ability to make the hulking brute behave. Spencer gave the young man a wink and dismissed him. "Thank you for your work here, Jenkins. An admirable effort. You may leave."

Jenkins scrambled from the chair, scurrying from the room like it was on fire.

Spencer waited until the click of the door sounded before he looked at Wallop. Placing both hands flat on the table between them, he met the man's belligerent gaze with a look as cold as iron and resisted the rage that rose inside him. His men here risked their lives, willingly, to keep England safe and knobs like Wallop, with their lives of comfort that they expected as their right—simply due to good luck in the game of chance at birth—weren't fit to shine most of these men's shoes.

Lucky for Wallop, Spencer Sweetman didn't rage. He calculated odds, formulated plans, and punished accordingly.

"Let me make one thing clear. If you ever come into my offices and speak to any of my men that way again, I will make you very, very sorry."

Wallop lowered his craven gaze to the table.

The room was silent save for a small, choking sound from Mitchell. Spencer cut him a look and immediately wished he hadn't. The young man's fist was pressed to his mouth, his face crimson with the effort of holding in his laughter. Spencer worked to still the trembling of his own lips. He counted backwards, willing Mitchell to hold it together. Mitchell's loud braying laughter that had him good-naturedly referred to as "the donkey" was contagious.

Wallop spoke, breaking the tension of the room, and Spencer released a long breath.

"As I was trying to tell your boy here, I know who killed Grendel. The same rascal who made off with my wife's tiara. I saw her in the hallway in front of Grendel's study."

Sliding Jenkins's abandoned scratchpad toward him, Spencer gazed at the notes scrawled in his inelegant hand. *Tick tock, Dukey boy*, the date at the top of the page seemed to holler at him. He placed his thumb over it and cast his eyes along the rest of the notepad.

*Tiara missing.* Underlined so firmly the paper had torn under the nib of Jenkins's pencil.

Spencer removed the fountain pen from his pocket and leveled a cool stare at Wallop. "Start at the beginning," Spencer commanded.

Wallop released a heavy breath. "Someone lifted the baroness's tiara a couple of weeks ago. And I know who it was, too." Wallop pulled his collar from his neck. "I saw her do it. I want her punished to the full extent of the law. This cannot stand."

Spencer's gaze rested on Wallop's fisted hand on the table. "You witnessed the theft of your wife's tiara, but didn't stop the thief?"

Wallop's eyes slid to the right. "I . . . I . . . I saw someone behaving oddly. It wasn't until we noticed the tiara was gone that I put two and two together."

"Behaving oddly?"

Wallop hesitated. "I encountered a woman. In . . . in the hallway."

"The hallway again?"

"Again?" Wallop's gaze shifted to Spencer's left ear.

Spencer tilted his head and forced Wallop to meet his gaze. "You said you encountered her in the hallway at the Grendel ball."

Wallop's fist came down on the thick oak table. "Dammit, man. I'm trying to report a crime. I am certain if you attend to this trollop's location, you'll find my wife's priceless tiara. Unless she has sold it, in which case, you can provide me with a report so my insurer can begin recompense."

Spencer leaned back in his chair. "Trollop? I thought you were reporting a theft and a murder. No one mentioned other less salubrious acts."

Another snort from Mitchell's direction.

Wallop scowled at Mitchell. "She's done away with her husband, too. I'm sure of it."

Spencer lifted his eyebrows. *Murder?* Now that changed everything.

"On what basis do you make that accusation?"

Wallop swallowed hard. "I know the man. Met him on the continent. Wanted to reconnect, but she didn't seem clear on where he was or when he would be back."

Spencer lowered his brow. Not knowing or caring about where your husband was, was certainly no crime. If it were, there wasn't a jail big enough to house the number of women who could be arrested on that charge.

"That hardly means she's done away with him, Wallop." Spencer placed the pen and notepad back on to the table.

"I mean it, Erleigh. I knew it was the Countess Von Dagga as soon as I laid eyes on her, even in that ridiculous Cleopatra outfit."

A pulse at Spencer's neck thumped.

Images of the whirlwind of a woman dressed as Cleopatra he had encountered that night flipped through his mind.

Even though the woman had been as perfectly coiffed and powdered as the other women, something set her apart from the rest. She had materialized beside him in a wash of golden light, not from the myriad candles that lit the room but rather *from* her. He had stood in stunned silence, his attention captured by the way her dress clung to her soft, womanly curves, the smooth gleam of her rounded shoulder, the way her lips had curled into a smile that seemed to be for him only.

Countess Von Dagga, Lady Grendel had called her. She had been unable to provide him any further information. Apparently, a nameless friend had pressed Lady Grendel to extend an invitation. Aside from her being new to town, and by her own admission sans husband, there had been little information to share with Spencer.

Spencer had watched as the countess had moved from the room, stopping to speak with a maid. She should have looked as thoroughly at home in the ballroom as the other ladies did, but something about her had his senses firing. It was the way she carried herself—like a child performing a task knowing a much-loved treat would be her reward.

As if feeling his gaze upon her, she had looked up and met his eyes. Her gaze had slowly run the length of his body before lifting back to his face. After a moment of perfect stillness, she had smiled. The room tilted and then she had turned on her heel and melted into the heaving crowd. Like Cinderella, only leaving behind the scent of jasmine instead of a shoe.

"You look into this strumpet, and you are going to find out she's bad news."

Spencer flipped the notepad closed. "We'll look into it."

Relieved at finally being taken seriously, Wallop's demeanor returned to its regular, overblown state. "I want her arrested. Throw the book at her." Wallop's brows lowered as he appeared to consider something. "I don't suppose when you arrest her, you'd let me search her rooms? I could . . . er . . . identity the tiara."

Spencer pushed his chair back. He'd given Wallop enough of his time. In one swift movement, he stood and strode toward the door.

There was more to this story. It was clear Wallop was not telling the entire truth. The man was a renowned womanizer, a liar, and a cheat. His eyes had focused intently on the back wall of the room, avoiding Spencer's gaze where possible.

And Spencer's intuition, which had served him well thus far, had prickled at the sight of the countess. That would explain his . . . interest in her. He paused at the door.

"I'm afraid if this person did in fact murder her husband, Lord Grendel, *and* steal the baroness's tiara, then she would be guilty of several serious criminal offences and would need to be approached with caution. By members of the police force only," Spencer directed to Wallop over his shoulder.

Wallop's indignant disembodied voice floated down the hallway.

"But I'm a baron!"

"Precisely your problem," Spencer muttered to himself.

He gestured with his head for Mitchell to join him on the walk back to his office. Heads bobbed up from desks, wary eyes watching as Spencer strode purposefully between the desks of the dim main rooms toward his corner office, overlooking St James's Park.

"What do you make of that?" Mitchell asked as they reached the door to Spencer's office. His doubtful tone told Spencer everything he needed to know about Mitchell's thoughts on the situation.

Spencer waved Mitchell through the door and shut it behind them. "Wallop is clearly not telling us all he knows about this. Get down to the gambling hells and find out if he owes money. I'll go to the clubs and see what's listed there. Who interviewed the countess today?"

Mitchell scanned a list of names. "No one. She was one of the attendees who left earlier in the evening, so we hadn't gotten to her yet. We'd focused our attentions on the people who were there when he was found."

Spencer tapped his fingers on the desk.

The accusation of a possibly murdered husband by a disgruntled baron was low on his list of priorities, but it would be remiss of him if he didn't at least look into the connection between the two cases.

"Find out what you can on this Countess Von Dagga. She seems to be in the wrong place at the wrong time one too many times for my liking."

Mitchell pulled a small flip pad and pencil from his breast pocket and began scribbling Spencer's directions. "Certainly, sir."

"Or perhaps we pay her a little visit ourselves. See what she has to say for herself."

Spencer couldn't ignore the flash of excitement at the thought of seeing that woman again.

# CHAPTER 3

The day had dawned dreary and dull, but for Albertine, it was as though it was lit by the brightest sunshine. She had woken with birdsong, refreshed and invigorated, despite her late entry into bed.

The parcel of letters, wrapped in a square of linen and stashed between her mattress and the slats, radiated a joyful, peaceful energy that lulled her into the best night's sleep she had experienced since Papa had died.

They now rested in her lap as she sat in front of the outdated dresser and its age-spotted mirror that had come with the house. Her hand stroked the packet of letters rhythmically, absentmindedly, as if she were petting a cat. She hummed the jaunty tune that had been playing at the ball as they'd left.

Joan removed the final hairpin from her mouth, pressed it into Albertine's hair, and let out a great sigh.

"Whatever is wrong, Joan?"

Joan met Albertine's eyes in the mirror. "I feel all queer. Like something's not right."

"Pish. You worry too much. Lady Roche's house is merely across the square. It will be a simple stroll."

"He might be waiting for us, Bertie. He'll want his letters back," Joan said.

Albertine rolled her eyes. "They aren't *his* letters, Joan. They are hers. He stole them. And I do hope I see the beastly man, I'd give him a bollocking. He was blackmailing her, after all."

Joan wrinkled her nose in response.

"He deserves everything he gets. And so do we." Albertine held the letters aloft. "We deserve the money these messages will fetch us. Lady Roche is one of the most powerful ladies in society. Our prompt retrieval of her letters will thrill her and, I am certain, she will recommend us to other ladies. This is why we are here, Joan. This is step one of our plan. If I can make some money, Franklin will have no power over me."

Joan looked dubious. "I'm not sure about that. He's still your next of kin."

"No. The *count* is my next of kin. A lady is the property of her husband."

Joan's dubious expression increased. "I suppose so. That is, if the husband exists."

Albertine smirked at Joan in the mirror. "No one but us knows the count is a figment of our imagination. And I, for one, rather consider him the perfect husband."

Albertine stood and smoothed the front of her dress. A giddy feeling welled up in her stomach. She longed to whoop and pump her fist in the air. But no, she would wait until the payment was in her hand. Hopefully Lady Roche would pay with banknotes. A check was rather difficult to cash when one had no means to identify oneself. Sharing her real name at this early stage of the game would undo everything. Perhaps she needed to hire a face for her business. Someone to take the checks and cash them for her. Although—her stomach twisted at the thought—there had been a decided lack of checks. She shook her head. There was no space for worries now. Worries were like house guests; you let one in and before you knew it, you were overrun.

As a treat, she would buy a ticket to the Anchor Dancing Booth. She and Joan had sat on the grass together their first week in London, and enjoyed the strains of music and frivolity from inside the tent. They watched the groups of well-dressed men and women clutching each other, laughing, filling the night air with their glittering excitement.

She'd promised herself that one day, soon, she and Joan would live a life so carefree and joyous.

Come this time next month, surely she would be inundated with clients and their money, and she would no longer have to jam the chair under the door handle of her bedroom when she slept, or search the street from the drawing room window before leaving the house. Perhaps the constant buzzing of anxiety that kept her awake until the early hours of the morning would finally abate, and her promise to her brother Algernon would be upheld.

Memories of lying on the floor next to Algie, their heads touching as they read the latest adventures of Algie's hero, Sherlock Holmes, flipped through her head like cards falling from a shuffled pack.

"When we're grown, we'll move to London together and solve mysteries. Real life Watson and Holmes," Algie said, every time they turned the final page of an installment. Even as his legs had begun to shake and wither, he planned and plotted their escapades as a detective duo living in London.

"We'll need more exciting names, of course. I rather fancy being a knight. Sir Dagger of the Ratiocination Realm," Algie said.

*Ratiocination.* One of Sherlock's favorite words and, therefore, one of Algie's. *The process of exact thinking. A reasoned train of thought.* A concept their logical papa encouraged in them both.

But even Papa's scientific brain, once lauded by The Royal Society as the brightest in Britain, was unable to find a cure for what caused Algie's muscles to spasm, shake, and ultimately, atrophy.

When he was no longer even able to sit, Albertine had spent hours beside Algie's bed and read the stories aloud, ending each one with their vow: "When we're grown, we'll move to London together and solve mysteries."

So here she was, living out their dream. Only without him. She breathed through the stab of pain. He would be so proud of her, she thought, imagining him egging her on. Living their dream brought him back to life for her.

A lightness bubbled in her chest, and she grabbed at Joan, hauling her into her arms. "This is it, Joanie. I can feel it. Thank you for coming with me and believing in me."

"Mmph." Joan yanked her head from Albertine's chest and peered up at her doubtfully. "Let's just wait and see."

Albertine released Joan with a little shrug. She didn't need to wait and see. Everything was falling into place exactly as she had dreamed. Skipping from the room, she held her arms out and twirled in a circle in the hall. The bag of letters danced in her hand as she swayed. "Let's go, Joanie. I am ready to introduce London to its newest lady detective—the Countess Von Dagga."

Even Joan's deep, weighted sigh and crossed arms could not dampen Albertine's spirits. There had been times of self-pity and self-doubt, not to mention countless tears, on this journey, but not today.

Today was the day they celebrated.

The park square that stretched between the rented abode of the Count and Countess Von Dagga and the fashionable town-house of Lord and Lady Roche was teeming. Governesses and their little charges, ladies in their best morning outfits, and dowagers with their teacup-sized dogs all milled about on the green despite the weather. The London season was about to begin, and it seemed every woman of marriageable age had descended upon the city. Which was perfect timing for Albertine. The ladies were generic types, similar in age to Albertine, all in recently made dresses in the *mode du jour*, all hunting for a husband. No one would question who she was, or what she was doing here.

She beamed at an older woman, strolling alongside two younger girls, clearly her daughters, all outfitted in brand-new dresses.

"Good morning. Lovely day for it."

The ladies murmured polite responses in return.

Although the rent had taken nearly every penny she had, it had been worth it for the upscale street address. Opinions in society were based entirely on looks, and if Albertine appeared to be a wealthy countess, then that is what people would believe. And if anyone ever wondered why they never encountered the count, well, they wouldn't be the first couple to enjoy their marriage by living apart.

Albertine patted Joan's arm, still linked with hers. She felt as light as a feather, as if she could float away on a warm summer breeze. She closed her eyes and tipped her face to the sky, savoring the insipid sun and ignoring the weak smatters of rain. Nothing could dampen her good cheer.

Joan glanced up at Albertine, her lips pinched and brow furrowed.

"Don't look so concerned, Joan," Albertine said gaily. "Lady Roche is about to shower us with gratitude, and all our cares will soon be gone."

Joan grimaced and gazed about darkly. "I've got a bad feeling about this, Bertie."

"Oh, tosh."

They had arrived at Lady Roche's front stoop, and Albertine straightened her hat with an impish grin. "London's most dashing and daring detective?"

Albertine could've sworn Joan rolled her eyes as she tramped up the steps toward the glossy black door. Joan was a good sport, really, despite her doubting nature. Albertine gazed out across the park. She had little experience with friends, Joan being her only one, but she was sure there weren't many who were willing to pack up and accompany their pal halfway across England. But Albertine was about to repay Joan for her loyalty. Of that, she was certain.

When they finished with Lady Roche, she would take Joan out for an ice to celebrate. Her meager savings hadn't stretched to such luxuries.

The door opened in response to Joan's knock and a short, elfin-looking man in the liveried uniform of the Roche household appeared. He studied the card Joan handed him with practiced indifference, his gaze sliding to Albertine. She met his look with what she hoped was a fearsome, utterly countessy stare in return.

"You may enter while I ascertain if her ladyship is at home." The butler opened the door further and stepped back to grant them entrance.

The sweet scent of hyacinths filled the reception room and a large, crimson Ming vase stood on a stand, strategically placed at the entrance to favor passersby a glimpse of the wealth and power of the Roches.

To the left of the hallway was a waiting room, and the butler ushered them in wordlessly. Albertine knew Lady Roche was likely standing behind the matching door to the right. They had agreed to reconvene the morning after the ball. A tingle of excitement zinged through Albertine's fingers as she pulled the ribbons of the small reticule that held the letters Lady Roche had been so desperate to retrieve.

Within moments, the butler appeared through the doorway again. "Her ladyship will see you."

Albertine threw a satisfied smile at Joan and took a deep, calming breath.

They crossed the hallway into Lady Roche's drawing room.

The woman in question was standing beside the window, peering out to the street below. She was a striking woman, a statuesque redhead with the milky skin of someone years younger than she was reported to be. The sun caught her hair, casting a golden glow like a halo about her.

As she gazed upon them with a frigid gaze, Albertine couldn't help but think of the indiscreet words this woman had written for her lover. How would it feel to be so infatuated by someone that you would compromise yourself? Risk banishment from society, contempt from all you knew and loved, just for the sake of a man. Albertine could not imagine ever being so foolish. No man would ever turn her head like that.

Lady Roche's elegant hands were twisted at her waist, and tight lines of anxiety marred her otherwise flawless complexion.

"Thank you, that will be all. Close the door behind you, if you please," she directed to the butler. Her cool green eyes lingered on Joan before flashing to Albertine's in silent question.

"Joan is an employee of my detective agency. The maid's outfit allows her admission to areas of houses that would be inaccessible to other detectives."

Albertine forced herself to stop speaking and kept her gaze firmly averted from Joan, whom she knew would be wearing a most incredulous expression.

Lady Roche nodded impatiently and waved them to the large floral chairs that faced the velveted chaise lounge. "The letters."

Albertine held the packet toward her, pride swelling in her chest. She really had done a superb job.

"Here are the letters, as requested." The spiel Albertine had practiced on the way over faltered on her lips as Lady Roche snatched the packet from her hands.

"Does he know they're gone?"

An image of the red-faced man, lolling slack jawed against the arm of the chair in his study flashed through Albertine's mind. Would he know what she had been after? How long would it have taken him to awaken and realize something was amiss?

The sleeping draught should have passed quickly. Judging by the way Lord Grendel had been slurring when he entered the room, he might just assume he had tupped her and fallen into a satisfied post-coital sleep.

"I do not believe so."

A smile twitched across Lady Roche's lips. "And is this all of them?" She untied the ribbon and shuffled the envelopes, counting them.

A wave of nausea clenched at Albertine's stomach. She had just grabbed a bunch of envelopes tied together. There hadn't been time to search the drawer for any remaining documents. Had there been any left?

Albertine smiled in a manner she hoped conveyed confidence rather than stricken panic. "Of course."

Lady Roche closed her eyes and clutched the letters to her chest, her lips moving in silent prayer. Taking a match from the mantle above the fireplace, she bent to the hearth. The smell of sulfur filled the room as she struck the match and held it to the letters. All three women watched as the orange flames licked at the paper, transforming the words, which had wielded so much power, into nothing but cinders.

Flakes of silver ash danced in the fireplace, and when the glow of the ember that had been the last letter faded, Lady Roche stood. She dusted her hands on her silk skirts as if they were little more than an apron.

"Your help was greatly appreciated, ladies," Lady Roche said, seating herself back at her desk.

She used a strange, dismissive tone, almost as if she believed their interaction was complete.

A cold sense of dismay unfurled in Albertine's stomach. She cleared her throat. Lady Roche looked up, an eyebrow raised.

Albertine met her gaze and the dread that had swirled aimlessly landed like a rock in her boots.

"There is the matter of the payment."

"Payment?" Lady Roche's lips pursed.

"Yes. Payment for services rendered. You . . ." Albertine licked her lips, her mouth suddenly dry. ". . . employed us to retrieve those letters on your behalf, which we did at considerable risk to ourselves."

Lady Roche's face was perfectly composed, save for the slightest twitch at her brow. "Which letters?"

Albertine held that emotionless gaze, her breath loud in the quiet room. Lady Roche was married to one of the wealthiest earls in the House of Lords. They were currently in a drawing room furnished with opulent silks and luxurious furniture. The desk she sat at would have cost more than Albertine's quarterly rent. She dug her nails into her palm as her lip began to tremble.

"We had an agreement. You gave your word," Joan burst out hotly.

A flush crept along the creamy flesh of Lady's Roche's artfully decorated décolletage. "Perhaps I can leave credit for you at my dressmaker's. I do not have access to money. My husband would want to know what it was for when I asked for it. I couldn't possibly tell him. And even if I did think of something, he wouldn't agree to pay a *woman*."

"But you agreed. We did the work," Joan's voice raised, and she stepped forward.

Albertine's stomach sank, but she placed a soothing hand on Joan's forearm. There was no point in making an enemy of Lady Roche.

Most women did not have their own money, as she well knew. Ladies were not permitted to open a bank account without their husband's permission. And Lord Roche's secretary would scrutinize any credit accounts at the month's end, ensuring Lady Roche could explain every penny. Not ideal when paying someone to retrieve love letters to your paramour.

Albertine shook her head at Joan's questioning look.

"Perhaps you can show your gratitude by sharing my services to any other ladies in your circle," Albertine said tightly, more for something to say than any belief this woman would help them.

Her mind was whirring like an automaton, but she couldn't grab hold of a thought to make sense of it.

Lady Roche's back stiffened, but she didn't look up from her papers. They were dismissed.

Clutching at Joan's hand, Albertine lurched from the room, like a sailor on a wet dock. Albertine and Joan trudged through the hallway in silence. The butler appeared out of nowhere and opened the door, flooding the reception room with blinding white light. A gust of wintry air blew through the open doorway, dislodging Albertine's hat and causing her to shiver. Sheets of newsprint wheeled through the street. Gray clouds clotted along the horizon. The street that earlier looked so welcoming now looked dark, dank, and dangerous.

She longed to cling to Joan and sob. *What were they to do now?*

Joan was stiff at her side, anger rolling from her in almost tangible waves. She was furious. And rightly so.

"So much for the upper class," Joan all but spat.

"Hush," Albertine returned. "It is worthless to be angry at her for a situation she cannot control. We are all in the same boat, are we not?"

Joan snorted and gestured to the vast, pristine house behind them. "We ain't in the same boat. Not by half. She's done us dirty. If you don't remember finely, we need that money."

Albertine remembered finely enough. But they hadn't come this far only to be felled at the first hurdle. No, she had managed that oaf Grendel just fine on her own, and she had retrieved those letters. She could do this. She had to. Her only other option was her cousin Franklin. She would rather die trying here in London.

"I ought to go back in there and give her a piece of my mind. Threaten to tell everyone about them letters," Joan said.

Albertine rested a pacifying hand on Joan's arm. She looked angry enough to do just that. "That would make us as bad as Grendel. No, this is a mere setback. Lady Roche will share my name in the drawing rooms. Money will come."

Albertine's voice was far surer than she felt. She tipped her chin to the gray sky. *What now, Papa? Any ideas?*

Albertine gazed out along the now nearly deserted street. The clouds parted and a ray of sun beamed down to the park in front of them. A man in an olive mackintosh rushed by, a battered bowler pulled down low against the rising wind. "What we need is a man."

Joan looked at her as though she had spouted another head and was doing a jig on the streets in her chemise.

"Ye've gone soft in the head," Joan said.

Perhaps she had, but all Albertine knew was she couldn't give up now. What awaited her back at Crawford House was immeasurably worse that what they'd find by forging forward.

No, she had to find a man to be the face of her business, and she had to find him fast.

# CHAPTER 4

A damp breeze that smelled like tar and the filth of the Thames blew along the street. Spencer flipped up the collar of his woolen coat. While it wouldn't dispel the smell, it would keep his neck warm. Although there wasn't much point in keeping his neck warm if the rest of him was as frozen as a block of ice.

He stamped his boots twice on the ground. "What do you think?"

Mitchell lowered the newspaper from his face, where it had obscured him from view. His head swiveled one way and then the other as he peered along the deserted road. A lanky man watched them from beneath a tattered hat. As he clocked both sets of eyes upon him, he turned and fled in the opposite direction. His long-legged gait was measured carefully until he reached the corner, whereby he broke into a trot.

"What's that then. The fourth or fifth?"

Spencer fingered the small piece of cork he had marked with his nail. "By my count, that was number eight."

Mitchell hummed. "Eight men in the last hour who have found themselves along this particular stretch of road, who fair turned tail at the sight of us."

Spencer nodded. "Curious."

Mitchell folded the newspaper in half and placed it on his knees. "Is it time for that chat with the countess? It's arctic out here, innit?" He blew on his hands and rubbed them together.

Spencer and Mitchell were sitting on the wooden bench in the park across the street from the current address of Countess Von Dagga. They had been there for most of the morning, as their nearly frozen buttocks attested.

Spencer nodded and stood. "You stay here. I'll go in alone. Keep it an informal kind of conversation."

Mitchell aped a terrified expression. "Alone? With a man-killer? A tiara-stealer? Will you be all right?"

The men chuckled, and Spencer dug his hands farther into his coat as another gust of frigid wind blew through the park.

"I think I can manage a countess, but by all means, keep a watch on that lower window. I'll wave my underpants if I need help."

"Believe me, sir, the sight of your pants will send me screaming."

Spencer smiled. "I'll have you know there's a bounty on my pants. Every eligible woman of marrying age in the ton is interested in them."

"I don't doubt they're great, sir. Ma always said, there's no pants like a duke's pants but no offence, I could live without seeing them." Mitchell shot him a wink as he pulled a small pocket watch from his coat and examined it. "Eleven fifteen on the dot."

Spencer removed his watch and nodded confirmation. "I'll meet you on the next corner at half past."

Mitchell tucked the paper under his arm and walked to the opposite corner of the park. Spencer's feet protested as his chilled blood began to move. As he tugged his bowler lower onto his forehead, Spencer's gaze ricocheted along the street, analyzing every opportunity for potential issues. A large, well-dressed man hovered at the end of the street, but he was too far for Spencer to make any sense of his features.

This street was one of Belgravia's finest, and the blank, regal faces of the buildings all turned toward the square of well-manicured greenery of the park in the center. Home prices, to buy or rent, in this area were not cheap. They were obviously not short of blunt, although his clerk had confirmed it was a rental arrangement taken for the season only. He had been unable to find any earlier rental records in London for the count or the countess.

Spencer paused at the steps of number thirty-six and gazed up at it, taking in the small collection of leaves building up in the corners of the step. The tiled steps were scuffed, and the giant brass knocker was tarnished with dark spots. Spencer lifted a gloved hand to rap at the door, but before his knuckles could connect, the door was wrenched open and a small, dark-haired woman in a maid's uniform appeared. There was something of the pixie about her. Her gaze traveled with a casual insolence along his body to his shoes and back to his eyes.

When their gazes met, she winked. "All right. You here about the ad?"

Spencer blinked once. "Er . . . yes."

That appeared to be the correct answer as the diminutive maid smiled, showing two dimples in the perfect apples of her cheek. "Yeah, I'd say you'll do," she said cryptically.

She gestured with her head for him to enter, watching him with an avid interest that made him feel off balance. He swiped his feet along the coir doormat before entering.

"I am looking for Countess Von Dagga . . ." He reached into his pocket for his calling card, which identified him as Scotland Yard Agent Sweetman, the title of Duke resolutely absent.

Before he could lay a hand on it, the maid had shut the door and was pushing him into the room.

"This way. Lemme take that coat."

She spun him around and yanked the coat from his shoulders. The fable his nanny used to read him about a girl in a red coat and a wolf sprung to mind. Spencer shuffled backward toward the entrance. She advanced on him. He shot a glance over his shoulder at the now securely shut door. His chance to signal to Mitchell was gone.

He removed his hat and held it against his chest like a shield. "Is the countess at home?"

"Sure is, luvvie. This way." The maid moved through the hallway briskly and pushed a wallpaper paneled door hidden in the hallway's wall.

Spencer stood frozen in the reception room. Was he to follow or wait to be announced? Where was the butler? He cocked an ear. The house was deathly quiet and still. It was highly unusual for a maid to answer the door and deliver a guest to the lady of the house, without even a glance at his calling card.

There was the rustle of silk, hushed voices—and a sweet smell wafted into the waiting room. Spencer sucked in a breath. The scent reminded him of his childhood at Trentham Hall. There was a small summer hut alongside the lake his great grandfather had installed as a gesture of undying devotion to his fifth wife. The banks that circled it were strewn with fragrant honeysuckle and jasmine. The only positive memories he had of that place were the summer days home from school lying along the banks of that lake, rowing and play fighting with his brother. His stomach flipped in its familiar way when he thought of Stephen, and he pressed his fist against his throat, clearing it roughly. He blinked at the ceiling, willing the rise of emotion to roll by.

The maid's head poked through the now open doorway, and she let out a short, sharp whistle one might use on a farm dog. "C'mon."

Spencer smiled. He couldn't remember the last time anyone had whistled at him, if ever. It certainly hadn't been since he'd inherited the Erleigh title, that was for certain. Still holding his hat in front of him, he strode toward the opening the maid had ducked through. He bent his head and found himself in a comfortably furnished and decidedly feminine room. A tidy desk and full bookshelf took up one wall of the room, and expensive-looking floral chairs faced each other in the middle of the floor. The room was well heated and the sweet scent he had caught a whiff of in the reception room was much stronger.

The woman he recognized from Grendel's ball, the countess, he assumed, stood in front of the roaring fire, one alabaster arm stretched along the mantel. She gazed at the window, appearing to be lost in thought. Spencer narrowed his eyes at her tense shoulders. A long moment of silence passed, and she turned, chin raised. When their gazes met, the haughty mask dropped. Her mouth dropped open and her eyes widened.

Spencer smiled. So she remembered him.

The countess moved to her desk, making some strange hand movements to the maid, who gazed at her with a puzzled expression.

"He's here about the ad," the maid said.

The countess paused, closed her eyes, took a deep breath, and addressed the wall behind Spencer's left shoulder. "You are?"

*The ad again.* He was most intrigued.

Spencer nodded. "Yes, the, er . . . ad."

She picked up a sheaf of papers and gestured to the oversized chair across from the desk. He remained standing. "Please sit . . . Mr. . . .?"

Spencer hesitated as his mind whirred. He wasn't certain what was happening here, but he would play along with it for as long as it led him somewhere. They hadn't been introduced and even if she asked about him now, it was unlikely she would connect his real name and the title she would have been told at the party. There was no problem in telling her the truth.

"Sweetman."

Her head lifted, and she gazed at him with a hard stare. "Sweet man?"

Spencer set his features and gazed back at her with wide eyes. "Spencer Sweetman at your service, madam. I believe we met, briefly, the other evening. At the Grendels' ball?"

Her lips twitched, and she turned her attention back to the papers on her desk. "Countess Von Dagga. I am afraid I don't recall meeting you. But I do attend a lot of events. I'm very popular."

*Liar.* And a bad one at that. She remembered him just fine.

"Pleased to meet you now," he said.

"I'm Joan." The maid moved toward him, placing her hands on his chest and nudging him into the chair.

The countess leaned back in her chair and fixed a cool gaze upon him. "Tell me about yourself, Mr. Sweetman."

Spencer gazed back, puzzled. *What on earth did she want to know?*

"What makes you think you are the man for the job?" She gestured to a folded newspaper on the corner of the desk between them.

Spencer rose from his chair and leaned over the desk, reaching for the paper. His hand hovered in the air above it. "May I?"

The countess inclined her head, as if to convey it was nothing to her.

The newspaper was folded to the advertisement's page. A bold circle had been drawn around a small, nondescript box in the column of advertisements.

*Man wanted.*

*Must be of youngish age, average height and looks, no distinguishing features. Strong and fleet of foot, hand, and mind.*

*Willing to work evenings.*

Spencer pressed his lips together and thought of the men he and Mitchell had watched stalk the street, only to turn tail at the sight of two officers of the queen staking out the very house they were intending to visit. Tricksters and cheats, the lot of them. What on earth was the countess trying to get herself into?

"We needs a man," Joan said from her position on the arm of the chair he had just vacated.

The countess glared at her. "Thank you, Joan, perhaps you could tend to the fire?"

"The fire is out," Joan responded without a shred of interest. "We needs a man, and ye look like you meet all our requirements. When can you start?"

The countess clicked her tongue. "This is an interview with Mr. Sweetman to ascertain whether he will be the right candidate for our position."

"You're our only candidate," Joan stage whispered to Spencer behind her hand. "No one else turned up."

"Joan," the countess scolded.

Joan smiled, utterly unabashed. "But even if they had, you look like you're the right candidate to me."

Spencer fought the urge to laugh. He half expected Mitchell to jump out from behind the door, laughing at the practical joke he had played on him.

"As I was saying . . ." Two high spots of color appeared on the countess's cheeks as she attempted to get the interview, if that was in fact what this was, back on track. "Are you good with your hands, Mr. Sweetman?"

The two spots of pink increased to red as he gazed at her. He cleared his throat and spun his hat in his hands to still his energy.

"That is, are you strong and capable? We might need things . . ." Her gaze dropped to his chest, and she swallowed. "Lifted. Or shifted."

"Here, why don't we give you a test?" Joan said, pushing off the chair and standing in front of Spencer with her arms spread. "See if you can lift me."

An incredulous smile burst upon Spencer's lips, but slowly died as he looked at Joan's expectant face. She was serious.

She nodded and lifted her arms above her head. "G'on then."

Spencer glanced to the countess, who was considering them with a tilted head. "You want me to lift you? In my arms?" he asked Joan.

She nodded vigorously.

*Good god.* What was the job they were recruiting for, exactly?

Spencer stood and placed his hat at the edge of the desk and returned the eager smile of the maid with a weak one of his own.

"Be gentle with me, sir," she said in a mock-coquettish tone.

He smiled genuinely at that. He had a strong feeling it was *she* that should be gentle with him. Spencer cut one last glance at the countess, who merely shrugged.

"We do need a strong man," she said, as if that was all the explanation one could need.

Joan's eyes were closed, and the absurdity of the situation suddenly struck Spencer. Bending at the knees, he swept an arm under the small woman's legs, knocking her backwards into his waiting embrace. Her eyes flew open, meeting his as he held her firmly. Giving her a slight jog, Spencer swung her up into his arms, sending her legs undulating into the air. She whooped loudly and despite the utterly bizarre turn of events, a bubble of something he hadn't felt in a long time floated in Spencer's chest.

*Joy.*

Since his brother's passing and his inheritances of the titles, his life had been devoid of any genuine pleasure or enjoyment. He had filled every hour of every day with task after task so that he fell into bed at night, exhausted into sleep. The prospect of giving up everything he had worked so hard for, just to spend his life on the Erleigh estates, hung over his head like a guillotine. But here, swinging a small-boned maid in his arms, under the amused gaze of a countess rumored to be a thief and a murderer, tiny buds of joy began to unfurl underneath the layers of ash he'd heaped upon them.

He cocked a brow at the countess. She pursed her lips and lifted an unimpressed shoulder.

"What do you think?" he murmured to the maid. "Do I pass?"

"Well . . ." The dimples in her cheeks danced.

He jogged her in his arms again and as she squealed with delight a tight, hidden place inside Spencer unlocked. Without stopping to think, he spun in a tight circle, lifting her higher and higher. Joan hooted and hollered as her skirts ballooned around them.

"Let me down. You'll do ya back," she cried between bursts of laughter.

He lifted her higher in his arms, as if considering her weight. "You weigh nary more than a feather."

"Ooh, a silver-tongued charmer, so you are."

He met the maid's laughing gaze and was surprised to feel his face erupt into a wide grin. It felt strange, as if all the muscles required to perform that action were waking from a hundred-year slumber.

"Have you quite finished?" The countess's tone was sharp.

Placing Joan on the ground, he waited until she steadied herself, then threw her a wink and adjusted his shirt cuffs crisply.

Joan leaned against the desk. "Ya got the job."

"Hang on a minute," the countess spluttered from the chair. "I haven't finished with my questions."

Spencer lifted his trousers at the knee and sunk into the floral chair. He leaned back and crossed one leg over the other. "I am an open book. Please, ask away."

"Are you married?" Joan interjected.

The countess groaned and placed her head in her hands.

"I am not." Spencer answered, ignoring the pinprick of discomfort that statement bought him. Were it up to him, he would stay that way, but five hundred years of the Erleigh name pressed upon him. Marriage was part of his duty, and duty was the air a duke breathed.

Joan peered at him through fluttering lashes. "You like women though?"

Spencer smiled. "I do, indeed. Very much so."

"The job is yours!" Joan cried, a hand to her breast.

"Joan," the countess exclaimed with exasperation.

"Yes, Ber . . . I mean, Miss Bertie?"

"I think I hear someone at the door."

Joan's gaze didn't shift from Spencer. "I didn't hear nothing."

"I'd like you to go check please. Now." The countess's tone brooked no room for argument.

Joan heaved a sigh, but backed out of the room, her gaze trained on Spencer.

A strange silence descended on the room in her absence, like the too-quiet ringing in one's ears after a round of gunfire.

"She seems . . ." Spencer blinked, unusually lost for words.

"Rather over-excitable, I'm afraid." The countess shuffled the papers on her desk, unconcerned. "Now, where were we?"

"You were explaining the position to me?" She hadn't been, but Spencer felt it was time to get a handle on what exactly was going on here.

"I run a somewhat . . . that is . . . it's a detective agency." She didn't sound too certain. There was a long pause, and she met his gaze. "There are times when we require the assistance of a man person."

"A man person," Spencer repeated, schooling his features.

"Let me speak frankly. While many consider me the mistress of disguise, if you like, there are times when a man is required. My husband, the namesake of the business, is currently on the Continent. While he is gone, I require someone to . . . well . . ." a number of emotions passed over the countess's porcelain face ". . . assume his identity."

Spencer covered his startled choke with a cough, pressing his fist to his lips.

"Madam, with all due respect, impersonating someone is highly illegal. I could go to jail. Not to mention what said man might have to say about the matter upon his return."

The countess's gaze swung to the door, and she bit her lip. Spencer followed her gaze. The doorway was clear. What, or who, was she so worried about?

"We do not need to worry about the count," she said, rather darkly.

Spencer raised a brow. "That's easy for you to say. It won't be you doing a stretch if he returns and kicks up a stink."

The countess smiled then and once more, Spencer was struck by how lovely she was. He steeled himself against the thought. It took more than a pretty face and the smell of his childhood to distract Spencer Sweetman from his job. No matter how sophisticated the con, Spencer was always, *always*, one step ahead. This was no different, beatific smiles and genuine laughter aside.

"Trust me. He won't be *kicking up a stink*," the countess said.

In Spencer's experience, men tended to get rather het up about other men assuming their identity, but the countess appeared resolute. Baron Wallop's words of concern regarding her missing husband echoed in his ears. Spencer narrowed his eyes at her. She, in turn, fixed her gaze on his lapel.

"When did you say he would be back?"

Her eyes widened, and she stood. "Oh, not for quite some time, I should think." She held a hand toward him to shake. Her hands were graceful, like a pianist's, but her nails were short and ragged as if she had chewed them to the quick.

"Thank you for your time. Please leave your details with Joan. We will be in touch about the position."

That sweet smell danced under Spencer's nose again and against his better judgment he wrapped her birdlike hand in his own. Her hand was soft and delicate and for the second time that day, Spencer acted without thought, and pressed her hand to his lips.

"Please do."

They made their way back through the house, unaccosted by Joan, and as the door closed behind him, Spencer felt a frigid breeze rip through him in a manner that no coat could warm against.

Nothing about that meeting had gone the way he had expected it to. Instead of finding out what Countess Von Dagga knew about Lord Grendel's death, he was utterly confounded.

And utterly intrigued.

# CHAPTER 5

Albertine closed the front door and turned the lock with a scrape. She leaned her cheek against the cool wood and inhaled deeply.

Hurried footsteps clattered along the hallway, and Joan burst into the reception room with a disappointed huff. "Don't tell me he's gone already? I wanted one last look."

Albertine straightened and leveled a stern glare at Joan. "Joan. You cannot behave like that with men here. City men are not the same as the guileless fellows of the village."

A slow smile spread across Joan's face. "I should hope not."

Albertine bit her cheek to stop herself from laughing. *Oughtn't one of them act sensibly?* "Besides, if we are all going to work together, then we must operate as professionals."

Joan nodded absently as she moved to the window and peered out, seeking one last glimpse of Mr. Sweetman, Albertine assumed. "Oh, yes. Professional. You can count on me."

Albertine coughed into her hand. Joan was possibly the least professional lady's maid in London. Which was par for the course, as up until three weeks ago when they had borrowed the dog cart from Crawford's stables and driven to

London, Joan had been an undermaid in the kitchen of Crawford House.

As Joan had been born in the village exactly one month before Albertine, her mother became Albertine's wet nurse. And after Albertine's mother had died when she was barely walking, the two girls had been raised as sisters. Their youth had been spent as thick as thieves, joining forces to perform pranks on Albertine's older brother Algernon and, far too often, experience his much cleverer and considered antics in return.

Albertine jumped as Joan rapped on the window, waggling her fingers at Mr. Sweetman when he glanced back.

Albertine winced. Lord only knew what the fellow thought of them. It was bad enough he was the only applicant for her advertisement. She had been so certain her notice would bring an overabundance of suitably unsavory men. Not crooks, no, that was a step too far. But she'd figured there were a number of men, well-bred enough to pass as a lower member of the ton, interested in a wage to do little more than pretend to be someone else. But not a single candidate other than Spencer Sweetman had appeared.

She sighed and kneaded her hands together. While the Grendels' party had been a crush, it had been full of upper-class members of the ton. How had he been invited? Was he a friend of Grendel's? What if he had been sent here to apply for the job with the intent to steal the stolen letters back? There was something about Sweetman that disturbed her. He was too good looking for one and for two . . . well, he was far too good looking. He wouldn't have been her first choice. The way he had picked Joan up as if she weighed nothing and practically flung her about the room, how his eyes had crinkled with amusement as he'd gazed down into Joan's laughing face. Something spiky and hot moved through Albertine's chest and she shook her head.

"Oh, jags," Joan breathed. "That blimmin' Wallop is back again."

Albertine straightened, her heart hammering in her rib cage. Her fingers scrabbled on the lock of the front door. She slammed it against the bolt, although she knew she had already locked it.

"Ohhhh." It was little more than a breath, but Joan's noise held a volume of meaning. "Sweetman's having a word with him."

Albertine bumped Joan out of the way with her hip. Sure enough, Baron Wallop and Mr. Sweetman were standing at the roadside.

Albertine sighed. There went her only candidate. Wallop would say all manner of untruths about her that even a desperate and down-on-his-luck man wouldn't be able to ignore.

The first response she had ever received to the handwritten notes she and Joan and nailed to the noticeboards outside the women's-only clubs in Mayfair had been from Lady Dufferin. An avid bridge player, she was convinced the Baroness Wallop was cheating at the weekly bridge game the Wallops hosted. Lady Dufferin had taken Albertine along as a guest to a game, where Albertine had discovered the baron was in the habit of bantering with the ladies as they played, refilling their glasses and talking general nonsense while using a small hand mirror to reflect their cards to the baroness. Who then, of course, cleaned the ladies out of their tokens.

Albertine had informed Lady Dufferin, who had denounced the cheats, and caused a considerable, and highly entertaining scene—at least in Albertine's viewpoint.

The weekly bridge game had been relocated to Lady Dufferin's townhouse, and the Wallops were considered persona non grata.

As compensation for a job well done, Lady Dufferin had offered Albertine a place at her club, which came with a substantial yearly fee that Albertine could not afford. Although it *had* been that job that had led to Lady Roche's request.

Which also hadn't resulted in payment.

Albertine heaved a sigh and returned her focus back to the men on the street.

Wallop's face was increasing in color, and he was gesturing toward the house with a pointed finger.

*Oh dear.*

Since she had outed the Wallops' scam, he had become fixated on her, loitering outside her house and appearing at the most inopportune moments. She'd taken to sneaking through the back window to avoid encountering him on the street. Another thing having a man about the house could fix for her.

Albertine chewed her index nail absently.

"What do you reckon Wallop's sayin'?" Joan asked.

Albertine bit down on her finger. She supposed he was warning Mr. Sweetman about the wicked ladies living inside this house, as he had hollered from the street every other day this week. They were lucky he had neglected to bring along a bucket of tomatoes as he had last week. It had taken them hours to clean the front of the house.

Sweetman held a hand up, and Wallop's demeanor instantly became submissive. He bowed his head and shuffled his feet on the rough roadside dirt. Sweetman leaned toward him and appeared to murmur something in his ear. Wallop's head shot up, and he turned toward the square. Albertine followed his gaze. The sky was gray and low and the park was empty save for a man in a drab, colorless coat reading a newspaper on the bench. The wind swirled around him, sending leaves cartwheeling along the gravel path and buffeting his paper. His hat was pulled low, probably to protect him against the chill. *Strange weather to be reading outside in,* Albertine thought. She turned her attention back to Sweetman as he clapped Wallop on the back and pushed him into motion along the road—then remained stationary, standing tall and watchful, as Wallop made his way down the street.

He turned to the window, as if he had been aware of their presence the entire time, and raised a hand to his forehead in a salute.

"Cor," Joan breathed. "What do you reckon he said to 'im?"

Albertine did not know. But she was going to find out.

The door was unlocked, opened, and her slippered feet flying down the steps of the house before she could consider her actions.

"Mr. Sweetman!" she called.

A frigid breeze rolled along the street, and she shivered. He paused and turned but made no move toward her, watching with a narrowed gaze as she approached.

She faltered when she got close to him, her question dying on her lips. What if Wallop hadn't been speaking of them at all? She thought of how the man appeared like a foul smell every place she attended. His threatening presence had begun to dog her every step, and she found herself checking the corners of the house when they returned from excursions. Between him and the near constant thoughts of Cousin Franklin, she never got a moment's peace.

"That man you were just speaking to. Do you know him?"

Sweetman knocked the brim of his hat with a knuckle to lift it from his forehead. "Not at all. He approached me." His gaze was wary, and as she looked into his eyes, for the briefest moment she had the strangest feeling she knew this man.

There was a gold ring around each of his pupils that made her think of the sun on the clearest summer's day.

Albertine licked her lips. "What did he say?"

His gaze held hers steadily, giving nothing away. "That if I were an honorable man, I would avoid having anything to do with you."

"Ah."

A corner of his lips lifted. "I told him I'm very happy to be a decidedly dishonorable man."

The hairs on Albertine's arm prickled.

"I will be frank with you, Countess. I would like this job very much." His eyes were earnest and clear.

Albertine shifted her gaze to the gray sky. A flock of starlings dipped with fluid grace. A sign? It didn't make much difference whether it was or not, as she had received no other interest other than this altogether too handsome man. She needed a man to front her business. Without one she didn't stand a chance at making any money. She needed to make money, and she needed it fast.

Her desertion had lost Franklin the monthly stipend the marriage he had arranged for her would have brought in for him. Although he was basically an imbecile, he was strongly motivated by money. It wouldn't take much for him to track them to London. Even in a city this size, there was only so long one could hide.

"How did you get an invitation to the Grendel ball?" she asked. *Damn.* Too late she recalled she had claimed not to remember him.

His eyebrows raised slightly and his gaze slid over her shoulder. She turned, but there was nothing behind her but the man in gray, still on the park bench.

"A *friend* invited me. I find sometimes being in the right spot, at the right time, can lead to very"—his lips quirked—"interesting situations. I like to follow them, wherever they may lead me."

*Interesting situations.*

Albertine thought of her experience at the ball two nights ago. The excitement of the crushing crowd, the thrill of seeking out the still and silent study, retrieving the letters, and outsmarting Lord Grendel. She smiled. For she had outsmarted him. And Franklin. Thus far.

*You're as sharp as a dagger, Bertie,* Papa had used to say.

Her smiled faltered at the thought of Papa. He had been committed to her education as much as her brother's—unusual for a daughter—and had always told her she was as smart as any man he had ever met. Had she been wrong to believe him?

She had spent all her money on getting to London and starting her and Algie's detective dream, but now she knew that she couldn't go any farther without a man to help her.

If this was the only man who could help her, then so be it—she had come too far to quit now. When she spoke, her voice was firm. "My business has found me with some people who are not quite as enamored of me as they could be."

Sweetman raised his brows. "Enemies?"

"Hush, no. Let's call them friends who aren't as keen on me as the others are."

Sweetman nodded. "I have a few of those myself."

"I need a man to be the front of my business. People, well"—she gritted her teeth—"they prefer to deal with men. Having a man as the face of the business would double my prospects."

"Forgive me, just the front?"

Albertine nodded. "Don't worry, you won't be required to do any of the investigating. I'll handle that. Just collect the money. And keep men like the one that you just encountered away."

His brow furrowed. "Has he been bothering you?"

Albertine glanced at the facade of the townhouse, with nary a tomato stain to be seen. "Nothing I can't manage, but he is becoming . . . bothersome."

Sweetman cracked his knuckles and winked at her. "Let me at him."

Albertine widened her eyes. "There will be no need for that. Simply keep him away. And any other men, should they . . . happen."

Sweetman raised an eyebrow. "I see. Is this all men or just a particular man that might *happen*?"

An image of Cousin Franklin sprang into Albertine's mind. His thick necked topped by a face ruddied by years of food and drink. The way his piggish eyes followed her, his leering laughter. She shuddered.

"That depends. I shall let you know."

"So." Sweetman bounced on his heels slightly, and the childlike gesture made her think of Algernon.

*What was it about this man that had her so discombobulated?*

"I'm to take the money and manage any men who might happen. All while pretending to be your husband, the Count Von Dagga until . . ."

"Until he returns."

"Ah, yes, until he returns. What's his name?"

"I beg your pardon?"

"The count. If I am to impersonate the man, it seems fitting I should know his first name."

"Ah. It is . . . Albert."

"His name is Albert?" Spencer huffed an amused breath. "That must be confusing."

"Not at all. We just call him The Count."

"You call your husband The Count?"

"Yes, that is his preference. He's rather . . . unique, is our Albert."

Spencer gazed at her wordlessly. Her heart began to thump so loudly she feared he must be able to hear it.

"The pay will be ten shillings. Paid monthly." Just naming the figure made her feel sick. It was far more than she could afford, but she must believe in herself. She had to. There was simply no one else to depend on. Her father and brother dead, her cousin out to sell her off to the highest bidder, and now this Wallop. No one was coming to save her.

Once her detective agency was up and running, she would be financially independent and Franklin would have no control over her. She would be in control of herself. The captain of her own ship.

She could do this, *would* do this.

Sweetman ran his palm along his jaw, and for a fleeting moment, Albertine thought he was laughing, but when he met her gaze again, his face was expressionless. "You have yourself a deal, Countess."

Albertine held out her hand toward him. "Welcome aboard, and please, call me Albertine."

Sweetman smiled as he reached for her hand, enveloping hers in his warm, dry one. "What a pleasure it has been to make your acquaintance, Albertine. I am Spencer Sweetman, but you may call me Count Von Dagga."

The playful bow he gave brought to mind the gaiety he and Joan had displayed in the drawing room. His smile had been deep and true, and something about it had wrenched at her heart. The expression on his face when he had set Joan to rights had been one of surprise, as if he hadn't smiled in a long time.

Not that she cared a jot; he was but a means to an end, nothing more. There was no way she would let a man distract her from what she needed to do here, no matter how attractive his joyfulness had been, or how her heart had fluttered when he had directed his open smile in her direction. No, Albertine Honeycombe had better things to do than that.

She needed this man for one thing and one thing only.

She yanked her hand from his and made a show of wiping it along the seam of her skirt. It felt chilled in the afternoon breeze.

"I will place an advertisement in the paper announcing our services with the hours when people may call upon us. You will run the appointment with them, ask the pertinent questions and lead them to believe that you will be the one to perform the work." She unclenched her jaw and tried to look serene. "And collect the money. Up front."

Sweetman gazed at her for a long moment. As if he was assessing her.

It was disconcerting in the extreme. Albertine forced her hands together at her waist to stop the urge to fix her hair, and met his gaze with wide eyes that she hoped conveyed trustworthiness.

"Would you like the job?" She swallowed hard.

He smiled, a slow upward lift of his lips that transformed his face. She could imagine what he had looked like as a young boy, playful, mischievous.

*Adorable.*

"I would not like the job, Countess. I would love it."

# CHAPTER 6

"What do you think?"

Mitchell had doubled around the block in the opposite direction to Spencer, meeting him on the roadside, one street over from the countess's house.

"I've somehow managed to find myself in the employ of our suspect," Spencer said drolly.

Mitchell shot him a searching glance, as if unsure whether he was joking or not.

"Say again? Being a duke ain't paying well enough?"

At the mention of the title, which had been his since his older brother's sudden death six months ago, Spencer's stomach knotted unpleasantly. He had yet to reply to his mother's last letter. It sat on the mantle above the fire in his drawing room, seeming to watch his every move. There had been some hope that it would accidentally find its way into the fire, but thus far, Spencer hadn't been so lucky. Although he hadn't had any luck for some time now. The thought brought a grim twist to his mouth. Even if the fire devoured his mother's missive, there would be another.

And another.

The Dowager Duchess of Erleigh was not one to take hints, preferring instead the cosh-over-the-back-of-the-head style of communication. He had better reply before she arrived on his doorstep. That was entirely the last thing he needed right now.

"She placed an advertisement in the paper this morning. That's what the men we saw must've been doing. Applying for the job."

Mitchell whistled an amused breath through his teeth. "Hold up." He pulled the newspaper from his breast pocket and flicked to the advertisements. Spencer pointed to the countess's advertisement. Mitchell's lips moved as he read the words, eyebrows flicking up once he got to the end.

"What's she up to then?"

A cloud passed over the sun, throwing the street into gloom. Spencer glanced over his shoulder. The road was bare, and the wind had picked up and fair tunneled along, lifting papers and leaves. He thought of the countess and the warmth of her drawing room, a warmth that wasn't only from the fire crackling in the grate. It had radiated from her. She was a mass of contradictions. Her open smile and guileless eyes the color of the toffee he and his brother Stephen had used to eat, handful by sticky handful, and yet . . . there was a guardedness that told him all was not as it appeared.

His boot hadn't even reached the last step onto the street when Wallop accosted him, demanding to know what information the countess had shared with him. The man was still highly strung and anxious about something. Not, Spencer suspected, his wife's missing tiara. No, there was something else going on. It was unlikely Countess Von Dagga and Baron Wallop were working together, but Spencer couldn't shake the uneasy feeling that there was something more simmering with those two.

Spencer had never been able to resist a riddle that needed solving. And the countess was the most delightful kind of puzzle.

"Wallop was here. Behaving rather oddly," he noted.

Mitchell nodded slowly. "I saw."

"There is something fishy about the situation with him. What did you find out about his debts?"

"He's in it up to his eyes. Are they in on it together, do ya think?"

Spencer mulled the question over. *Did he?* No, he was certain they were not working together, but there was a link between them, of that he was sure. Albertine had been frightened of him. Maybe she owed him money?

"Anything is possible. She's offered me the job as the front of her business. It would be a good idea for you to interview her, see what you make of her."

He couldn't help but smile at what Mitchell would make of the small maid and her contagiously cheerful disposition. While he couldn't imagine Albertine or her maid involved in murdering a man, his time at Scotland Yard, and society, had taught him that people often conducted themselves in ways one could never anticipate.

"Oh, and she wishes me to impersonate the count."

Mitchell's mouth dropped open. "Ye what?"

"She wants me to act as her husband while he is *abroad*."

Mitchell whinnied.

Spencer scowled at the younger man. "In name only. She seemed rather fixated on claiming the money for their services up front."

Mitchell nodded thoughtfully. "Is she on the make? Planning to take the blunt and scarper, like?"

He thought of the expression she had worn when she offered him the job—there was strength there, but a sadness too.

"Perhaps. Although they are still here. It is more likely that she is taking on jobs as a 'detective' and not performing the task."

"A detective?" Mitchell brayed with laughter. "A woman? For sure, who would hire a woman to do detective work? Never."

Spencer shook his head. The boy had a lot to learn. "Not never. There are times when a woman might wish to use another woman to perform certain tasks for her. Regarding sensitive matters that cannot be discussed with a man."

Mitchell screwed his face up and stared into the distance. He chewed his lip as he thought. After some time he said, "Like what?"

Spencer lifted his shoulder. *Who could say?* "Women's business is far beyond the realms of my understanding, Mitchell. Pay her a visit and find out what she knows about Grendel's death. I will follow her for the next week or so, and see what I can find out."

He pumped Mitchell's hand and waved down a passing hackney. It had been a long time since he had been fooled by someone, and he would not let that happen now. The countess and her funny little maid were suspects and nothing more.

And if his investigations proved she wasn't involved in anyone's death, she was still a married woman, however remotely, and he didn't have any interest in dallying with that.

★ ★ ★

The door of Erleigh House opened before the carriage had even pulled to a stop. Spencer let out an irritated sigh at the sight of his butler. Did the blasted man sit at the window the entire time Spencer was out, like a loyal spaniel awaiting his master's return?

The low afternoon sun lit the face of the whitewashed building and cast a golden glow upon it. There were few passers-by who did not tip their faces toward the facade of the mansion as they walked by. As well they should: It had been designed to awe, to impress, to intimidate. Their expressions were often filled with envy and longing. He couldn't blame them. In this light Erleigh House looked inviting—as if a large and happy family lived between its walls, untouched by sorrow or troubles, unlike the regular man's.

It was a lie.

Erleigh House was nothing more than a beautiful prison.

Blaine, the thin-lipped, hollow-cheeked butler-cum-spy who worked for Spencer's mother more than he did for Spencer, stood in the doorway ready to dog his every step within the confines of the house. *Would Your Grace like a bath? Would Your Grace prefer to sit in the study like the previous duke, your father, your brother, had preferred?* Reminder after reminder that his kin were dead, and he, through a series of unfortunate events, was now the duke, and his life was now to be dedicated to nothing but his duty to the Erleigh title.

His coat was whisked from his shoulders and a footman kneeled at his feet, untying his bootstraps, replacing them with a pair of warmed house slippers. A silver tray bearing a mountain of envelopes was presented.

"I have taken the liberty of organizing your missives into importance, Your Grace, and provided your secretary with the ones that appear to be little more than invitations."

As if he could not manage his own diary. Like he was an imbecile unable to even determine which event he wished to attend. Spencer scrubbed his hand along his face.

"Thank you, Blaine," he ground out between gritted teeth.

"No need to thank me, Your Grace," Blaine responded, as he did without fail, every time Spencer thanked him.

It grated him enormously, but he would never cease thanking the insufferable man. Spencer might have been forced into the claustrophobic box of a dukedom but he refused to compromise his values. He prided himself on treating every single member of his employ with respect and humility.

"I have stoked the fire in the study," Blaine continued hopefully.

Spencer shook his head. "I'll sit in Mother's drawing room."

"Your Grace—"

"Good day, Blaine." Spencer's tone brooked no room for argument. He strode along the hallway toward the west wing of the building, which was traditionally reserved for the Erleigh duchesses.

With no duchess in attendance, Spencer saw no reason to leave the smaller and more comfortable rooms unused. His brother's and his father's vast, masculine chambers were ice cold, and Spencer found it impossible to concentrate while surrounded by reminders of them.

He walked the seemingly never-ending hallway, a gallery dedicated to the wonders of the Erleigh linage. The right side of the hall was home to life-sized portraits of every Duchess of Erleigh since the inception of the title. And on the left, from which he averted his gaze as he always did, the dukes. The pictures made him feel quite queer. Under the unblinking gazes of his ancestors, he imagined he could feel his collar heat up and tighten like the manacles he used on the men he arrested, criminals about to lose their freedom. He quickened his pace, not releasing his breath until he had entered the drawing room. Leaning against the closed door, he allowed himself to close his eyes and simply listen to the silence of the room.

He inhaled a deep breath, and the scent of talcum assailed him. He sniffed again.

Definitely talc.

His stomach dropped, and a cold chill overcame him.

"Mother," he said.

"Spencer."

He didn't need to open his eyes to see her disapproving look. It dripped from every letter in his name.

He was going to throttle Blaine for not warning him. He would wrap his hands around Blaine's twig of a neck and squeeze until it snapped.

Spencer forced his lips into a smile. "How delightful to see you."

"Your labored sigh indicates otherwise, my dearest Duke."

Steeling himself, he opened his eyes slowly.

Mother sat in a floral armchair, her posture impeccable. It was as if she had a backbone forged from the purest iron, although, Spencer reflected sourly, she was made of far tougher stuff than mere iron.

Hair impeccably coiffed, skirts artfully arranged around crossed ankles, and expression blank, she was the epitome of the perfect lady.

Lines spread from her lips like lines on a map—a map of disapproving looks and disappointments not voiced.

Her hair showed a smattering of gray, far more than the last time they had met, and the hand upon her rosewood cane was wrinkled, almost gnarled. His heart thumped. She was aging before his very eyes. Well, not quite before his eyes, because he had been studiously avoiding her for six months.

Her imperious stare skewered him to the spot.

Mother didn't do a thing without reason. Better to get it over with. "To what do I owe this pleasure?"

"Does a mother require a reason to call upon her only son?"

Spencer twisted his mouth into a smile at the sharp reminder. "Of course not. Shall I call for some tea?"

Then he could set about breaking Blaine's neck.

He drove his finger into the small button on the wall and held it there. A distant burring sounded throughout the house, but Spencer didn't release the knob. The traitorous figure of Blaine appeared in the doorway. He bowed toward the dowager duchess before turning to Spencer. They stood facing each other, Blaine an entire head shorter than Spencer. His beady eyes flicked from Spencer's face to his finger on the bell, once, twice, but Spencer still did not lift it.

"Your Grace?"

The words were like a dash of cold water in Spencer's face, and he released the button.

"Blaine. What a thrilling surprise for the master of the house to find his mother lying in wait for him. It is an indescribable joy to see my mother, Blaine, as you can imagine, for an unplanned, *unannounced* visit." Spencer felt as if a tooth might crack, he gritted them so hard.

Blaine's Adam's apple bobbed as he swallowed.

"My mother would like some tea, Blaine. As would I."

"Certainly, Your Grace." Blaine bowed again and stepped around the door.

Spencer gripped the edge as the other man tried to close it. "Actually, Blaine. I would like a whiskey. A lot of it."

"Certainly, Your Grace."

"And Blaine?" Spencer waited until the other man met his gaze. "If you ever pull a stunt like this again, you will find yourself following Her Grace back to the dowager's cottage. On foot."

Spencer watched with grim satisfaction as a number of emotions, foremost dismay, flitted across Blaine's face before it settled into the mask of blank politeness it always held. His mouth opened to speak but Spencer got there first. "Let me save you the bother. *Certainly, Your Grace.*"

Blaine nodded once and removed himself. For once, he was smart enough not to speak.

Spencer released the door and turned back to his mother, pasting a smile on his face.

"How splendid it is to be in your company again, Mother, truly. And what an honor that you've called upon me for no reason other than to share your undying affection."

Spencer threw himself onto the velvet chaise opposite his mother, grinning at her expression as he flung his booted feet over the arm of the lounge.

Silence drew in on the room. Spencer was a patient man. He listened to the quiet ticking of the mantle clock. . . fourteen, fifteen, sixteen . . .

His mother cleared her throat delicately. *Aha.* Here was the guillotine, sharpened and ready to spring.

"You have not replied to my letters, Spencer."

Spencer ran through his collection of excuses. Pretend he hadn't received them? No, as the most recent missive was on the mantelpiece behind his mother in this very room, he doubted that would work. *I have been busy?* That would be akin to lighting dynamite in a brandy factory.

He settled on honesty. "I have not."

"I believe you are still *working*." She whispered the word, as though it were some unspeakable act that would bring nothing but shame.

"It is not appropriate. Trentham Hall needs you, Spencer. You are now the duke. I will not allow five hundred years of hard work to be undone simply because you wish to play little spy games in town."

His mouth twisted at his mother's words.

Hard work? She had no idea. He worked alongside men who toiled all the light hours of the day, putting their lives at risk to feed their families, to keep London safe.

To keep people like his mother and her cronies safe.

No one had cared what he had done when he wasn't the duke. Now his job was shameful, childish, irresponsible.

As the "spare," the just-in-case second son, Spencer had been dismissed his whole life. Although he understood he was luckier than most and that there was liberty in the uninterested gaze of his parents. All eyes on Stephen had allowed Spencer to hammer out his own path.

And forge his own way he had. He had willingly sunk into the dimly lit, sweltering gambling hells. There was freedom to be found in the filthy lanes, the crowded, louse-ridden pubs full of sozzled patrons seeking relief in gambling, debauchery, and thieves' games. Secrets had been easy to extract, treachery, thievery, sleight of hand exposed, and all of it had thrilled him.

Spencer had never felt good enough. Never as bright or as smart as Stephen, but in the seething mass of the underworld he had found his own niche, one that hadn't been carved by his brother before him, as everything else in his life seemed to be. He was willing to put his body on the line in a way that most men of his standing were not. And the work excited him and made him feel as if he, too, finally, was worthy.

The mere idea of giving it all up to do little more than manage expenses and improve the family coffers left a sour taste in Spencer's mouth. He had never asked for this. Never wanted this. This should be Stephen's job. Had always meant to be.

But to refuse would be impossible.

"Lord Grendel was murdered." He spoke baldly, hoping to shock his mother—but her face remained as impassive as ever. "Murdered, Mother. In his own house. During a ball." Irritation spurred him on. What would it take to make his mother show a skerrick of emotion?

Mother clicked her tongue. "What does this have to do with Erleigh, Spencer?"

What did it have to do with Erleigh?

*Everything and nothing.*

He let out a deep sigh that was a mere octave away from being a groan.

"As regards our last discussion, you need to attend to our estates. You are now the duke. The tenants rely on you. The servants rely on you. You are now a cog in a large machine that is far, far more important than your little games here."

She leaned heavily on her cane and stood, taking her unopened letter from the mantle.

"You will also need a wife. Inside this envelope is a list of appropriate matches. Choose one before the season is over, or I will choose one for you."

Spencer sat up abruptly, his boots thumping on the floor.

His mother's features shuffled, and she presented him a look, more pursed lips than smile, and dropped the envelope into his lap.

"Do I have your assurance that you will end all this non-sense and assume your position as the Duke of Erleigh?"

Spencer's mouth watered the way it did moments before he was going to toss his boots, a skill he had all but mastered in his youthful heyday.

*Tick tock, Dukey boy.*

"Yes, Mother. This is my last job. As soon as I have located the perpetrator, I will give it up and come to Trentham."

"And how long will this *task* take?"

For some reason, the toffee-brown gaze of the countess flashed through his mind. He had a sense that however long he spent in her company would never be enough.

The door opened and Blaine entered, saving Spencer from having to respond to his mother.

"Blaine, I will attend to my mail in the duke's study after all."

"Very good, Your Grace."

Spencer turned once he reached the doorway. "However long it takes is however long I will take, Mother. Lovely to see you. Now, if you will please excuse me. The work of a duke is never done."

He bent into a curt bow and strode from the room.

# CHAPTER 7

The front door slammed so heavily that Albertine's teacup rattled in the saucer. Joan appeared in the doorway, panting, a newspaper clutched to her chest.

"Oh, Bertie. We be done for."

Joan's eyes were wild, her hair had come loose from its pins and now curled about her head like she had been dragged through a bush. Backwards.

"What is it?" Albertine leaped to her feet and made her way to the window, searching the street below. It was bare, the dank, yellow fog keeping London's people indoors this afternoon. "Is it Wallop?"

She'd hoped the earlier conversation with Sweetman had done the trick, as the roadside had been free of him since.

Joan handed her the newspaper, her hand trembling. "I wish it were. It's Lord Grendel. Bertie, you've killed him."

*Impossible.* Albertine snatched the paper from Joan's fist. Noise roared in her ears, and her eyes could barely make sense of the headline of the paper that screamed at her.

She groped for the chair behind her and sank into it.

*Lord Grendel found murdered in own house.*

This was not good, not good at all.

"Read it, Bertie. The boy was yelling it out on the corner, and I couldn't believe my ears. I fair snatched that paper and ran all the way home. Oh, jags, read it!"

As children, as soon as their school lessons had begun to cover the things a well-bred lady should know, but also science—Papa's passion—Joan had left the schoolroom and begun her duties as staff. The two girls had still spent evenings together, and it became commonplace for Albertine to read aloud to Joan, her friend's own reading never progressing much beyond recognizing letters and some simple words.

Albertine licked her lips. "London is agog to hear the news of Lord Grendel's murder. Found by his servants, during one of the infamous Grendel balls, considered just on the right side of scandalous for their excess, splendor, and frivolity. The annual fancy dress ball held by Lord and Lady Grendel was attended as usual by the crème de la crème of society. So, it was with some surprise that a servant discovered the stiff body of Lord Grendel, dead, in his study."

"Ohh. That's you done." Joan sank in the chair opposite Albertine and wailed. "Hung, you will be. Dead!"

The paper shook violently in Albertine's hands. The words swam in her vision, but she pushed on. "Calm yourself! I did not murder the man."

Joan removed her hand from her brow and glared doubtfully at Albertine.

"I didn't! Don't you see? It wasn't me. Someone else must've found him passed out in his study and murdered him!"

*Seems unlikely*, Joan's twitching eyebrow said.

The idea that she could have killed him hit Albertine with the shocking force of a fist. What if she *had*? For a moment she couldn't breathe, the weight of the realization a heavy rock pressing against her chest. The man was a horror, it was true, but she had never thought to murder him. Just give him a good night's sleep and retrieve Lady Roche's romantic notes.

Which had all come to naught anyway, as least as far as getting paid.

"Does that paper say how he died?" Joan demanded.

Albertine swallowed hard and peered at the shimmering newsprint. The letters danced in her vision. She shook her head. "No, no mention of it."

"But what if someone did see you with him? They'll think for sure you did it," Joan said.

"No one saw me with him. I am positive of that." She swallowed against the dryness of her mouth, because in actual fact she wasn't positive at all. What if he had a weak heart? Had the double draft of the sleeping potion been too much for him?

The metallic rap of the door knocker rang through the house. The women stared at each other. Albertine's heart began to pound unsteadily.

"What if that's the peelers? Come to arrest you, like?"

"For the last time. I didn't murder the man! I have nothing to fear."

Joan looked doubtful. "I know you say didn't, but what if you did and didn't notice, like?"

"One does not accidentally murder a man." Albertine sounded more certain than she felt. Had she murdered him? Surely one would notice something like that.

The door knocker rapped again, and both ladies jumped.

Albertine stood and attempted to fold the newspaper back into its tidy shape. Her hands shook and the pages twisted and stuck, refusing to settle into their previous position.

"Answer the door, Joan, please."

Joan pulled a horrified face. "Why me?"

Albertine repressed a sigh. Surely there were staff who responded to their employers' requests by doing as they were asked *and* without comment.

"Because you are currently employed as the maid here and it would look exceedingly odd for a countess to answer the door. It's bad enough we have no butler."

"Employed?" Joan's nostrils flared as if this was the first time she'd heard of the notion.

"Just while we're here. Doing this." Albertine gestured around the room weakly. Whatever *this* was. It no longer seemed of any importance.

Joan huffed an indignant breath. "Oh, well, if I'm to be *employed*," she spat the word as if it were a curse, "I'll let them peelers in. It will be my pleasure to show them through to the countess."

With another huff that told Albertine exactly what she thought of being employed, thank you very much—fair enough considering that she was drawing no salary—Joan threw open the door and swept from the room with a dramatic flair to rival those of any actors treading the boards in the West End.

Albertine abandoned the recalcitrant newspaper on her desk and rushed to the window, pushing it up as high as it went. Her toes lifted from the ground as she leaned out to get a glimpse of who was knocking on the door in such an alarmingly persistent manner.

She was still halfway out the window when Joan's voice sounded behind her.

"Countess, it's the police here to see ya, like."

Joan stood in the doorway, wringing her apron in a manner that suggested she had known it was going to come to this and, quite frankly, was washing her hands of the whole sordid business.

"Inspector Mitchell," she added darkly. "From Scotland Yard."

Albertine wasn't sure what was more concerning, the fact there was a man from Scotland Yard in her rooms, or that Joan, always on the lookout for a likely looking man, wasn't trying to garner his attention in some way.

"Will you be wanting tea, then?" Joan rounded on Albertine with suspicion.

Albertine fought a smile. "That would be greatly appreciated."

Joan sniffed in response. "I'm sure it would be."

She turned to Mitchell, who was watching their interaction with an amused expression. He was a handsome young man, his plump and cheerful face framed by a shock of bright red hair that was smoothed back and parted with a line seemingly sharp enough to slice bread.

His amused look transformed into a smile as he met Joan's gaze.

"And you?" Her tone was markedly warmer as she addressed him.

"A tea would be greatly, greatly appreciated, bostin," he returned.

Albertine's heart sank to her boots. The word *bostin* was used only up north, and his accent was rich with the musical inflection of the northern counties.

Joan froze. "Ye from Birmingham?"

Mitchell offered her a wide smile. "Close. Wednesbury. And you? Is that a Black Country accent I hear?"

Wednesbury was the closest village to Crawford House, and Cousin Franklin had a small house in the center of that village. Albertine eyed the young man. He was unfamiliar to her, and he was surely too young to have encountered Franklin, but it was a small town.

Joan turned to Albertine with unsubtly raised eyebrows, jerked her head at the inspector, and spoke with a decidedly non-Black Country and utterly inauthentic accent. "Nooooooo. Arm fram roond 'ere."

Albertine closed her eyes and pinched the bridge of her nose. "Tea, Joan. Please."

Joan scurried from the room, and Albertine fought the urge to apologize for her.

"Wednesbury. How lovely. How long have you lived here in London?" Albertine sat and gestured for the inspector to do the same.

Mitchell leaned forward and placed his hat on the floor at his feet. "A long time now. Left the Black Country years ago, but the accent lingers, don't it."

He grinned at her, and Albertine fought the urge to hug him as one would a young cousin. There was something so utterly cheerful about him, she almost forgot he was an inspector. Her stomach, which had churned unpleasantly a moment ago, now soared jubilantly. Surely a jolly young boy from the country would be no match for her.

"What can I do for you, inspector?"

His wide grin did not dim as he gazed about the room guilelessly. "I assume you have heard about the recent death of Lord Grendel?"

Albertine gasped and thrust a hand to her breast. "I say. Who? No, I hadn't heard. What terrible news. What a shock."

A gust of wind sailed through the still open window, rustling the discarded newspaper on the table, where it lay between Albertine and the inspector. Albertine watched in horror as the breeze flipped the pages until the large print headline announcing Grendel's death was visible.

She met and held Mitchell's clear blue gaze. "He was rather getting on, though, wasn't he?"

The inspector's eyebrow knitted together.

"I mean, I assume he was getting on a bit? Never met the man, as I said."

The newspaper continued to flap in the wind, like a siren on the rocks, performing for the inspector's attention.

"Wonders!" Albertine exclaimed, pointing at the empty doorway.

While his attention was diverted, she bustled over to the window, whipping the traitorous newspaper from the table on her way and tucking it under her arm.

"I thought I heard something." She glanced out the window, letting out a little shriek as the beady gaze of Wallop met hers.

He stood on the roadside, arms crossed, staring up at the house. He pointed a finger at her menacingly.

"Wench. You owe me money." His voice rang through the room, as loud as if he were within it.

Her fingers fumbled with the latch as she scrambled to close the window against the barrage of abuse from the street below.

Mitchell rose from his chair. "Is everything all right, Countess?"

She grimaced. "This area is not what it used to be. I must speak to the landlord."

As she reached up to snatch the curtains closed, the newspaper fell from her armpit.

She watched with mounting horror as the paper cartwheeled through the air, landing on the boots of the inspector.

*Lord Grendel Murdered*, the headline screamed. The inspector bent with agonizing slowness to retrieve it.

Was now the moment to faint? It would be rather difficult to question someone if they were unconscious, feigned or otherwise. She raised her hand to her head.

"Har we are den." Joan entered the room with a clatter of crockery. "Tay for two."

Albertine squeezed the bridge of her nose. Presumably the pirate's accent Joan had just acquired was supposed to hide her own Black Country accent. She loved Joan like a sister, she truly did and was well aware she couldn't have achieved half of what they had done without her, but sometimes did wonder if parenting the farmer's fifteen children as Cousin Franklin had arranged would be easier.

Fingering the bangle on her wrist, Albertine glanced at the teapot and back to Mitchell—who was now watching her with an unreadable expression, all signs of good cheer vanished.

Her heart lurched as her fingers connected with the beadless bangle.

She needed to get inside the Grendel home, and back into Grendel's study to retrieve the beads. If they were still there. As soon as possible.

*No*, she told herself, *no, they couldn't trace those back to her.* Could they? It was always better to be safe than sorry, though, particularly when wanting to avoid being associated with a murder.

"Lovely, tea. Thank you, Joan. That shall be all." Albertine gestured to the seat that Mitchell had stood from. "Please sit."

Mitchell held the paper out toward Albertine, now traitorously folded into a tidy little parcel. "I see the papers have gotten wind of Lord Grendel's passing."

"We saw that. But it's naught to do with us," Joan exclaimed hotly, all accents abandoned. "Naught at all. She just meant to—"

"Joan!" Albertine hadn't meant to yell her name quite so loudly, but one was never entirely sure what would come out of Joan's mouth at the best of times. And this certainly was not the best of times.

The silence in the room swelled, and Albertine was overcome with the sense that things had well and truly gotten away from her.

Mitchell raised a no longer quite-so-cheerful brow. "I have a few questions I would like to ask you, Countess Von Dagga."

She gazed at the window longingly. She would fancy her chances at making it out and down onto the street before him, if only it weren't for Wallop guarding her front stoop.

Albertine clenched her teeth into what she hoped would pass as a smile. "Certainly, inspector."

After all, wasn't that the sort of thing one said when one had a perfectly clear conscience?

★ ★ ★

Albertine leaned against the door to her study, her ear pressed against the heavy wood and a hand pressed to her heart.

The front door banged closed and Joan's footsteps beat a rapid tattoo through the hall. Albertine leaped out of harm's way as Joan thrust the door open.

They stood staring at each other in silence for a moment.

"Well?" Albertine asked with a tentative smile.

"Well," Joan replied blackly.

"I thought that went rather well. All things considering." Albertine tried to sound positive and failed.

To her gratification, the inspector had asked questions that were easily answered and showed no sign of considering her an actual suspect. Standard procedure, he had assured her, to check if guests had noticed anything that could help them with their investigation. He had appeared to believe her story of a headache that called for their early departure from the party, which she knew would be recorded alongside everyone's coming and goings in the butler's house book but he had not told her how Grendel had been murdered. There were really only so many times one could ask before appearing suspicious.

Her stomach clenched at the thought that she might have inadvertently killed the odious man. And her beads. *Wonders.* She had to get to the Grendels' house and retrieve the beads before anyone discovered them.

"Oh aye, considering he was here to determine if you'd murdered a man. Rather well, my foot."

Albertine rolled her eyes. "Honestly, Joan, if you are going to be unhelpful, then . . ."

Joan raised both eyebrows in a manner that told her she'd gone too far. "Then what? I can just bugger off back to Crawford House, can I? Leave you here on your own, will I? Oh aye, you'd be fine. Can't even boil a pot of water. It's you that should be back off to Crawford, missy."

Albertine blinked. She knew that Joan was right—she needed Joan far more than Joan needed her. Joan could return to Crawford House any time she wished and resume her work without question. Her mother would ensure there was always a job to be found for her. It wasn't Joan that Cousin Franklin was hunting the countryside for.

She shuddered and reached out to grasp Joan's hand, rubbing it between both of hers to warm it. "You are right. I need you far more than you need me, and I know it. Please let's not argue. You are all I have."

Joan huffed a breath, a stubborn set to her shoulders that Albertine was well acquainted with.

"Perhaps we should go to Hyde Park," she suggested. "We could get an ice and take a wander? Would that make amends?"

Joan's scowl lessened. Albertine knew only too well how powerful a sweet tooth Joan had. "I shan't even make you share. You can have one all to yourself."

On their way to Hyde Park they could call on Lady Grendel and hopefully be able to get back into Lord Grendel's study to find those beads.

"Fine." Joan crossed her arms across her chest. "But Wallop is still out on the road out there."

Albertine pulled her shawl from the hook on the wall. Frankly, after the visit from Inspector Mitchell, Wallop was the least of their worries. "Don't you worry about Wallop."

\* \* \*

Albertine opened the back door, cocked an ear, and waited for the two raps that would signal the coast was clear. When they came, she lifted her skirts and took off down the four concrete steps that led to the back parcel of land. Taking care to step only on the flat stones she and Joan had laid to avoid grass stains on her slippers, she ducked under the overgrown yew tree in the corner. Lifting the loose timber fence paling in the corner of the yard, she sucked in a breath, threw her hat over the fence, and squeezed through the gap, careful to ensure her skirt didn't catch on the exposed nail of the rail.

Donning her hat again, she adjusted her skirts and took off at a sedate pace through the backyard of Lord and Lady Aspices.

"Good afternoon," she called to the startled-looking servant emptying a bucket of slop water into the grass.

As soon as she rounded the corner of the house, she picked up her pace, trotting out on to the roadside. Her eyes scanned the street for a hansom cab. Unusually for this time of day, the road was bare.

"Oi!" A footman had appeared from the back of the Aspices' home and was storming toward her.

Albertine glanced back along the street. It was still empty.

Perhaps there would be a better chance of hailing a cab at the intersection. She took off toward the corner of the street. *Blasted skirts and silly heeled shoes.* She felt as if she were waddling like a wind-up toy.

The monstrous figure of Wallop appeared on the corner, with Joan rushing behind him, gesturing frantically to Albertine behind his back.

Albertine spun around, only to find another, larger footman had joined the first. Both were standing at the iron fence speaking in furious, hushed tones.

The welcome sight of a hansom appeared in the distance, but it had to pass the footmen before it could reach her. She cast a glance over her shoulder at Wallop, who was closing the space between them, with Joan now hanging from his arm.

"I am your neighbor," she gestured vaguely behind the men. "I was looking for my cat. Pumpkin."

They watched her with wary eyes, and she widened hers and pointed at Wallop. "I think this man has done something to it."

The hansom neared, but still wasn't near enough for Albertine to determine if it was empty or had a passenger. She was going to have to take her chances.

The footmen looked over her shoulder at the nearing Wallop.

"Stop, thief!" Wallop bellowed along the street.

The footmen glanced at each other and wordlessly came to some agreement. They advanced upon her.

She held her hands up at the men. "That man is unhinged. You can't trust a word he says."

"I'm a baron," Wallop hollered.

This was not going the way she had envisioned it. But Papa had always told her she was as sharp as a dagger, and she would have to prove that to be true.

The thud of the horses' hooves increased as the hansom cab bore down on them. Holding her gaze on the footmen, she took a backward step on to the road. As it neared, the jangle of the horses' bits, the thud of their hooves, the clatter of the carriage increased. She turned, lunged forward, and gripped the iron handle of the hansom as it passed by.

For one heart-stopping moment, her boots were lifted from the ground as the carriage continued its unrelenting way down the street. She scrambled her feet onto the mounting platform and dove into the cab, landing on the battered leather seat with an inelegant "Oof."

"Bloody nora." The driver pulled the reins and turned toward her. "What in the blazes are ye doin'? Yer could've bin killed."

"I shall double your fee if you do not stop. Keep going. As fast as possible, if you please." Albertine adjusted her hat and smoothed her skirts, as though it were every day she performed acrobatics into hansom cabs and her heart wasn't about to leap out of her chest.

Wallop charged toward the carriage. The footmen remained on the path, watching with dazed expressions.

"And do not let that man on under any circumstances."

It only took the driver a couple of seconds to decide, the promise of a double fee too appealing to resist. "Rightio, luv."

He flicked his ponies with a practiced wrist and urged them on. Wallop came close to intercepting them, red-faced and panting, and reached out a fleshy hand toward the taxi. The driver yanked hard on the reins, sending the cab veering sharply to the right. Albertine feared for a moment they would tip, but the carriage righted itself and they were suddenly rattling along the road, Wallop free.

Albertine whooped a delighted laugh and turned in her seat to look through the back window. Wallop rested his hands on his knees, breathing hard, his face an alarming shade of crimson.

Joan was already on the move toward the square.

Albertine sat back against the cool leather of the bench seat. "Jolly good show."

The driver doffed his hat with a knuckle, a small smile tilting his lips. "What's next, then?"

Her stomach twisted. If only she knew.

One thing at a time. "Stop here," she commanded as Joan sprung out onto the footpath, arms waving. She had cut a diagonal path through the park and popped out on the corner.

The carriage pulled to a stop beside her and Joan jumped on with a breathless laugh. "Crisps almighty! That was a close one."

Albertine strangled out a small smile, her heart still beating far too fast.

Joan turned surprised eyebrows toward her as she gave the driver the Grendels' address.

"I left the beads from my bangle in Grendel's study. I need to retrieve them."

Joan leaned back against the cracked leather seat and let out a noisy breath. "If they find those, then ya done for."

"Joan!"

She shrugged. "Just sayin'."

"Yes, well thank you for your helpful commentary. I am simply going to pop in to pay my respects to Lady Grendel and nip into Lord Grendel's study and find them. I'll be in and out within five minutes. It's hardly a big thing."

Joan's expression remained blank but her eyebrows quivered doubtfully. "So if your potion didn't kill him, what did?"

Albertine pressed her lips together. That question had been keeping her awake at night. "I think someone came in after I left, and killed him. He was enormously unlikable, there was probably a queue of people who wanted him dead."

Joan nodded. "Makes sense. But you better hope no one saw you going in to his study nor finds those beads. It don't look good."

"Luckily I have nothing to worry about. I am certain no one saw me and once I retrieve the beads there is no proof I was ever in his study—" The rest of her sentence died in her throat as she looked at Grendel's front door. Three black-suited men stood on the step, notebooks and pencils in hand.

"Oh jags," Albertine muttered as Inspector Mitchell tipped his hat back and turned to peer into the approaching carriage.

"I've changed my mind, we won't be stopping here after all," she directed to the driver.

She turned away from Joan's smug eyebrows.

As the Grendels' house shrank from view, Albertine's confidence that everything was quite so rosy went with it.

# CHAPTER 8

"Where do you want me?"

Albertine looked up from the newspaper she was reading with an open mouth. She blinked at him a few times before worrying her lower lip with her teeth as a rush of pink spread along her cheeks. Spencer's body tightened at the movement of her lips, and he fought the urge to groan.

"I beg your pardon?"

"What does the man of the business do daily?" Spencer straightened his collar and tilted his head in what he hoped was a jaunty manner. It had been quite some time since he had felt lighthearted enough to do anything in a jaunty fashion, even less so since his mother's visit.

There was a rustle of fabric as Joan advanced on Spencer at great speed. Albertine flicked a warning glance toward her, to no avail.

"I've got a coupla things you can do for me." Joan was staring at Spencer as if he were a tasty-looking slice of cake.

Spencer took a step backwards as she stepped up close to him.

Albertine sat up straight in her chair and slapped the paper onto the desk. "Thank you, Joan, but I would like to run through my business with Mr. Sweetman. Show him the ropes, as it were."

Joan turned and glared blackly at her. "Oh, your *business*. Aye, show him all the work you do." She let out a short, explosive *Ha!* "I suppose I'll make the tea again then, will I? Dust about in here? Tidy up?"

Albertine shook her head at Joan with a warning glance that only seemed to incense her. Spencer's gaze darted between the two of them. The looks they gave each other were loaded with meaning he didn't understand.

Albertine's flickering gaze landed on Spencer and her demeanor changed immediately.

"Any more talk like that and you'll find yourself without a position," she addressed Joan woodenly.

Joan lifted a corner of lip, more unconcerned than Spencer had ever seen a servant after being threatened with the loss of their job. "Oh, aye? Who will cook ya dinner, then?"

Albertine's lips pressed together, and she forced a smile that was more a grimace. "One would imagine the *cook* will."

"And help you dress?" Joan had crossed her arms across her chest and was glaring at Albertine darkly.

Albertine dabbed at her top lip, where a sheen of sweat had broken out. She lifted her chin. "My, er . . . my other maid. Countesses have a lot of maids."

Joan responded by tilting her head and raising an eyebrow. Albertine glared back.

Spencer hadn't seen or heard another soul since stepping into this house. He paused and listened. Apart from the clattering of a horse out on the road, there was no sound or movement. Was it just these two women living here alone?

"You don't do all those things, do you, Joan?" Spencer asked lightly, hoping to break the tension.

"All on my own?" Joan didn't shift her gaze from Albertine. "No—"

Albertine launched herself from her chair toward her. Albertine covered Joan's mouth with one hand and gripped her shoulder with the other.

"Joan!"

Spencer watched as the ladies grappled, Joan squirming to free herself from Albertine's grip and Albertine holding tight. But just as Spencer felt he might need to step in to ensure Joan wasn't smothered, Albertine released her, placing her hands on her shoulders and squeezing gently.

"That will be all, Joan. Please."

They stood as still as statues, staring into each other's eyes for a long moment. Joan's eyebrows pulled tight, Albertine's expression pleading.

"Please," Albertine whispered.

Joan whirled on her heel and stormed from the room.

Albertine cleared her throat and moved to her desk, ignoring his astonished gaze. "I have received a response to my most recent advertisement." She opened a desk drawer and shoved the newspaper into it, but not before Spencer caught the headline. *Killer Party! Police Believe Member of Ton Killed Lord Grendel. Interviewing Party Guests.*

Albertine picked up a thick cream note paper from the desk and waved it toward him. "Lady Cobham. She has lost her dog. She believes a gang of dognappers have taken it, and she would like us to retrieve it."

Spencer's stomach dropped.

Lady Cobham was a right old battle axe. Once one of the most powerful ladies in society, and a close associate of his mother's. There was no way he could show his face at her residence without blowing his cover. Gossip was the life force that maintained her ancient blood at the freezing temperatures required to keep her immortal soul on earth.

Albertine held the paper out to Spencer, and he cast his eyes over it, fighting a smile as he read her outraged accusations aloud.

"A sign that England, in general, is in a state of decay, Mayfair has fallen prey to the influx of degenerates, the French and middle class, and we are now at risk from dognappers."

He burst out laughing at that. The middle class? God forbid.

He remembered Lady Cobham's dog, Fancy. She was never seen without it. The wiry mutt had piddled against furniture inside all the best homes in London. It was of no surprise that someone had finally done away with it.

"Has she received a ransom note?" He handed the paper back to Albertine. Their fingers brushed and a bolt of electricity shot through his hand. Her skin was soft and lush. She expelled a tiny huff of breath and licked her lips. His gaze followed her lips, and he released a breath of his own. For a brief moment he imagined what it would be like to wind his fingers between hers, to feel her hand on his bare skin.

"Not that she mentions."

"Eh?"

She waved the letter. "She doesn't mention receiving a ransom note."

*The dog.*

He'd forgotten all about it. This was most unlike him. Since his mother's appearance, he had been discombobulated.

*Who was he kidding?* It wasn't his mother disturbing his equilibrium, it was this woman.

There was something about her that set him off kilter. He had never been so aware of another's body. The tiniest movement held him captivated, the way one corner of her mouth lifted before the other when she smiled, how she bit her lower lip when she was thinking, that she smelt like ripe blackberries in the sunshine. Perhaps it was simply that he had too much time on his hands. Working at Scotland Yard required a lot of him, and he had been too busy for anything more than a brief dalliance for months. This was the most time he'd had on his hands in years. Maybe a visit to his last mistress was in order. The thought dissipated like smoke as he met Albertine's warm gaze. Her eyes were the most intriguing shade of brown. Deep and rich. No, it wasn't that he needed a woman, it was that he desired this woman.

*Blast it.* That inconvenient thought had no place here. Not to worry, he would tamp that thought down and ignore it, much like he did any other unwanted feeling that dared appear. His parents had well versed him in that particular skill. He had a pedigree in it. Five hundred years of Dukes and Duchesses of Erleigh had taught their children how to stuff their emotions and deny their very existence.

"She wants me to find out who stole the dog and have it returned to her," Albertine said.

He nodded. *Focus, man.* This was the perfect opportunity to find out what kind of scam she was running.

"Unless we receive a ransom note, there isn't a lot we can do. Unless I get payment up front and . . ." He waited for her to offer any indication that she intended to fleece Lady Cobham out of her money.

Albertine pulled her lower lip between her teeth, and he dropped his gaze to the untidy desk.

"I think not. Not this time."

At his questioning look she said, "As you said, it's unlikely we will find her dog unless this imaginary gang contacts us. I'll attend this meeting with her while you and Joan speak to the servants and see if they know anything. I don't want to promise her something I can't deliver."

Spencer studied her. Her gaze was direct, there was no fidgeting, no telltale flush or sideways slip of the eyes. She was either telling the truth or a phenomenal liar. The thought burned.

"Fair enough," he said.

What was her game here? This was the perfect opportunity to get him to take the money up front and pretend to search for the dog for months. Maybe she was playing a bigger game, looking to keep Lady Cobham distracted while Joan gained access to the inside of her residence and did away with her jewelry. Like the tiara Wallop had accused her of taking.

"I shall ask where he was and when he went missing, but London is a big city. It's easy enough for a person to get lost here, let alone a dog."

Was he imagining the slight hitch in her voice at the word *lost*? Perhaps he had. She was as clear eyed and cheerful as ever.

She smiled at him, and he couldn't help smiling back. They stared at each for a long moment until she looked away, cheeks flushed.

He needed to find out what she was up to and move on. Before he did something utterly stupid. Like give in to the need that burned through his hands to reach out and tuck the wayward strand of hair behind her ear, to imagine pressing his lips against her neck, to run his palm along her—

"Let's go."

She was standing at the door, waiting for him to come to his senses. What remained of his logic demanded he put as much distance as possible between him and this woman—*now*.

But he stood, adjusted his trousers, and walked toward the delectable Countess Von Dagga.

Logic be damned.

★ ★ ★

The servant's entrance at Lady Cobham's residence was hidden from view at the bottom of a set of plain concrete steps. Because they were narrow and steep, he and Joan took them single file. As they descended, the heat and light of the day dissipated as if a blanket had been draped over a lamp. While clean, these steps were worn and scuffed, in marked contrast to the glistening tiles at the main entrance to the house.

They paused in a small, dank portico.

"Stick close, Sweetman. Servants in a house like this can be a pack of wild dogs." Joan waggled her eyebrows at him.

He smiled. "Can they just?"

She stepped close. "Oh, aye. No fear though. I'll show ya the ropes."

"Joan, I don't doubt you have a lot you could teach me."

Although it hadn't rained recently, the stairs were damp and lichen grew in the cracks of the flagstones.

"Take care on that moss," he said.

She hopped nimbly over the thick patch. "You'll catch me if I fall, won't you?"

Joan fired a wink at him and pushed her finger on the silver button marked *Trades*. "If there's anything to find out, we'll find it out down here. Servants love a bit of gossip at the expense of them upstairs. It's the only way they can release their frustrations about the job."

Spencer thought of Blaine. Did he glide silently through the halls of Erleigh House only to close the door to the butler's office and scream into his kerchief? Perhaps a well-timed eyeroll or a *tsk* was enough to satisfy his frustration at Spencer's unwillingness to fold himself into a shape that matched the empty space in the Duke of Erleigh puzzle.

He doubted the man had the bollocks or brains to dare break his composure, even in the privacy of his rooms.

A soot-covered face appeared in the glass panel of the door, peering at them with suspicion.

"Yeh?"

"Our mistress is calling on her ladyship."

The dark face disappeared, and the door opened. The small figure trotted along the hallway without so much as a second glance. Joan seemed unbothered by the unwelcoming greeting. *What a difference one staircase made.* Should Spencer have rapped at the main door, a well-dressed butler would have greeted him and, upon hearing Spencer's title, shown him through into the reception area and offered refreshment. It was, Spencer realized with a shock, the first time he had ever been *downstairs.*

Gambling hells, brothels, docks, and gang headquarters. But never the servants' quarters.

He smiled in wonder. It had been a long time since he'd had a first experience.

Even though it was Joan's first time in these particular servants' halls, she strode confidently along the walkway. A weary-looking woman popped out of the door to their left.

"Help you?"

"Our mistress is up visiting with Your Ladyship." Joan gestured to Spencer, including him in the conversation.

The woman rolled her eyes. "Och aye, good luck to her. Go through to the hall and get a cuppa."

Joan made off down the hallway and Spencer followed, taking in the rounded corners, worn floors and smoke-filled rooms. The noise was constant: people calling out orders, the clatter of pots and pans, footsteps scurrying along the stone floor. Indeterminate cooking smells and steam flooded the hallway.

They followed the hall until they popped out into a large room, bare save for a mammoth wooden table in the middle.

"All right?" A small, narrow-faced girl looked up from her darning.

"Our missus is up there, visiting," Joan said with a flick of her head to gesture upstairs.

The girl nodded, turning her attention back to the lace shawl in her hands. "Help yaself to the pot."

She gestured with her needle to the tin kettle atop the stove.

Joan poured two cups and handed one to Spencer before throwing herself into one of the uncomfortable-looking chairs.

"Ahh, that's better. Bin on our feet all morning, ain't we." Joan was addressing Spencer, but her eyes were trained on the young maid at the other end of the table.

As soon as she glanced up, Joan pounced. "We work for a lady detective. Your missus has hired her, like."

The girl gazed at her with wide eyes and swallowed hard.

"I'm Joan and this here absolute cove is Mr. Sweetman."

The girl shot a glance at Spencer, then back to her darning, two spots of color burning at her cheeks. "Elsie."

"Hectic ol' day," Joan said conversationally. "Lots of detective work to do. Our lady is busy, but she's taking on this job for Lady Cobham. Wants her help to find Fancy, the dog. Thinks it's been stolen, like."

Elsie bit her lip and jabbed at the fabric in her hands.

"You know anything about it?"

Elsie nodded, an unhappy turn to her lip. "She's wasting her time. She won't find it."

Joan wiggled her eyebrows at Spencer—*here we go*, they said.

Elsie put her darning down. "It weren't no one's fault. Not really. That dog was a horror. Always yapping and pishing everywhere. She used to make us take it outside for a walk every two hours, but when you got a million other jobs to do, we didn't always have time."

Spencer noted the past tense.

Joan stroked her chin and nodded. "Got the hump and did away with it, did ya?"

"Wot? Nah. We'd leave it out in the courtyard until one of us found a minute. It was nice sometimes to get some fresh air but other times. . . well, the graft don't stop because a dog needs a jipper. One morning the milk boy comes and leaves the door open, don't he."

Joan shot Spencer a look, which told him she had worked out what was coming.

"The devil of a thing was always making for the tradesmen, but Johnny was already in the cart. By the time he saw it, it was too late."

Joan breathed out a sound of concern. "Why didn't you just tell her?"

Elsie's eyes widened and her mouth dropped open. "Tell her?" She shook her head. "We'd all lose our jobs. The milk boy would lose his job. The horse driving the carriage would lose its job too. She loved that dog more than she loves her kin."

To be fair, Spencer hadn't liked the dog at all, but he liked it more than he liked her kin, having been at school with them both. Her kin was two sons: a weak-chinned man who referred to himself in the third person and spat when he talked, and one who had fled to the Continent to escape a scandal involving a young boy.

"This way is kinder." The chatty maid went on. "She thinks someone's snatched him up for being so adorable. Sleeping on someone else's bed, eating someone else's food. He used to eat better than we did. Two meals, Cook had to make. One for her and one for that mutt. His favorite dessert was crème brûlée," she said with disgust.

Eccentric figures like Lady Cobham were nothing new to Spencer. Society was full of them. People with unlimited funds, limited real-life education, surrounded by people who could not, or would not, tell them no. It was not unusual for their outlandish behavior to seep into the lives of their staff. Not unusual, but it still angered Spencer. That a dog ate better than the staff keeping this large house running, for one lady no less, seemed the ultimate in unjustness. Which is why he wanted nothing to do with society and its nonsense. He would not participate in it. The senseless rules, the snobbery, the gossip, the sheer bloody stupidness of it all.

Only now he had to. He pulled at his collar, suddenly feeling very hot.

A bell rang out. The girl jumped as if jabbed with a hot iron and let out a deep, heartfelt sigh. She pressed the heels of hands to her eyes for a moment.

"Please. Don't tell ya missus. We'll lose our positions without a letter of recommendation."

"Of course." Joan nodded, and the girl bolted from the room.

Spencer lifted the cup to his mouth, grimacing at the mouthful of cold tea. He and Joan were finally alone. Now was his time to find out just what the countess was up to.

"What do you think she'll do when we tell her this?" he asked.

Joan rolled her eyes. "Hard to tell what she'll ever do, to be honest."

"I suppose she could take the payment and pretend to look for the dog."

Joan shot a fierce stare. "Oi. We don't work like that. We do the job, and we gets paid fair for it." She gazed off into the distance and took another sip of her tea. "Only we ain't getting paid fairs," she muttered. "Too bloody soft she is."

"Who? The countess?"

"Albertine." She said her name like a correction.

He thought of Albertine. There was something soft about her. When their hands had touched earlier, she had been soft to touch, but soft *in* touch too. There was a callousness in the men he usually dealt with, a hardness. They'd lie to your face, promise never to break the law again while their hand was rummaging in your pocketbook. But not Albertine.

Under what circumstances could a woman so soft murder a man? Or two?

"She is unusual," he said.

Joan turned to him with a sharp look and searched his face. "Aye, she is. You won't find another like her, that's for sure. And that's what makes her so special." Her tone was forceful and held a note of warning.

So, all staff enjoyed sport at their employers' expense, except Joan?

"How long have you worked for her?"

Joan took a gulp of her tea and gazed around the room. "A while now."

He waited, but she offered nothing further.

"She's a good person. But . . . it's hard, innit. It's all right for you lot."

He jolted. Had she worked out who, and what, he was?

"My lot?"

"Men. And even better if you're one of them up there." She jerked her head upward to indicate upstairs. "Then you can do what you like. Not us. We have to do what we're told. Sometimes . . ." She blinked at the ceiling. "Sometimes it's nice to think that you might be able to do what you want. Even for a little bit. Have some fun, do things outside the box we're shoved in."

Spencer nodded. He understood that feeling all too well.

"Is that what London is? Fun? Without the count?"

Joan sighed. "Yeh. Just supposed to be a bit of fun before . . ."

"Before what?"

"I don't know, Sweetman. Before I'm too old and crippled to have fun. Or I find someone like you to marry." She winked at him, but it felt forced, as if she had lost her cheer.

"What about the count and countess? Do they have a happy marriage?"

Joan smirked. "I'd say it's the happiest it's ever been."

"They enjoy being apart?"

That smirk again. What did Joan find so funny? "Oh aye, it works best for them."

"And when will he be back?"

"Who?"

"The count. Albert."

Joan laughed. "Albert, is it? Who can say? He marches to the beat of his own drum. Very much like Albertine. Very much."

Spencer studied her averted face. A flush had begun its way up her neck. "Where is the count now?"

The housekeeper they had met on their way in popped her head into the doorway. "Your lady is leaving."

Joan winked at him, and he couldn't help but feel as if she were relieved to have their conversation interrupted.

They moved through the rabbit warren of hallways in silence. Spencer blinked into the tepid sunshine, sucking in deep breaths of the air he usually tried to avoid. He never thought he would describe London's air as *fresh,* but he hadn't fully realized how oppressive the dimly lit, polluted rooms of the servants' areas had been. The smells of the kitchen seemed to hang on his clothes, in his hair. He imagined he could even smell it on his breath.

They trudged back up the damp stairs. Albertine was standing on the roadside, tapping her foot. Her face erupted into a smile when she saw them.

"Am I glad to see you two." She linked her arm through Joan's and strode off along the street.

"She is awful. Truly, the most terrible person I've ever met. She fires her staff so frequently that she calls them all Mary so she doesn't have to learn new names. I think the dog saw an opportunity for freedom and made a break for it. Ugh."

She unlinked her arm and shook her hands in the air as if ridding herself of a sticky substance.

Upon seeing the looks Spencer and Joan were giving her, she stopped walking. "Oh, dear. What did you learn?"

Joan looked at Spencer expectantly.

*Thank you, Joan.* "The milk boy ran the dog over," he said. No point in beating around the bush. "Have you any other jobs? This one is a dead end."

Both ladies looked at him and burst into laughter. It took a moment for him to realize what he'd said, as unintentional it was, but was soon smiling himself. Their laughter was infectious, and the bubble in his chest expanded.

"Excuse the pun."

"Wonders." Albertine sighed and gazed up at the white-faced house. "I have a feeling she wasn't planning to pay me, anyway. Doesn't believe in women working."

"Onwards then," Spencer said.

Albertine continued gazing up at the townhouse. "Not so quickly. I feel for her. She really loves—loved—that dog. While she is possibly the meanest lady I've ever met, I do still wish there was something I could do for her."

"Uh oh," Joan said as she elbowed Spencer. "See that look. That means hold on to your hat because she's about to convince you to do something you would've sworn you'd never do."

Albertine smiled at Joan, and when she turned her gaze to Spencer, it was as if time stopped. That smile did something funny to him. She had a beautiful smile, all straight teeth and full lips, and a small dimple in her left cheek.

He pressed his fist to his chest. The tip of her tongue appeared between those distracting lips, and she raised her eyebrows at him.

"Are there many things you've sworn never to do, Spencer?"

He dragged his gaze from her mouth. What the hell was happening to him? He was short of breath, winded, as if he'd run a race.

"Not many things, no." He was dazed into telling her the truth.

The answer seemed to please her, and suddenly all he wanted to do was please her. *To see that expression in bed, her hair untied and in his hands, whispering sweet words that made her smile.*

"Hopefully pretending to find a missing dog, but actually finding one that looks similar to a dead one and passing it off as the dead one isn't on that list."

His mouth dropped open as she spun on her heel and continued her walk along the street.

Joan looked at him with resigned eyebrows and linked her arm through his. "Told ya so," she said with resignation. "Looks like we're finding a dog."

# CHAPTER 9

Number Sixty-five Piccadilly was a nondescript, drab shop. At the shabby end of the popular road, the store sat glumly amongst matching dingy shops. Their windows were grimy, or patched with wood, black with soot.

Gone were the lively customers, ducking in and out of the market stalls. Even the cramped traffic appeared to have abated. This part of the street had a curious, still air about it . . . as if it was waiting.

Albertine lifted the curtain of the carriage and peered out.

The window announced: *John Taylor, Shoemaker.* It was as if one man had said to another *Make a shop, and make it cheap.* Everything about it, street front to the signage, was cursory— from the darkened window, which was unusual for a shoemaker, to the poorly executed sign hanging drunkenly from its hook. Usually shoemakers sat in the window to complete their work. This let them utilize the natural light, saving their eyes, but also served to showcase their skill.

But John Taylor's window was plastered with old newspapers. Why on earth was he advertising himself as a shoemaker if he was an animal market? She gazed at the dilapidated building.

Something smelled fishy, and not just the large piles of manure that lined the road.

"It looks closed. Is the address correct?" Albertine brought her nail to her mouth and chewed.

Spencer's face was as shuttered as the window. He appeared displeased, although she couldn't fathom why. His usual jovial nature had dissipated the closer they had gotten to the address on the note they had received.

They had rushed home from Lady Cobham's house, Albertine's mind whirling. An advertisement she had seen in the newspaper that very morning while checking for further news of Grendel's death had sprung an idea on what to do about Fancy.

She swallowed at the lump in her throat at the thought of the newspaper. It had announced that police were certain the murderer of Lord Grendel was an attendee of the party and were closing in. Naturally she supported the police in finding murderers, but she couldn't help but take the printed words personally.

Her heart began to pound and she took a deep breath. She ran her thumb along her bangle. The thought of the beads being found in Grendel's study rang through her mind like a catchy tune. She had to do something. But what?

She would think of something, she always did, but right now focusing on finding a fake Fancy was the only thing giving her any relief.

The advertisement that had given her the idea had read: *Pedigree dogs available. All breeds, all sizes. Bring home your next plucky pal. Contact John Taylor of Taylor's Animal Market.*

She had dashed a note off, asking the John Taylor of the advertisement if he had any white and black terriers; she had included the professional photo of Fancy that Lady Cobham had provided, dressed in a tiny waistcoat and perched on a tasseled cushion. He had returned a note promptly stating that it was just her luck, as he had one that looked much like it, found homeless and wandering the streets that very morning, perhaps it might be the one she was seeking?

"That'll be it." Spencer's tone was flat.

A small shiver crept along Albertine's spine as she gazed at the street. Market carts toiled slowly along the street, groaning under the weight of its cargo. The road beneath them was filthy, strewn with rubbish and rotting cabbages. Rustic-looking men, who were as familiar as the men on the estate of Crawford house, walked beside the carts, pulled by donkeys instead of horses.

For a moment she could imagine herself back in Wednesbury, that these men were the tenant farmers making their way into the little village she had called home.

The door to the shoemaker opened, and a slight man in a tall top hat stepped out. He carried a small terrier in a wire cage and had a strangely shaped canvas bag over his shoulder. The red of his waistcoat flashed as his leery green coat flapped around him.

"Jack Black," Spencer said with a narrowed gaze. "The Queen's rat catcher, if you believe everything he says. Which I wouldn't. Rather famous around this area."

She didn't ask him how he knew who or what was famous in this area. She supposed this kind of thing was Spencer's real life. The West End theater shows bought out a whole range of people. Pickpockets, and easy women working together, preying on the swells that ascended on the area. Was Spencer part of a gang that stole from drunk and foolish swells? Perhaps he worked with a beautiful woman who slipped her hands into drunken men's pockets while he distracted their women with those leonine eyes and perfect visage. To avoid the strange knife of pain in her chest that thought bought her, she turned her focus back on to the rat catcher.

He waddled along the street, unbalanced by the yapping dog in the cage and the oddly shaped canvas bag slung over his shoulder. The bag was lumpy and appeared to be . . . moving?

"Is that bag," she swallowed, "full of rats?"

Spencer nodded as he picked up his hat from the bench seat and placed it on his head. "I don't think this John Taylor is entirely who he says he is. I suggest you stay in the carriage."

Albertine looked at him, aghast. She had been certain he was joking, but his usually good-humored face was now utterly humorless.

"I appreciate your chivalrous offer, but I decline. You are employed to be the face of my business. This does not mean you actually are in charge. I am more than capable of handling myself."

He met her gaze. She flicked her head and met his gaze with what she hoped was an arch one. How dare he? She was more than capable of purchasing a dog from an animal market.

They held each other's gaze for a long moment until Spencer broke the tension with a smile.

"As you wish."

He opened the carriage door and vaulted out with the bounce of a man years his junior. Blasted men and their trousers, she thought.

Albertine allowed him to assist her from the carriage, their gloved hands grasped tightly. His hand was warm and strong. He didn't release her until he had checked she was safely positioned on the roadside. For a common street criminal he really did have impeccable manners. She ran an assessing gaze along his outfit. He was very well put together; his boots sturdy and well shined, the hems of his trousers didn't appear to have been turned, and his clothes were not patched. Despite this he must be rather down on his luck to have accepted their position. The man hadn't even tried to negotiate his wage!

Spencer gave Albertine a questioning look and she realized her hand was still clasped in his. She released it with a small pang of reluctance. How strange that she should find his presence so comforting. Perhaps it was due to the nerves she'd suffered ever since she'd seen Inspector Mitchell at Grendel House. She'd meant every word said to Joan—she truly didn't believe that her sleeping draught had killed Grendel, but her mind wouldn't stop whirring with possibilities. Perhaps he'd slept so deeply that he'd fallen and cracked his head? that he'd fallen and cracked his head? She needed to find out how he had died—but how?

Spencer hesitated at the door to John Taylor's shop. It took a moment for the smell to hit Albertine and she gagged—the air was humid and smelled of wet dog and excrement.

Lots and lots of excrement.

Rummaging in her reticle, she pulled out her handkerchief and pressed it against her face. Only then did she dare to breathe again.

The room was dingy and dim, bursting with dogs of all shapes and sizes.

A cacophony of barking and howling had begun at the jangle of the bell above the door.

"Shuddup." A voice roared over the din.

A door on the back wall opened and an enormous man stepped through. Clad in a patchy velveteen jacket with dirty ivory buttons, a striped waistcoat, and a faded and stained neckcloth tied in a great bow around his neck, the man stopped and stared at Spencer and Albertine. She could almost see the cogs of his mind cranking like the tin soldier Papa had built for her when she was a child. When she cranked the handle, the toy's arms and legs would jerk about, causing her and Algie to laugh, no matter how many times she cranked it.

The moment he clocked who they were, his posture changed. He stood straighter, puffed his chest, and his irritable expression morphed into a crawling, ingratiating smile that turned Albertine's stomach.

A wave of gratitude for Spencer's large, comforting presence overcame her and without thinking, she placed her hand on his arm. His gaze slipped from her hand to her eyes and whatever he saw there caused him to place his hand over hers and squeeze gently. His grip was firm, but his touch tender.

"We's Mister and Missus 'olmes," Spencer said in a low voice that gave her a little thrill. His accent had changed, the vowels flattened and rougher. "We sent over the note, 'bout the dog.'

Albertine tried not to smile. He was good. Very good. *What luck had bought such a man to her doorstep?*

The robust, square man moved toward Spencer with an outstretched hand. "Yes, yes. The Holmeses. About the dog. I remember. Ya looking for a certain type of dog."

The men shook hands, and the man nodded in welcome to Albertine.

"John Taylor, at your service."

Taylor, or at least the man calling himself such, had a bulbous nose and wet, fleshy lips. His light gray eyes were sharp and glinted with cunning. His hair hung in greasy locks over his neck and ears. Everything about him was disturbing in the extreme.

"Come closer to the fire and we'll talk about this dog, eh?"

The last thing Albertine wanted to do was to walk further into the stench, but it appeared she had little choice. Shooting her an apologetic look, Spencer released her hand and gestured to the corner of the room, where a feeble fire burned.

The dogs restarted their barking as they entered into the room and Taylor kicked a cage with his ancient Wellingtons, sending it scuttering along the floor.

"Shuddup," he growled again.

Albertine tensed, as did the dogs, all quietening in their cages, watching her and Spencer with distrustful gazes.

There were twelve cages stacked against the wall, filled with sixteen dogs, but not a single one would have passed as Fancy.

Fumbling in his pocket, John Taylor took out a pipe and spent an inordinate amount of time lighting it. His cheeks rounded as he puffed to ignite it. When finally satisfied, he let out a long plume of blue smoke and showed them his teeth, or what was left of them.

"Yous looking for a terrier?" he confirmed.

Spencer nodded. "A small black and white one."

Taylor scratched his head.

"My boy can find you one. But terriers. Hmmm." He puffed on his pipe with an air of consideration. "Costly."

Albertine fought the urge to roll her eyes.

"I reckon we could find you one for six guineas."

Albertine choked a startled cough. Six guineas! She didn't have six guineas, let alone six to spare. Beside her, Spencer didn't so much as move an inch. Not a flicker, not a twitch. He could have been made of stone. Again, she was struck by his acting skills. He was a formidable ally.

"Your needs are particular, are they not?" Taylor said with wide-eyed innocence. "That's a lot of running around for my boy. Hard to find, those terriers."

"You said in your note that you already had one."

He turned his sharp gaze on her and Albertine resisted to the urge to take a step away from the man.

"They is popular, so they is."

Albertine knew that they could tell Lady Cobham Fancy had been found and was being held to ransom, and she would pay it to ensure his safe return. She had said as much herself. All she wanted was Fancy home, unhurt. But six guineas was a lot of money and Albertine couldn't help but feel once Lady Cobham had paid the ransom, she wouldn't feel the need to pay Albertine as well.

If she had ever intended to pay her.

Lady Cobham had turned a critical eye upon on Albertine and informed her that she disapproved of women working. Pretending to be a wealthy countess really put her in a sticky spot. On one hand, as a wealthy countess, she shouldn't need money, but on the other, she desperately needed money. Her eyelids fluttered with frustration. She had hired Spencer to avoid working for free, but here she was, now paying employees but still not making money.

But there was something about the way the old lady's voice had quivered as she spoke about the little dog, her only friend. How she had glared furiously at Albertine as her eyes had started to fill, denying their existence by blowing her nose and complaining about the dust in the room. It was clear that her heart was broken, and her refusal to give up hope that Fancy was out there being cared for had reminded Albertine of herself. There was nothing wrong with believing in the impossible— sometimes it was all one had. Albertine knew what it was to be alone in the world. In some way finding a new dog for Lady Cobham to love was akin to Albertine finding love for herself. If Lady Cobham, as nasty and unkind as she was, had someone to love, then surely Albertine could as well.

"They are," Spencer agreed. "But six guineas for a stray you've picked up off the street is a lot. We'll give you four."

The door to the street banged open, and the bell clanged loudly, setting the dogs off their barking again. A filthy boy of indeterminate age appeared in the doorway, pulling a strange wheeled cage contraption behind him.

Mr. Taylor smiled around his pipe and puffed with a self-satisfied air. The boy bought in a burst of welcome fresh air, but also a new smell. Albertine pressed her handkerchief back against her mouth.

"I got you that terrier," he said to John Taylor.

In the wheeled cage sat a white and black spotted terrier. Although brown and black would have been a more accurate description. A layer of smut clung to the dog's body, from paws to mid body. It had clearly been lifted from the street. Its fur was matted and filthy and while it wasn't a replica of Fancy with a wash, a brush, and some food, it might pass. Depending how bad Lady Cobham's eyes were.

Taylor bared his teeth around the pipe. "Six guineas."

"Four," Spencer replied in a hard voice.

Taylor eyed Spencer with a narrowed gaze. Even the dogs had stilled. The only sound was the quiet hiss of his pipe as the man sucked on it.

"Put him in the river," he directed to the boy.

"Wait!" Albertine cried.

He glared at her and Albertine saw the true hardness of him. He wasn't pretending in the hopes of getting two more guineas out of them. He would kill the dog simply as a business decision.

"Wait. You can have your six guineas," Albertine spat.

Spencer grasped her hand. "Missus 'olmes. Six is daylight robbery."

It was. She knew that. The bigger problem was she didn't have six guineas. They would have to go across town to inform Lady Cobham that she had found Fancy, who, as she had feared, was being held to ransom. If Lady Cobham didn't happen to have six guineas lying about, they would then need to wait until she had attended to her bank to withdraw the funds and trek back across town.

In that time, she feared that the despicable Mr. Taylor would change his mind and on their return charge more for the dog. She looked at his smug countenance as he puffed on that foul-smelling pipe. He was more than likely intending to do just that. If she managed to squeeze six guineas from Lady Cobham, she could hardly go back asking for more. And then

Albertine would be further out of pocket. But what was she to do?

"Does the missus want her dog or not?" Taylor said.

Spencer's hand was still wound around hers and she squeezed it, grateful for the comfort. As if his hand had given her strength, she came to a decision.

"She does," Albertine answered.

"Then it's six guineas. Or this fella takes a little swim." He gestured to the dog in the cage. The dog sat up, ear pricked as if listening to the conversation, but at Taylor's gesture to him, emitted a loud sigh and lay down on, as if their conversation had grown tedious.

"Tell ya wot. I'll even throw the cage in," Taylor said.

The urchin's head whipped around to Taylor. "Oi, that's my cage."

The cage was roughly made; scavenged pieces of different types of wire woven together and tied together with twine. It wasn't worth a shilling, let alone six guineas.

Spencer pulled on Albertine's hand lightly and they moved over to inspect the dog. Albertine bought her hanky back to her mouth. The dog smelled like the Thames. It cracked one eyelid as they neared, but didn't sit up. Albertine put a finger to the cage.

"Hello there, boy." She looked up at Taylor. "It *is* a boy?"

*That* she wouldn't be able to fool Lady Cobham with.

"Have a look for yaself. Know what ya looking for?" he said with a mocking laugh.

Albertine raised an arch brow at him. "It's not *always* difficult to find."

The boy laughed and Taylor shot him a dark look, lurching forward with a raised hand. The boy jerked out of reach.

"That's enough."

Even Albertine started at Spencer's tone. It was firm and masterful. She bent her head to hide her smile. From the corner of her eye, she saw him pull something from his pocket and drop it into Taylor's hand with a rattle.

Guineas?

Where on earth did Spencer Sweetman find six guineas?

Greed shone in Taylor's eyes as he lifted each coin to his lip and bit each one to check they were real. When satisfied, he nodded toward the dog.

Taylor opened his mouth to speak but Spencer flicked his coat, holding it open as if showing Taylor something inside it. Whatever Taylor had been about to say died, and he took a step backward.

"There ya go. Hope he enjoys a long life with ya. If ya ever need another doggy, you know where to find me."

Albertine hoped they never saw this man as long as they lived.

Spencer fastened his jacket and grasped the rope that formed the handle of the cage. He gestured to her with his head. "Let's get outta here, Missus. It's time to go."

She couldn't have agreed more.

They burst out the door, sucking in deep gulps of fresh air. Albertine fought the tears that welled in her eyes. Spencer watched her with the expression she imagined all men had when confronted with tears—a mixture of helplessness and a desire to run as far away as possible.

"Those poor dogs." She turned to him and clutched his arm. "I wish there was something we could do for them." She bit her lip in thought. "Perhaps we could come back this evening and break them all free?"

Spencer sighed and, for a moment, looked as if he were considering it. "Then what? All those dogs on the streets? With nothing to eat? They have a better chance of getting a home there with him."

She leveled a hard look at him. "Those dogs are off to the butchers, not loving homes."

Spencer grimaced and looked back at the shop. "You're possibly right, but we are here for Fancy."

As if it could sense they were talking about it, the dog growled and lunged at Spencer's hand through the cage.

"Poor thing is scared."

Spencer looked at the dog with distaste. "He smells. Appallingly."

"Oh hush," she said. "He can hear you."

"He speaks English does he?"

"Of course, he does," she said with a wrinkled nose. "Anyone can see this is a clever English doggo."

Spencer's gaze dropped to the filthy dog, a doubting cast to his expression. "French, German, I'm not bothered. All I care about is that he can pass for Fancy."

They crossed the street to the waiting carriage, the prickle of watchful eyes at her neck. Spencer handed the dog to the driver.

"What are you doing? He can't sit there out in the cold," Albertine exclaimed.

"He is not sitting in here with us. He smells."

"He'll be scared." She gazed at Spencer with wide, pleading eyes.

He closed his eyes and pinched the bridge of his nose. "Albertine. Up until a minute ago, he was a stray dog wandering the streets and scavenging for food. He will cope with a carriage ride outside."

She considered her options. He had a point. The dog did smell.

"Fine." Albertine began to unbutton her coat.

"What are you doing?" He watched her fingers move over her buttons with a look she couldn't decipher.

"I'm removing my coat to put it over the cage to keep him warm."

Spencer stared at her a long moment before shrugging out of his coat with a resigned expression. "Please get in the carriage. It's freezing out here."

She smiled at him brightly. "You have a soft spot for him already, don't you? I can tell."

He dead-eyed the dog. "You really cannot, because I really do not."

Albertine continued to smile. She had noticed how he had carefully checked the cage was securely fastened before laying his coat over it.

The coat jogged her memory.

"What's in your pocket, Spencer?"

"Hmm?" Spencer busied himself with opening the carriage door.

"I saw you show Taylor something. He seemed scared. I thought he was going to demand more money and then . . ."

"Oh, that," Spencer shot her a wink. "Just my flintlock revolver."

Her eyes widened but before she could say anything further he bustled her into the carriage, threw himself into the seat beside her, and shut the door.

Spencer Sweetman was an enigma. A riddle to solve. That was the only reason her nerve endings were performing a polka. That was the only reason she couldn't take her eyes off the way his jacket clung to his broad shoulders, or how his thighs strained against the fabric of his trousers. She ripped her gaze away from him and stared out the window, fanning her face with her glove.

Yes, it was that he was a puzzle. That, and only that.

# CHAPTER 10

Albertine clapped her hands briskly. Both Spencer and Joan glanced at her but she was looking at the dog.

"Are you going to be a good boy for me?" Albertine crooned.

The mutt stood on his back legs and nipped at Albertine. She scooped him up in her arms and allowed him to lick her face.

Spencer's skin began to heat as the dog nibbled at her ear, and she laughed in delight. "Ooh," she moaned, "you saucy little boy."

Spencer had to look away. *Think of something else, man.*

Still. The way she tilted her neck and laughed with pleasure was doing strange things to his insides.

Albertine placed fake Fancy back on the ground and straightened, meeting Spencer's gaze. Her eyes were bright with excitement.

"Are we clear on what we're all doing?"

Spencer smiled. He organized teams of men, in dangerously perilous situations, life or death situations, but he would be hard pressed to have found a man as organized and passionate about a task as Albertine was about this.

"We are rehoming this little . . . fellow . . . to Lady Cobham, where he hopefully lives a long life full of crème brûlée."

Albertine had sent a note to Lady Cobham informing her that the dog had been found, and under pressing from both Joan and Spencer had added a note that the ransom had been six guineas.

They'd received a note an hour later, delivered by one of her footmen, demanding Fancy's immediate return. The note had also included six guineas, which Albertine had handed directly to Spencer.

He was more confused than ever about what was happening here. She must be playing a long game. A missed opportunity to increase the ransom and skim a bit of cream off the top, she had pressed the coins into his hand immediately. He was yet to see any evidence that she was anything other than a lovely, kind-hearted, attractive woman.

Mitchell had informed Spencer that during his visit Albertine had been reading a paper about Grendel's death, but had completely denied knowing anything about it—much like she had denied remembering meeting him at the ball. She had lied, it was impossible to deny, but she seemed to approach everything else in her life with complete honesty. Spencer was never confused, and he didn't like the new sensation. It was as if the ground kept moving around him, and he was unsure where to place his feet next. His intuition, which he had relied on for so long told him one thing—that this woman was no killer, but that same intuition told him something wasn't right here either.

"I must admit, I will quite miss this little doggo," she said as she patted fake Fancy on the head.

Spencer watched with mounting horror as the dog pawed at her skirts and began humping her leg.

She smiled fondly. "Do you want to dance, baby dog?" Grabbing his paws, she began to do a little jig. "The Dance of Life, my Papa used to call that."

Spencer swallowed, his mouth suddenly dry.

Albertine let out a peal of delighted laughter. "Your expression! Yes, I do know what it is he's doing. I grew up in the country."

Spencer clung to the small nugget of information to take his mind off the "dance of life." "I'm a county boy myself. Where did you grow up?"

"You're a country boy?" She narrowed her eyes at him. "I would not have guessed that at all. You seem so . . . well versed in the ways of the city."

He nodded. "I grew up in the country, but I love the city. I have lived here since . . . well, for many years."

"Do you?" She wrinkled her nose. "I much prefer the countryside. There is no birdsong here, and some days it seems there is no light either. It often feels as if you can't ever get a moment alone. Even"—she gestured out the window—"the parks are cages."

Something twanged in his chest.

She went on. "I love the smell of the forest after rain, the freshness of the soil, the sounds. The smell of grass, flowers, trees. Here I wipe my face with a handkerchief after being outside and it comes away black."

Two pink spots brightened her cheeks as she spoke. She looked particularly beautiful, he thought, when she was passionate about something.

"Why are you here then?"

She let out a sigh that seemed to shake her whole body. "Here is merely a carriage stop along my true path."

"Where to?"

"Freedom," she muttered.

"Beg pardon?"

"Cornwall. The Cornish coast is the most beautiful place I have ever seen in my life. Papa took us there once."

He stiffened. Cornwall. Trentham Hall was on the coast of Cornwall.

"It's the last time we were all together and happy. That is where I want to live. I want to spend my days walking the coastline, tending to my garden, and enjoying the sea air."

Spencer grimaced. The idea of spending his days in Cornwall felt very much like a noose around his neck.

"It is bitterly cold in winter. The fog will make it impossible to see a foot in front of you, let alone the coastline. You'll spend months damp, cold and restricted to your rooms as outside is intolerable." His shoulders had risen toward his ears, much as his voice had.

Albertine blinked at him. "What on earth did Cornwell ever do to deserve your ire?"

He thought of Trentham Hall, the gothic ducal palace he had grown up in. How the windows rattled in their frames. Frigid air blustered through hallways and the damp seemed to chase you, regardless of how many fires were lit, or how many layers of thick fabric they draped over the windows and called furnishings.

He'd hated coming home from school once he had escaped to Eton. While other boys longed for home and the comfort and privacy it provided, he had missed the sounds and warmth of the other bodies in the dormitory. His room at Trentham was located at the back of the west wing, overlooking the woods that surrounded their property. He'd hated moving from the nursery into the gargantuan room on the third floor of the house. Stephen had been three doors away, separated by two dressing rooms, but it had felt like miles.

His childhood memories were of lying awake at night listening to the house chatter away with the sounds of mice, wind, and trees. Stephen, as the eldest, had left for school first, and the nightly check-ins between them had stopped. Spencer learned it was easier to keep busy, to distract himself then expect anyone at Trentham to care about how he felt.

And once he had left, he'd sworn he would never go back.

Spencer ground his teeth. There was no point in thinking about all that. It had all happened how it happened and thinking about it served no one.

Least of all himself.

"Where are you?"

He startled. Albertine was staring at him with a tilted head and a quizzical expression.

"Where did you go just now?"

"Go? I was right here, Countess." He took a breath and forced his shoulders down.

"You looked as if you were miles away. And not in a particularly happy place."

He felt exposed. She didn't miss anything. He lifted a shoulder dismissively. "Just woolgathering."

The dog in her arms looked up and bared its teeth. "I was thinking about how appropriate this awful dog is for Lady Cobham."

The dog barked and squirmed in Albertine's arms as if taking offence. Let me at him, his yap demanded.

Albertine rested her head against the dog's wiry fur. "Hush now. That mean man is just making sport, weren't you, Spencer? Say sorry, you've hurt doggy's feelings."

"Sorry, little chap. All in good fun, eh?" He held his upturned palm out to the dog, who shied away from it dismissively.

*Good god.* He was apologizing to a dog for hurting its feelings. He needed to wrap this case up and get away from this woman. She was bad for him. She bought out too many feelings. Imagine if one of his men saw him now. They'd have him committed.

And he'd deserve it.

"I cannot imagine why you've taken such a dislike to this little doggy. He's just lovely. Aren't you, Fancy? Just divine."

Spencer looked the dog over. Albertine and Joan had given the dog a wash and a brush, and while it was certainly more presentable, it was no more agreeable. Its fur was wiry and oddly shaped. Hair drooped over its mouth like a sad little moustache. Its body was as wide as it was long and its legs were far too short. It was one of the ugliest animals he had ever seen in his life, and that was before one got to know its aggressive personality. There was little, if anything, that was divine about this dog, apart from the fact it looked close enough to the real Fancy to, hopefully, pass as it.

Frankly, he wanted to get rid of this dog as soon as he could.

Albertine snuggled her face into the dog, who let out a growl of pleasure. It hated everyone, except Albertine. There was something about her that even animals couldn't resist.

She pressed her nose against the dog's damp one, murmuring sweet nothings, and a realization crashed over him.

Whatever was happening between her and her husband, she was no murderer. She couldn't have had anything to do with Grendel's murder. He was going to head to Scotland Yard and have Mitchell remove her name from anything to do with the Grendel case.

He made a show of pulling his timepiece from his pocket. "I have an appointment I must attend. I won't be able to come with you to Lady Cobham's."

It was far too risky to go to her townhouse. He had gotten away with it once, but she was sure to be watching and waiting for the carriage with Fancy and he wanted to speak to Mitchell as soon as he could.

"But you won't get to say goodbye to Fancy." Her eyes were wide and filled with disappointment.

She walked to the window and Fancy glared at Spencer over her shoulder with watery eyes and bared his teeth.

Spencer bared his teeth in return. "So long, Fancy. Hope not to encounter you again. Toodle pip."

"You can take the rest of the afternoon off. After we return this dog, Joan and I are going to pay Lady Grendel a little visit." Her voice was stilted.

Spencer's stomach dropped. "Lady Grendel? Why, exactly?" he asked, Mitchell's report ringing in his ears.

*She's up to something*, Mitchell had said after interviewing her.

Albertine continued to stare out the window. Spencer stood behind her and joined her vigil. Mitchell sat on the park bench, a newspaper on his knees, his face turned toward them.

The hulking figure of Wallop leaned against a lamp post farther along the street.

Spencer shifted his gaze to the countess. Mitchell was yet to find anything out about her yet. She had just mentioned Cornwall and her father, which would have been the perfect opening for him to ask who her father was, if she had grown up near Cornwall, but all he could think about was how soft the tendrils of hair that framed her face looked. There was something about those little curls that made him want to reach out and tuck them behind her tiny shell-like ear. Her face was tipped back but when she turned to face him her eyes were strangely glassy, as if she were fighting tears.

"Countess . . ." His questions about her family died on his lips.

"I'm going to tell you something, Mr. Sweetman. Something rather irregular."

Spencer didn't speak. He had found over the course of his career that the less a man spoke, the more the other was encouraged to do so. He studied her face, the smattering of freckles along her nose, and suddenly he understood why women might be obsessed with bleaching creams and staying clear of the sun. The light smattering of freckles were enough to make him completely forget he was supposed to be investigating her.

"I need you to help me out the side window."

All thought of freckles evaporated. "I beg your pardon?"

"The window. I need you to assist me out it."

"Why?" Spencer all but spluttered.

"Why indeed, Mr. Sweetman, why indeed."

Silence stretched on between them. He waited for her to provide the answer to his question but she continued to stand there and stare at him as if he were the queer one for asking.

"Do you mind terribly if I ask why you're leaving the house out of a side window instead of the door?'

Albertine took a great breath as if steeling herself. "There is a man."

"A man?" She must've seen Mitchell and worked out she is under surveillance? Damn the man's shock of bright red hair. It was like a beacon.

"Yes, a man. Not a very nice man. Who is . . . unhappy . . . with me."

"Is he bothering you?"

"Yes, he is." Albertine's face was impassive but her lids blinked rapidly.

"The man I encountered on the street the day I got the position?"

"Yes."

*Wallop.* "I believe that one of the tasks you hired me for was to protect you against any men that *might happen*?" He raised his eyebrows at her and she smiled.

"Why don't you allow me to perform my task and remove this man?"

Albertine licked her lips in an utterly distracting manner. God, she was beautiful.

"Could you?"

Her bronze eyes gazed up at him, and he had the over-whelming desire to protect her at all costs. This woman was incapable of murdering a man. Of that he was certain.

"I absolutely could. Why don't you give me a couple of moments, and I shall ensure the coast is clear of any *happening men*, and you shall make your way to return this darling dog."

The smile Albertine gave him hit him like a train right in his chest. *Oh, this woman.* He was in big trouble.

★ ★ ★

The air was cool on Spencer's face as he strode down the front steps of Albertine's house.

Baron Wallop was resting his bulk against an iron lampshade, his head turned toward the lit window of what he knew to be Albertine's drawing room. A burst of anger shot through him.

"Wallop."

Wallop jumped at his name, so engrossed he had been in studying the window.

He pushed off the iron lamppost that had been supporting his cumbersome frame and Spencer fancied he heard it groan in relief.

"What are you doing?"

"I saw you go in and I . . . I wanted to know if you found the tiara. I was waiting for you, Your Grace."

His eyes slid back to the window as if a compulsion curse had been put upon him.

"I don't believe you." Spencer took a step toward him and Wallop stepped back.

"Is there a law that denies me the right to stand on the roadside here?"

Spencer lowered his eyebrows at him and uttered words he never thought he would, in a tone he almost never used. "*Your Grace.*"

"I beg your pardon?"

"When you speak to me, you will use the correct form of address." His voice was as hard as an iron bar. He would use that hateful moniker if it meant this man left Albertine alone.

Wallop stuck his tongue into his cheek and glanced back at the window. "Your Grace."

"Thank you. There is, in fact, a loitering law that stipulates no man may loiter in front of this particular square, and if my memory serves me"—he narrowed his eyes—"I can assure you my memory is sharp and very, very long, that same law states when an officer of Scotland Yard tells you to leave a suspect alone you should stay as far away as you possibly can."

Spencer took another step forward but this time Wallop didn't move. His breath was sour, like day-old brandy and ill health. He placed his finger on the poorly folded cravat tucked into Wallop's shirt, but when he saw the stains upon it, quickly removed his hand.

"If I see you around here again, I will have you arrested for interfering in a police investigation."

Wallop scoffed. "You can't arrest me, I'm a baron."

"I think you'll find I can do whatever the hell I like. I'm a duke."

The older man exhaled as if Spencer's words were a sharp jab to the stomach.

"Let's not fall out over this, Wallop." He placed his arms around Wallop's immense shoulders and turned him away from Albertine's house. "Let me do what I need to do. And trust me, I know what I'm doing."

Wallop's face reddened and he chewed his lip, as if considering how to respond. With one more glance to the window, his shoulders rounded and he nodded. "Right you are. It's just—" He cleared his throat. "I need that ruddy tiara back . . . Your Grace."

Spencer set his features. He doubted this tiara really existed, so what was it that Wallop wanted with the countess? Was it some sort of rejection/projection situation? Had she rejected Wallop, causing him to become obsessed with her? Spencer couldn't deny her attraction himself. She was a whirlwind. There was something more to this. While he was here with the countess, he would get Mitchell to look into Wallop further. Find out exactly what the connection was.

"Tell you what. Why don't we meet at my club?—wait, on second thought, we should go down to my offices tomorrow." There was no way Wallop would get into his club. They had five hundred years of standards to uphold. "And Mitchell will run you through the case."

Wallop looked up, his eyes shining. His chest puffed out and he stroked his chin. "Good show."

Spencer placed his hand on his back and pushed him into a trot. "Off you go, and leave this to us before you blow our chances at having a despicable criminal locked up for good."

"Good show. Good show. Yes, you're the man for the job. If anyone can do it, it's you, Your Grace."

Spencer stood and watched Wallop until he was out of sight. He turned toward the park. Mitchell raised his newspaper in the signal they had agreed up on earlier that indicated they were to convene around the corner.

Mitchell must have something he needed to speak to Spencer about, and he needed to inform Mitchell that Albertine was planning to call upon Lady Grendel, for reasons he couldn't quite understand. There had been a moment when he had forgotten himself, so certain that Albertine had nothing to do with Grendel's murder. But why was she planning to go see Lady Grendel if that was the case? There was something afoot here.

He had told Wallop that he knew what he was doing, but as the faces of the countess and the irrepressible Joan appeared at the window beside the door, he wondered if that was true at all.

# CHAPTER 11

"Crisps on toast. I am nervous about this, Joanie." Albertine's palms were damp and sticking unpleasantly to the fur on the underside of fake Fancy's body.

Joan raised an incredulous eyebrow. "Nervous? About this? Faking an old lady about her dearly departed dog? Ye will break into a man's drawers—"

"Shhh," Albertine hissed, gesturing toward the driver of the carriage. "His desk, Joan. Not his drawers. I'm not that hard up."

"You will be, coz she ain't going to pay," Joan warned darkly.

Albertine sighed. Joan was only reiterating what she had known from the moment she took the job. Lady Cobham would not pay. But that wasn't what this case had ever been about. Joan knew that she was a cranky old so-and-so, but there was something about the way she had talked about the missing dog that told her it was more important than she was letting on. She was awful, that was true, but that didn't change the fact at the heart of it, she was a lonely old lady with no one but her dog for company.

And Fancy, the fake one, didn't stand a chance out on the streets. Albertine rather felt like a matchmaking mama.

Knowing that the new Fancy was now looking at a life filled with treats and luxury gave her a warmth that she knew wasn't just about Fancy.

Is that what she dreamed of herself? For someone to pull her into their lap and hand-feed her chocolates? Suddenly an image of Spencer sliding a warm chocolate into her mouth popped into her head. *Where did that come from?*

"Why are you smiling?"

Joan's accusatory voice jolted Albertine back to the present. She shook her head. She didn't have time to think like that. No one was coming to save her; she had to save herself. And if saving this ugly homeless dog took her mind off the conundrum of who or what killed Grendel, then what harm was it?

She turned thoughts of Grendel's death over and over like a stone in her palm. One minute she was convinced it had nothing to do with her, the next she was terrified that the timing of him imbibing her draught and then dying could not be coincidence and she should leave London on the first available boat. To anywhere.

"Oh, nothing really, I was just thinking that Fancy has more chance of dying of too much love now. He doesn't know how lucky he is."

Joan eyed the dog with a curled lip. "I'd say. He's ungrateful about it really. Now, what are you going to do about that?"

Albertine jolted, her thoughts still on Grendel's death. "About what?"

"His terrible personality. Albertine!" *Were they talking about Grendel?* "You cannot pretend that you haven't noticed the dog tries to bite everyone that goes near it except you. You can't give Lady Cobham a dog that bites her! She'll know straight away."

A sigh of relief. They *were* talking about the dog. "I'll just say I got it wrong and take him home. I'd love you to come live with me, wouldn't I?" She addressed the dog in her arms. Fancy licked her face and she held him against her breast for a moment. She really would miss him.

"It's time for you to go to your new home," Albertine murmured to Fancy. "Be a good boy, please. This is a chance that millions of doggies would kill for. Don't mess it up. You can bite anyone you please, but not Lady Cobham. She might bite you back."

Fancy gazed up at her through cloudy blue eyes, panting as if in agreement.

"This is it, pal," she said softly. "Your one chance. A chance at a life you could never have imagined. All you have to do is give the love I know you have in your heart. She needs it."

Fancy lurched forward and licked Albertine's face. *I will*, his enthusiastic licking seemed to say, *I definitely will*.

"Shall we take him across the road to relieve himself first? Save him doing it on the carpet and losing his position before it begins?" Joan asked.

Albertine gazed across the road to the fenced park. There was a large iron railing around its perimeter, with a row of tall yew trees pressed along it for privacy. The gate on their corner currently stood open and Albertine knew there was a matching gate at the other end of the park.

"No, I can't take the risk of something happening. Let's just get him in there and get out."

The carriage door opened and Lady Cobham's footman lowered the step. He studied the dog, sitting studiously in Albertine's lap.

"Not bad," he said, nodding toward the dog. He lifted a hand to his forehead. You even got the . . . ear."

Albertine nodded. "Shoe blackener. Someone will have to reapply it every couple of days. And any time he gets wet."

The footman reached toward the dog to take him from Albertine's lap but snatched his hand away quickly as the dog bared his teeth and growled. The footman nodded and took a step backwards. "Got his personality right, too."

The dog yapped at the footman as if to hurry him along.

Albertine scrambled from the carriage, trying to manage both her skirts and the dog at the same time. The footman grasped her elbow as she stumbled down the step. Fancy lunged at him again, hanging on to his shirt sleeve.

The footman screamed and shook his arm, which only made Fancy hang on tighter. Albertine tumbled down the last remaining step. The footman waved his arm about and the dog clung on, swaying in the wind like a macabre ribbon.

Finally, he flung him off and fake Fancy landed with a thud on to the pavement.

There was a moment of perfect silence as they stared at the dog lying still on the pavement.

"Crisps, you've killed him!" Albertine yelled.

"He bit me! He's ripped me jacket," the footman yelled back indignantly. She knelt on to the pavement, running her hands over the dog's wiry fur. His little chest rose and fell and Albertine let out a sigh of relief. As if her expelled breath held magic, the dog lifted his head and gazed her through one watery eye. He sprung up and darted across the road, dodging the wheels of a passing carriage.

The three of them stood, mouths open watching the dog run like his life depended upon it. All the way across the park.

"Are you going to go after it?" Joan asked.

Albertine sighed, suddenly exhausted. Why couldn't one thing, just one thing, work out for her? She was vaguely aware of the footman extending his hand to her but she stayed on her knees, swaying slightly like a candle in the breeze. And that is how she felt. One puff of air away from being extinguished.

"Look. Here comes Sweetman."

Joan's voice held all the delight that Albertine knew hers would hold if she had seen him first. A wave of relief washed over her. Spencer would know what to do.

Clutching the footman's hand, she yanked herself from the ground, ignoring the pain in her knees.

"Was that . . .?" Spencer didn't need to finish his sentence.

It was as if he and Albertine understood each other perfectly well without words.

She nodded. "It was."

Spencer raised his eyebrows and tilted his head slightly in the manner he did when he was considering his next move.

"This dog will be the death of me," he muttered.

"He bit me!' The footman exclaimed, clearly appealing for more attention that he'd received from the ladies. "Ripped me jacket."

Spencer shrugged off his overcoat and held it out to the footman. He was wearing a crisp white shirt that made the green in his hazel eyes sparkle.

Joan intercepted the coat and hugged it to her body as though it were a baby. "He's gone, there's no use going after 'im. Cor, this smells good." Joan pressed his jacket to her face.

Spencer laughed, his teeth shining in the dim afternoon light.

*What was wrong with her?* Albertine thought. What was wrong with him? It was if he shone today, everything about him danced, glowed, or sparkled.

"Rightio, see you shortly. Hopefully with that blasted dog." Spencer doffed his hat at Albertine with a wink and tossed it to the footman before taking off across the street.

His hair had grown since he had first arrived on her door-step and Albertine watched as it bounced as he turned his head each way before taking off at a clip across the road. He was as fluid as water, all strong, boundless energy. His stride was long and easy and his shirt clung across his broad shoulders. There was something youthful about his movements and Albertine found herself wondering what kind of child he had been.

A rascal, she would place any money on. In a moment of levity she had seen a look pass across his face, almost of won-der, as if he couldn't quite believe he was smiling, having fun. Perhaps he'd had a hard life, a lonely life.

"Do ya reckon he'll find it?"

Joan's voice bought Albertine back to the present, and she exhaled a sigh through her nose. If anyone could, it would be him. Her belief in him surprised her somewhat. Since Papa and Algie were gone, she'd had only Joan to rely on. Now Spencer too, it seemed. She considered the tree-lined fence that surrounded the park. It was entirely possible that the gate on the opposite side of the enclosed park would be open and that the dog would run straight for it but something told her it wouldn't. If the dog was in that park, Spencer would find it and retrieve it.

"Do you know, I really rather do."

"Do you think we should go help him find the dratted thing?" Joan's tone told her she absolutely did not want to.

"Yes, I suppose we should."

Joan groaned.

"Don't you breathe a word of this to anyone," Albertine said in warning to the footman, who was still nursing his sleeve.

He looked up at her with wide eyes. "Me? I like my job, I ain't saying a word!"

She didn't think he would. It was interesting how awfully Lady Cobham behaved, renaming the maids to suit herself, treating her servants as one person, rather than individuals with their own lives and needs. She was a tyrant and yet . . . Albertine thought about the pact of silence the servants had seemed to have taken about the fate of the dog. She ran her gaze along the footman's uniform. A young, strapping lad he was, but cheerful and pleasant in a way that told her he was happy enough in his position.

Her only frame of reference was the servants of Crawford House. Who to her were more like part of the extended family. Papa had happily included Joan in Albertine's early learning and paid for the butler's son to attend the local school, written references, and given gifts to staff on births of babies and birthdays. Generations of the same family had worked at Crawford House for years, happy with their lot in life.

She eyed the footman again, who was now laughing with Joan over something. He seemed cheerful, the surly snobbishness of servants she had encountered in her time in London absent.

Albertine had assumed the silence about Fancy was designed to protect the servants and the milk boy, but now she wondered. Was it actually about protecting Lady Cobham? She loved that dog, and it appeared the dog was the only thing in the world that wasn't being paid to spend time with Lady Cobham.

Spencer appeared across the road with Fancy tucked beneath his arm like a bag of shopping. He crossed the road back to them and held Fancy out toward her.

"I found him with his head in a picnic basket." He glowered at the dog with a curled lip.

Albertine rubbed at a spot of jam on the dog's moustache and searched him for damage. All this dog had to do was live and her job was done.

"Thank you."

As she looked at Spencer, the sun moved from behind a cloud, filling the sky with bright, vivid color. It seemed to light Spencer. His hair shone, his skin sparkled and when he smiled back at her, her heart began to beat unsteadily.

"Wonders," she groaned.

"Sorry?" he looked at her, an eyebrow raised.

She cleared her throat. "Time to deliver this god. I mean dog. I shall meet you both at the park when the job is done."

Turning on her heel, she strode up the stairs. She needed to put some space between her and Spencer.

She had accused Joan of being naïve, but here she was acting like she had never seen an attractive man before.

But the truth was, she hadn't ever met someone like Spencer. His good cheer and comforting presence made anything, everything, seem possible.

*The way he had handled John Taylor.* She hadn't felt a moment's fear with him by her side. She turned back to him when she reached the top of the stairs.

He tilted his head as he gazed back at her. He looked awestruck, like a boy watching the stars, wondering about the mysteries of the universe.

*Is that how she looked when she gazed at him?* She definitely felt it. Something moved between their gazes, an acknowledgment of some sort. *I see you*, his eyes seemed to say. *I see you too*, hers said in return.

"All right then, off you go. Get rid of that mutt," Joan directed to Albertine as she threw Spencer's jacket at him. He caught it without taking his eyes from Albertine.

"Sweetman?" Joan jogged his arm.

He shook his head as if to clear it and nodded. "Yes, best of luck. Toodle pip, Fancy."

He raised a hand in farewell, and it was with a start that Albertine realized she had the dog in her arms. She'd completely forgotten about it.

★　★　★

Lord and Lady Grendel lived in an elegant four-story, crisp white villa on an exclusive street in Mayfair. Not on *the* most exclusive street, but due to being wedged between two very exclusive roads, it was able to claim the benefits of the fashionable address at a reduced price. Glossy black rails fenced off the servant's steps below and four gleaming marble steps led to a large door, the top half brightly colored stained glass. The brass hardware on the door shone in the dim spring sunshine.

Albertine sighed. As expected, Lady Cobham had not paid her. She'd not even stood as Albertine had entered with Fancy, but simply held her arms open for the dog. Albertine had found she hadn't minded after all as she'd watched the older lady bury her face into the dog's fur and sniffle. Fake Fancy, thankfully, had lapped up the attention, licking her face and yapping as if he had missed her too. Albertine had let herself out quietly before Lady Cobham could notice anything usual about her dog.

It wasn't just the dog that had her feeling discombobulated.

The conversation with Spencer back at her house had stirred up thoughts of Crawford House and the woodlands around it that, in her childhood, seemed to stretch on forever. She and Algie had spent days, months, years of their lives tramping alongside the stream, with a picnic lunch packed by Cook. Her collecting flowers, him examining the undergrowth for unusual and medicinal mushrooms and plants. It had never occurred to her that things would change.

That one day her brother wouldn't be around.

Hot tears filled her eyes, and she dug her nails into her palm.

So many of her daily thoughts were of conversations with Algie. Everything she knew about society, about London, about how someone could live on their wits, had come from him and his voracious reading habits.

"See here, Bertie, it says Sherlock was based on a real man, Dr. Joseph Bell. You just need to pay attention to the small things. The things people think don't matter. He worked for Scotland Yard," he'd said, awe coloring his voice.

"We'll go," she'd said. "When Papa discovers a cure for you, we will go to London, and we will go and see Scotland Yard, we will watch the men running about solving their mysteries. One day you'll be one of them."

He'd nodded but the happy light had died from his eyes. His body, once so strong and energetic, had begun to fail him, and it was becoming clear to all of them that no amount of science could help.

"Promise me you'll go, Bertie. Go to London and start your own detective agency. Solve mysteries like this," he waved the latest Holmes installation at her. "Like we said we'd do together. For me."

She had rested her head on his lap to hide her tears and promised him.

She shook her head and brought herself back to the here and now. *No more thoughts like that.*

"Right. Spencer will call upon Lady Grendel to pass on condolences. Joan and I will attend downstairs. Joan, you distract the servants and I'll sneak upstairs. I want to get into his study."

Joan nodded but Spencer looked unconvinced. "What do you want in his study?"

"The murderer might have left a clue." Didn't the man realize this was a murder investigation?

The oddest expression crept over his face, and he ran a hand along his jaw. He rather looked like he was trying not laugh.

"I dare say it is. Only one would hope Scotland Yard has searched his rooms and found any clues left behind."

"Yes," she said airily. "One would hope."

Only one *didn't* hope because one had only gone and dropped the dratted beads off their bangle somewhere in the dratted study and needed to try and retrieve them. With any luck the beads had rolled under some furniture and hadn't been found. Or found and deemed to be of no importance and tossed in the garbage. Her fingers worried at the bangle on her wrist. Perhaps she should dispose of the bracelet?

Only she couldn't. Algernon had made it for her, spending hours on it once he had been confined to his chair. Every detective needed a place to stash their emergency potions, he had said.

"What will you do if the study door is locked?" Spencer was looking at her curiously.

"Don't you worry about me, Mr. Sweetman."

*What a naysayer,* Albertine thought as she gazed at his doubting expression.

"Well, then, tally ho?"

"Aye," Joan asserted.

Bless her—Joan, at least, sounded as keen as mustard.

Spencer alit from the carriage and extended his hand to assist the ladies. Albertine thrilled at the feel of his large hand in hers—even through their gloves she could feel his warmth.

"Oops."

Instead of reaching for Spencer's outstretched hand, Joan had launched herself out the door at him. Her arms entwined around his neck, knocking his hat to the ground. Something black and oily twisted in Albertine's stomach as the two of them performed a little dance on the footpath, Spencer's head thrown back.

"Ooh you're so strong, so ye are," Joan jested. "Thank goodness."

Spencer groaned theatrically, "Ohhhh, my back. My back!"

Albertine screwed her face as Spencer hoisted Joan higher into his arms with an enviable ease. He took a step backward, and pretended to stumble as if under a great weight.

"Oh please, won't someone help me," he called out into the street.

They swayed and Joan's squealing laughter sang out into the air.

Albertine picked up Spencer's hat, working to keep a smile on her face. There was something about their easy humor that irritated her immensely. She didn't begrudge Joan a bit of fun—lord knows she deserved it after everything she had sacrificed. It was just that she often felt on the periphery with their easy repartee and laughter. There was something about Spencer that made her feel tingly and nervy, caused her to turn every word she might speak over and over as if a stone in her palm. She could never have thrown herself into his arms, and deep inside she knew if she did it wouldn't have been in jest.

She was jealous, she realized with a start. *Albertine wanted to know what Spencer's arms felt like holding her tightly.* What his chest felt like pressed against her, what it would feel like to have her legs wrapped around him.

"Put her down immediately." Albertine's tone was sharper than she had intended. "You are making a scene, and it is inappropriate."

It was as if she had doused him with ice water. Spencer's back straightened and he all but dropped Joan to the ground. His face was shuttered and he did not meet her eyes as he took his hat from her hand.

"My apologies," he said woodenly.

Joan, still laughing, straightened her dress and adjusted the tendrils of hair that had escaped from under her hat. "None from me. That was the ride of me life."

Stiff silence met her proclamation. Spencer lifted his chin and gazed blankly into the distance, his back ramrod straight, hands clasped behind his back.

"We shall reconvene around the corner in an hour." Albertine's tone was pinched. Emotions warred inside her. She was embarrassed about ruining their fun with her jealousy, but she couldn't very well admit that to them.

Spencer adjusted the brim of his hat, and straightened his sleeves, his face impassive. "Right you are."

He moved to the front door, and Joan and Albertine made their way down the servant's stairs.

"Joan, you can't act like that with him. He's a cracksman."

Joan shot her a disbelieving look. "A crook? Nah. I don't judge no one for being a bit down on their luck with the blunt." She raised a pointed eyebrow in Albertine's direction, "Nor should you. And anyway, he's one of the good ones. I can tell."

Albertine fought the urge to roll her eyes. Joan's exposure to men was limited to Albertine's father and brother; Walkens, their ancient butler; Jones, the gardener; and his son, a dim-witted and easily startled boy. And there was Joan, speaking like she was some sort of brothel owner who had seen thousands of men come and go and could make character judgments on sight.

"Well, I sincerely hope that is the case, however I do not want you to act like that with him. You might give him the wrong impression."

"The wrong impression?"

"He might think you have . . . intentions."

Joan burst into raucous laughter. "That's the right impression then, innit?"

She was still laughing as Albertine pressed herself into a dark corner of the basement entrance. Joan raised her hand and knocked on the servant's door twice.

Albertine crept up the servant's stair, Joan's voice decreasing in volume as she made her way up the bare, creaky staircase. Several doors punctuated the stairway, each leading to various parts of the building. Grendel's study was on the first floor, toward the back of the house. With Spencer keeping Lady Grendel busy and Joan in the servants' quarters, Albertine was hopeful the chance of running into someone was slim.

The hallway leading to the study was dim and quiet. There was a strange smell in the air, a mix between metal and caustic soda. Albertine tried the door handle but—as Spencer had predicted—it did not budge. She knelt at the door and pulled her lockpicks from her reticule and flipped aside the lock's privacy cover. The lock released quickly but Albertine did not allow herself a moment of excitement until she was inside the study with the door closed and locked—she'd learnt that lesson—behind her.

The study was almost exactly as it had been the night she had been in there on the night of the ball. The walnut veneer of the desk gleamed in the sunlight streaming through the open curtains. A leather writing pad sat in the middle of the desk, an ink pen leaned drunkenly in its holder. It looked as if Grendel had popped out and would return at any moment. She ran her hands along the back of the one floral chair—its matching partner, the one Grendel had sprawled out on that night, was missing. Where that chair had been was now a blank space. The large Turkish tapestry rug was still in place in the center of the room. The smell of caustic soda was so strong that she began to feel quite lightheaded. The room had been thoroughly scrubbed. There would be little to find here.

She studied the room. The whiskey bottle was still on its silver tray, although only one glass remained. Had the other been removed for testing? She sucked in a breath and gave herself a moment to consider. Had Grendel drunk the entirety of his glass? She hadn't, but that was all she was certain of. It would take any chemist worth his salt the work of a minute to determine her compound in his drink.

*Although.*

She looked over at the whiskey bottle. The whiskey bottle had not been removed, which would indicate they didn't suspect anything wrong with it. Perhaps the glasses had been merely removed for cleaning and hadn't been returned yet.

She tried the top drawer of the desk, and was surprised when it slid open easily.

It held nothing more than an old pen and a glass paperweight with a butterfly trapped inside. The second and third drawers were empty. Perhaps it was her imagination, but she fancied she could still smell the scent from the letters in that bottom drawer.

Albertine hadn't opened any of the other drawers when she had taken the letters, but it felt odd they were all empty. Had Scotland Yard taken the contents? What were they looking for? Her fingers tingled as she thought about Lady Roche's question: *Is this all of them?* Had Albertine retrieved all the letters or had she left some behind?

She shook her head to clear it. There was no point in thinking about things she could not change: What was done, was done. What she needed to do now was make sure there was nothing in this room that could tie her to Grendel's murder. If someone had seen her enter or exit the study, it was merely their word against hers—but not if there was proof she had been in here. It was imperative she found the beads.

Closing her eyes, she turned toward the whiskey and its tray, visualizing the trajectory of the small beads. There had been no noise made as they dropped, but she had not seen them on the tray or the sideboard the tray sat upon. One could safely assume the beads fell on to the rug under the desk.

She couched onto all fours and swept her hand under the large, wheeled chair and the far corners of the desk, to no avail.

Albertine froze as the thick thud of feet moving along the hall reverberated through the floor.

The footsteps neared and paused outside the study door. Albertine held her breath. She had locked the door, but what if whoever it was had a key?

The door handle turned once and the wood creaked as whoever was on the other side of it pushed against the door. The handle rotated in the opposite direction. There was a moment of pure silence.

Albertine fancied she could hear soft breathing from the other side of the door. It wasn't her breath—hers was trapped deep in her chest.

After what felt like an age, the footsteps moved off down the hall.

She scrambled off the floor. Dust prickled at her nose as she lifted the edge of the thick velvet drapes beside the desk, letting out a squeak of pleasure as one dull brass bead of her bangle glinted mutely in the afternoon light. She snatched it up and placed it carefully in her reticule.

Lifting the thick curtain and giving it a shake, she was disappointed not to find the other, but if it had been this difficult to find when she was specifically looking for it, hopefully whoever had spent their time in the room looking for clues hadn't consider it worth keeping. If they had found it.

In any case, she told herself fiercely, it was impossible to trace it back to her. Or improbable. Difficult. Challenging at the very least.

She shook her head. There was no place for doubts. If she allowed one doubt to creep in others would follow, overwhelming her with the enormity of what she faced. No, best to ignore it all and push on. She reminded herself of Papa's words—she was as sharp as a dagger, and she would live up to his words, no matter what it cost her.

Creeping to the door, she pressed her ear against it, listening for sounds of movement on the other side. Hearing nothing, she unlocked the door.

The lock clanked as loudly as a shotgun in the silence. She was in the hallway, back against the door when the footsteps returned. Fumbling in her reticule, her hands felt thick, as if she were wearing mittens. It was too risky to try and relock the door. Hopefully by the time anyone noticed it was unlocked she would be long gone. Albertine checked twice that the bead was inside her bag before she pulled the drawstring tight and walked toward the sound of the nearing footsteps.

A tall, gaunt maid appeared around the corner, shrieking at the sight of Albertine. The tray in her hands wobbled precariously.

"Sorry, madam." The woman attempted a curtsey while working to keep the tray upright.

"Silly me, I appear to have taken a wrong turn. I was looking for the water closet."

The maid gazed at her with a dark look, her narrowed gaze flicking from Albertine to Lord Grendel's study.

"Grief affects us all in different ways, doesn't it? I am just so distraught over my dear friend's passing. And in such a manner. Tell me," Albertine continued conversationally. "Did you see the body?"

The maid blinked at her. "The undermaid found him."

"And?" Albertine prompted. "Blood everywhere I suppose?"

The maid took a step backwards. "Blood, ma'am? No, there were no blood."

"No blood? Well, how on earth did the man die then?" Albertine stuck her tongue out the corner of her mouth and crossed her eyes, putting her hands to her neck as if being strangled.

The maid took two more steps backwards, glancing behind her as she did. "I . . . I . . . couldn't say, ma'am."

"Couldn't say? Did his face look peaceful?" Albertine raised her voice as the maid turned and walked briskly in the opposite direction.

The maid's footsteps picked up pace, the clattering of the crockery on her tray indicating great speed.

*Jags.* She'd learned precisely nothing. Hopefully Joan had better luck with the servants downstairs. Albertine wondered how Spencer was doing. She turned and walked along the hallway in the opposite direction to the disappearing maid. She would give her a minute or two to make it down the stairs before following her.

"Can I help you, Madam?" The disapproving voice of the butler sounded from behind her.

"Silly me, I appear to have taken a wrong turn. I'm looking for my dear friend Lady Grendel."

The butler's pursed lips and doubting eyebrows told her what he thought about her skulking about the halls of Grendel House, but he was too well trained to say it aloud.

"How did you enter? I do not recall admitting you."

She really should have asked Spencer what name he would be using. "You were admitting a dear friend, a different one, and were distracted." Albertine smiled widely, fearing it was desperate, rather than reassuring.

"His Grace, The Duke of Erleigh?"

"Yes, yes, of course. Him." Albertine waved an impatient hand. "Could you point me toward him? These large houses can be so confusing."

The butler's eyes flicked to the second door on the left and Albertine launched herself at it before he could reach it and announce her. The last thing she needed was for him to inform Lady Grendel she had been found wandering the halls of her house and in the middle of a murder investigation no less.

She opened the door and slipped into the room, firmly closing the door behind her and leaning against it.

Lady Grendel sat on a crimson chaise, a tray of tea half drunk and discarded on the small table at her knees. Albertine had expected her to be drawn and wan, but the only sign of mourning was her black dress. Her eyes were bright and two peach-colored circles sat high on her powdered cheeks. Her lips were stained a deep pink.

"Lady Grendel, my condolences on the tragic"—Albertine clutched her chest and gazed about the room—"truly tragic passing of his lordship."

The room was filled with flowers of every imaginable variety. The scent of them all mingled together unpleasantly in the overheated room.

Lady Grendel smiled and stood, kissing Albertine on both cheeks in welcome.

"Hello, Countess. The Duke of Erleigh should be back any minute," she declared as if Albertine hadn't mentioned her dead husband at all.

Albertine waited until Lady Grendel sat before lowering herself into the seat across from her. "Oh?" She wasn't sure what response the woman expected from her.

"Oh, yes." Lady Grendel fanned at her breast. "The man has the face of an angel and shoulders of Atlas."

Albertine twittered. "Delightful." The man sounded interesting at least. Had he gone somewhere with Spencer? Men were always skulking off together to places that excluded women.

Hopefully Spencer was able to hold his own. Although, he had seemed to cope marvelously the night of the ball. She opened her mouth to ask Lady Grendel where Spencer was when she spoke, her eyes closed in rapture, "Deliciously delightful."

There was a long pause that Albertine didn't quite know how to fill. Lady Grendel roused herself from her beatific stupor. When she opened her eyes she jolted, as if surprised to find Albertine sitting across from her, and busied herself pouring Albertine a cup of tea.

"How are you holding up?" Albertine asked. "You must have had such a terrible shock."

Lady Grendel smiled with alarming suddenness. "How would you feel if I told you that you no longer had to attend the opera?"

Albertine blinked, baffled by the swift change of subject. "The opera?"

Lady Grendel nodded. "You do attend the opera, don't you?"

"Of course, yes, I enjoy the opera so very much."

"No one *enjoys* the opera, darling. Oh, we certainly enjoy it ending. My god, all that wailing." She ran a practiced hand along her elaborate hair do. "We attend the opera because it is the thing to do. Because everyone else is going and we can't bear the idea of missing out. We go to get dressed up, see and be seen. What is the point of doing anything, if no one is there to see you do it?"

Her tone was decidedly neutral but she held Albertine's gaze with an intensity that was unnerving. Her statement felt pointed. Was she trying to tell Albertine she had seen her the night of Lord Grendel's death? Surely that was impossible, Albertine had entered the ballroom and found her in conversation with Spencer.

Albertine took a deep swallow of her tea, gasping as it scalded her throat.

Would it be insulting if Albertine asked Lady Grendel to open a window? She breathed through her mouth. A bead of sweat tickled at Albertine's hairline. It was hotter than Hades in here but Lady Grendel appeared not to notice.

"Lady Grendel, did you see anything the night of his Lordship's, er . . ."

"Murder?" Lady Grendel's tone was bored. "It's quite all right to say it. Between you and I—" She leant forward as if she were about to impart a secret but did not lower her voice. "It's really rather lightened things up around here. I had concerns this season was going to be unutterably dull, but we've started things off with a bang, haven't we?"

Her eyes glittered. "I mentioned the opera because that is how one feels about marriage. Unfortunately, one is required to attend, but in all truth, it's an event one could do without."

Albertine stared at the widow. "Lady Grendel, forgive me for being so frank, but I don't suppose you have any ideas who would have, or could have done such a thing?"

Lady Grendel gazed at Albertine over her teacup. "Are you asking me if I murdered my husband, Countess?"

Albertine took a moment to consider the woman in front of her. Bold and original, was she the type to do away with her husband? Risk death by doing away with him? Most marriages in the ton were marriages of convenience, and once the required heirs were produced both parties were happy to go their own ways with whomever they chose. However, Albertine thought back to the way Lord Grendel had born down upon her in his study, his bullish, cruel demeanor. It would have been difficult to accept your "lot in life" if that was the sum total of it. She was certain Lady Grendel could handle blunt speak.

"Did you?"

The tip of Lady Grendel's tongue moved around her top lip. "No, but thank God someone did. My life stretched out ahead of me like a noose around my neck. I had imagined I would never be free, destined to suffer this pitiful, empty life. I prayed to our good lord to release me from this dreariness and behold! He has."

Albertine blinked. "Well . . ." She was uncertain what to say to that.

"There's such freedom in widowhood. I can barely wait to get started." Lady Grendel clapped her hands with joy. "I'll be required to take up residence in the dowager's house, but think of all those delicious men I wasn't able to partake of, now available. And who doesn't love a merry widow?"

"I'm glad you're feeling so . . . at ease with the matter, Lady Grendel. Just one more thing—I don't suppose anyone has mentioned how his Lordship died?"

Lady Grendel took a sip of her tea. "Hmm? Oh, they think someone drugged and throttled him." She smiled again. "Nothing my dear husband didn't deserve."

# CHAPTER 12

Spencer stood two doors down from the Grendel Townhouse at the allocated time but the women were nowhere to be seen.

He worried at the seam of his glove. He was very rarely uncertain of the next course of action, but for the first time since he could remember, he found himself at a loss about what to do. Spencer had offered his condolences to an exultant Lady Grendel, who had immediately propositioned him. That had been surprising, considering she was a widow whose husband was not yet in his grave.

He had asked to use the water closet and checked on Grendel's study. The door had been locked and there had been no sign of Albertine. Instead of taking his chances with Lady Grendel again, he had simply left.

What was taking them so long? Had Albertine been caught sneaking about the halls of the mansion? Movement on the street caught his eye and his stomach flipped as Joan and Albertine made their way toward him. Joan was gesticulating and appeared to be berating Albertine about something. Her head was tilted toward the indignant Joan, her gaze cast to the ground. They were an unlikely pair, those two. He'd never encountered a relationship between staff and employer like it. It wasn't in anyway like the relationship between him and Blaine.

It often felt like Blaine was the one in charge. Blaine, although not born into aristocracy, cared far more than Spencer about the rules and duty that went with the Erleigh title. Spencer's work required him to spend time with men who were considered leagues below him on the rungs of society, where he had found men with greater honesty, more decency, and kinder spirits than the men of his station.

When, God forbid, tragedy befell one of their men, it was not unusual for the wives of the colleagues to send in baked goods and meals to pass on to the grieving family. Food, Spencer was certain, they could not afford to part with. And yet they did it. The people of the lower classes seemed to understand one another better, care for each other better, understand the importance of family and friends.

When Stephen had died, many of Spencer's friends had simply acted as if it hadn't happened. As if Stephen had never happened. At Stephen's funeral, men who had long known Spencer had instantly begun to refer to him by that dreaded title. As if Stephen had never even existed, or had simply been a cut-out inserted into the place of duke—generic and easily replaced. It made him furious, even now. He scuffed his foot along a crack in the footpath. Not that it mattered. No matter how often he had felt like grabbing a man by the scruff of his neck and demanding he cease referring to him as the duke, demand he pay his condolences, or say something, anything, to remind them that Stephen had existed, it wouldn't bring him back. For Spencer, Stephen forever would remain Stevie, his dearest, older, and only brother, long after he had been resigned to a footnote in Erleigh history books. The one he had always looked up to, fearing he could never measure up to.

And now never could, never would.

Sucking in a deep breath, he forced the feelings back down into the abyss that was his chest. It felt endless, a black hole that could swallow any feeling, and ensure he would never have to feel it.

The women ceased speaking as they reached him, both watching him with wary expressions.

"There you are," he said, setting his face into polite blankness.

He searched Albertine's face. She appeared to be avoiding his gaze, her head turned back toward the Grendel residence. Her averted face exposed the creamy skin of her neck, the small hollow beneath her ear. Would it feel cool to the touch, like the marble it looked like, or would it be warm?

She turned back to him and their eyes collided. There was something in her eyes, not fear exactly but something like it. Something that reminded him of the deer that stalked the edges of Trentham Halls woods. *Wary, watchful.* No matter how many times they had seen him quietly sitting beside the lake, regardless of the offerings he left for them, they never allowed him near. Even while grazing they had watched him warily from the corners of their eyes, bolting at the slightest movement from him.

His father had held a party, a group of men from London. Dukes and lords arrived *en masse* for a weekend. The weekend had been punctuated by gunshots and hunting calls, dogs barking, the raucous laughter of the men of the House of Lords.

Spencer had never seen the deer again. He clenched his fists.

"Ladies." Spencer gave a little bow. "Did everything go to plan? Find anything?"

Albertine's face remained impassive, but her hand gripped at the small bag looped around her wrist.

"No clues. Thankfully Scotland Yard did a thorough job. They probably have arrested the man responsible for this already."

"Oh, aye, it was a man. They said so downstairs." Joan didn't shift her gaze from Albertine.

"What did they have to say downstairs?" Spencer was genuinely interested. Servants being naturally suspicious of the authorities, it was usually difficult to get any information from them.

Joan tucked her hand into the crook of Spencer's arm. "You take me for an ice at Gunter's and I'll tell you."

Spencer couldn't help but smile. "An ice sounds like just the ticket," he said at the same time Albertine scolded, "*Joan.*"

"What?" Joan countered.

"That is not proper." She widened her eyes meaningfully.

"I don't mind sharing if he can't afford two."

Spencer bit his lip. Joan was worried he couldn't afford two ices. Her concern touched him.

He patted Joan's hand on his arm. "I think you are worth an ice all to yourself, Joan. Shall we?" He crooked his elbow to Albertine, who merely gazed at it suspiciously.

Her upturned lip stung a like a slap.

"It is a lovely day, let's walk through the park to Gunter's," he suggested.

They ambled along the roads of Mayfair toward Berkeley Square. Despite the recent blustery cooling weather, today's sun was warm and bright. Albertine walked alongside Joan, her arm tucked through Joan's, and the two of them bantered and joked. Had Spencer stopped to consider, he might've wondered why his heart felt buoyant. The sound of Joan's musical accent and Albertine's quick-witted retorts amused him—the entertaining repartee between the ladies was infectious.

"And let me tell you about the time she tried to save a robin. Scrambled up a tree only to find she couldn't make it down. Too proud to admit it, she stayed up there until it begun to dark."

"I wasn't stuck! I was simply enjoying the view," Albertine responded indignantly, in a manner that told Spencer this story had been told for some years.

"Oh aye, enjoyed it so much, Algie had to carry you down on his shoulders!"

Their laughter was infectious and although Spencer hadn't been there, he felt their amusement as if he had.

"Who is Algie?"

A strange silence met his question. Joan reached for Albertine's hand and squeezed it. Albertine's lids fluttered and she pressed her lips together.

"Algie. Algernon. He was . . . *is* . . . my brother. He . . ." Albertine didn't finish her sentence, but instead twirled her hand in the air.

*Ah.*

Spencer didn't need her to finish her sentence. He understood only too well what the stumbling over past and present tense meant. Her hand gesture said more than any words could. How impossible it was to force the words out and retain a straight face, how your lips began to tremble at the mere thought of speaking them aloud. How announcing the death of your brother made it real somehow. That by not saying the words you allowed your brother to remain in your memories, as if he were simply out of town. That your lack of communication was the usual absence between adult siblings each with their own busy households to uphold.

Spencer understood more than he cared to. The dread that came with encountering an acquaintance who might inadvertently ask after your family, the awkward silence that followed as you watched the emotions you remember only too well play across their face. Shock, pain, followed by embarrassment.

"I'm sorry to hear about your brother," Spencer said. "I'm sure you loved him very much and miss him greatly."

Albertine met his gaze with a furrowed brow. Those eyes held him captive, so wide, so trusting. The damn deer again.

"I do," she said simply.

"I lost my brother recently, so I understand." The words appeared in the air between them. He certainly hadn't had time to think them or consider if he would say them. He never spoke about Stephen and had never offered the information willingly about his death before.

The one benefit of being part of a gossiping society was that he had never needed to inform anyone of Stephen's death. The newspapers and social chatter had taken care of that.

Joan's hand clasped his, squeezing briefly in a gesture he found enormously comforting.

To his greater surprise, Albertine ran her hand lightly along the back of his arm, rubbing like a mother's hand along her child's back. Not that his mother had ever rubbed his back in comfort. Perhaps he'd seen a nanny do it in the park. He wasn't sure where the image had sprung from, certainly not from experience. His nanny had been a sour woman who believed children should be seen and not heard, and certainly never touched.

"It is the most difficult thing to endure," Albertine said plainly. She tilted her face up to the bright white sky. "But look at us, still here. Still breathing. Still . . ." She stopped walking, sucked in a deep breath, and closed her eyes.

Joan and Spencer stopped. Joan wrapped her arms around Albertine. "I miss him too."

When Albertine opened her eyes, they were glassy but she smiled. "Although it was so very painful, I am grateful we got to spend the time together that we did. He got sick," she said to Spencer. "The doctors knew what was happening but we couldn't stop it. But we had precious months to cherish our time together and say our goodbyes."

Spencer closed his eyes. That was the most painful part for him. He hadn't spoken to Stephen in months. Both were busy with their lives: Stephen with the estates and Spencer in London. *He had assumed they would always have time.*

"I didn't get to say goodbye to my brother. He fell from his horse. He was an experienced rider." Spencer shook his head. "He knew what he was doing, but that is the thing about accidents. They just seem so bloody senseless. Perhaps the horse got spooked by something, or . . . I don't know. The possibilities will drive you mad. The horse appeared back at the house later that afternoon and by the time a search party had been mustered and found him, it was too late."

Perhaps if they had gotten to him sooner. Perhaps if he hadn't ridden out alone, although he'd been riding since he was old enough to walk. Perhaps if the day hadn't been so misty. Or if he'd taken another route.

*Perhaps, perhaps, perhaps.*

It was enough to drive a man mad.

Albertine blinked against the tears building in her eyes. "I'm so sorry. It must have come as such a shock."

He nodded. It had been a shock. It didn't take much to recall the knock on the door the following morning. A messenger from the local village had been sent with a note. From his brother's secretary, he had assumed. It hadn't been his mother's handwriting.

He'd been awake and breakfasting. He didn't keep a butler, preferring the ease and intimacy of a smaller household, and the housekeeper had bought in the envelope. It had seemed harmless and he'd opened it with one hand while the other continued to fork eggs into his mouth, his mind fixed on the day's tasks ahead.

The housekeeper had found him later that morning, in the same position at the table, the food long cold, when she'd come to clear the plates. He still remembered the small sound of surprise she made when she'd found him sitting there. The silence in the room had led her to believe he'd left.

He had stood when she entered, the sight of another person waking him from his stupor.

"Pack my trunk, please," he'd said, "I will be returning to Trentham Hall. My brother has had an accident."

"The duke? Oh, my days." Her hand had moved to her heart and her brow had furrowed as she studied his face. "Is he all right?" She had paused then and peered at him with a look that had almost undone him. "Are you?"

"No," Spencer had said, in answer to both her questions, listing like a drunk man as he walked from the room. That was the last time he had been in that house as Spencer Sweetman.

He returned as Duke of Erleigh.

Joan reached for Spencer's hand, and he was grateful for the small comfort.

They walked like that for some time, their steps falling into unison. Joan's hand upon his, her arm around Albertine's waist.

Albertine's arm around Joan's shoulders, her hand resting on Spencer's shoulder.

It was simple thing, a woman's touch. But he had never felt so protected, so nurtured, so alive.

They reached the large brick columns that indicated the entry to the square and slowly, as if they all regretted it, untangled themselves. A lightness came over Spencer as he watched a young boy holding the string of a kite take off across the grass, his face lifted toward the sky, a smile wide enough to split his face.

"Let's race. The last one to reach Gunter's buys the ices."

Joan whooped and took off at a trot without a backward look. He turned to find Albertine standing still, her nose lifted slightly. Spencer ignored the pang of disappointment at her lofty attitude. What had he been thinking? It was a childish and unseemly thing to suggest. Not the sort of thing a duke should be partaking in at any rate.

Albertine began to walk toward him but stumbled, reaching for his arm to steady herself. She removed her shoe and checked it over for damage. Spencer looked to the footpath, searching for what had caused her to stumble. There was nothing unusual or out of place.

He turned back to find her removing her second shoe.

"Catch." Throwing both shoes in the air, she shot him a wink, lifted her skirts, and took off across the green in her stockings.

He watched, open mouthed, as her shoes thumped to the ground.

*Minx.*

He collected her shoes and sprinted to catch up with her.

They ran across the green, dodging perambulators and small children, dowagers and their dogs.

Albertine's laughter floated in the air back to Spencer and it was as sweet as morning birdsong. A feeling began in his chest, as light as a bubble and with every step he took, the wind on his face, the sound of Albertine's laughter, the bubble grew and grew and Spencer's lips began to twist at the ends and the bubble grew until it burst and a sound rumbled from his chest.

*Laughter.*

The sound of his own laughter was so foreign to him that it took him a moment to realize what it was. Joy had been absent in his life for so long he barely recognized it. He gained on Albertine and slowed his stride, matching her pace effortlessly.

"Nice try, Countess."

"It's these blasted skirts. It's all very well and good for you in your trousers," she puffed.

"Joan seems to have managed."

She had, although he knew that was an unfair comparison. Joan's uniform was gathered at the waist but loose and flowing around her legs, allowing her to kneel and complete her physical tasks, whereas Albertine's skirt was tightly fitted along her hips, flaring out into what appeared to be, at least to Spencer's eyes, an ocean of fabric, as was the latest fashion ideal.

Albertine grunted dismissively but picked up her pace all the same.

Unsurprisingly, Joan reached the sweets shed first and leaned against the small fence that sectioned off the outdoor dining area with a triumphant grin.

Spencer slowed, allowing Albertine to reach Joan first. They huddled together, panting and laughing.

"Well done, team, it looks like I owe you both a scoop," Spencer said.

A group of ladies hovered at the entrance to the shop. Their cool gazes flicked over Albertine, scanning her disheveled hair and flushed face, before landing on her shoeless feet. Spencer's stomach dropped. It was early enough in the season and he hadn't been the Duke of Erleigh long enough to be instantly recognizable to every person of the ton, but he knew there were some ambitious mamas who made it their business to know every eligible man with a title.

He pulled his hat low on his head, angling his face away from the entrance to the shop. "Your shoes, my lady."

Albertine reached for the shoes but Spencer steered her to a wrought iron chair away from the watchful eyes of the women. "Sit. Allow me."

She smirked but sat. Lifting her leg, she arched her toe toward him. "Oh, your Highness. Will the slipper fit? Am I to be a princess after all?"

Her words, although said in jest, cut Spencer like a thousand little knives. He felt like a cad. For the first time he felt dishonest, dishonorable.

He found no honor in his deception toward her. He knelt at her feet, careful to keep his face averted. He brushed her stockinged feet—a small twig was stuck at an angle to the toe of her stocking and he pulled it out, brushing small pieces of grass that clung to her sole.

She huffed a breath and pulled her foot from his grasp.

Their eyes met and he raised a brow in question. "Ticklish?"

She rolled her eyes. "Hardly. There was a . . . bee."

"A bee?"

"Yes, it was rather close to your face actually." She flicked her foot toward him with an impish smile, stopping just before making contact with his chin. "You should take care."

He gripped her ankle, the bones beneath his hand delicate and ran a finger along the sole of her foot. "Another bee?"

"Indeed."

He ran his palm along the flat of her foot, dragging his thumb along her big toe first, moving along the rest of them until he came to the smallest one, which he caressed with a light touch. Albertine released her breath with a sigh that caused his stomach to tighten. Her foot flexed beneath his hand and he pressed his thumb into the soft pad of her foot again. He glanced up at her, her lips were parted, head thrown back, eyes closed. God, she was the most beautiful thing he'd ever laid eyes on.

He slid his hands along her feet until he reached her ankle. Cupping it, he leaned as if to kiss her toes.

They both froze, and Spencer stared at her stocking. He had completely and utterly forgotten himself.

What had begun as an action to avoid the eyes of onlookers had become more intimate than anything he'd ever experienced.

He slipped her shoe onto her foot, pushing on the wooden heel slightly to ensure its fit. Brushing his hands against his trousers, he stood and came face to face with Joan, watching them with a black expression.

"How about that ice, eh, Joan?"

For a moment he thought Joan wasn't going to answer him. She stared darkly at Albertine, who was studiously avoiding her gaze, face flaming red.

Finally, Joan turned her gaze to him and smiled, her expression as open and cheerful as it ever was. Perhaps he had imagined the murderous glint to her eye. "I won, so I reckon that gets me two scoops."

He laughed and held the door open for her, nodding at the dandy that strolled out of the shop. "Two scoops? I think that effort calls for three, wouldn't you?"

Joan walked into the shop and Spencer turned back to Albertine. "Coming?"

She nodded and stood, but kept her eyes averted from his.

As she brushed past him to enter the store, he caught a whiff of her scent.

He needed to get to Scotland Yard and tell Mitchell that she was no longer a suspect. Hadn't that been what he'd been planning to do? The buzzing sound in his head increased. He couldn't remember anything except how her foot had felt in his hand, how he longed to run his hands over it again, without the woolen stocking between them.

He must have nodded and spoken in all the right places because he suddenly looked down to find a bowl of ice in his hands and Albertine and Joan looking at him expectantly.

★ ★ ★

They took their bowls of ice outside and Spencer steered them toward a table at the outskirts of the alfresco area.

He pulled out the chairs facing the crowd, ensuring that he got the seat that would show only his back. They ate in silence, enjoying the sunshine and their flavored ice. Spencer focused on the chill of the ice in his mouth; the initial sting, swiftly followed by the burst of sweetness. Anything to take his mind from the feeling of Albertine's foot in his hands.

"I found out some interesting information," Albertine announced.

Spencer looked up from his ice, careful to keep his expression neutral. "Oh?"

Albertine glanced over her shoulder. "Lady Grendel informed me that Lord Grendel was strangled."

Joan let out a sigh, pressed her hand to her heart and leaned back in her chair. "Oh, thank goodness."

"Thank goodness?" Spencer asked.

Joan yelped and rubbed at her leg. She shot Albertine an accusing look, which was returned with wide-eyed innocence. "I just meant . . . thank goodness the peelers know it weren't poison or nothing."

"Poison? Why would they think he was poisoned?" Spencer watched as Joan's gaze darted from his to Albertine's.

She shrugged. "Dunno. Just thought that would make sense."

"Him being poisoned makes sense to you?"

"Nah, only that you know now you're looking for a fella, right? A lady couldn't strangle a big man like that."

"That's right." Albertine sat up urgently in her chair. "A ladies' hands are surely too small and delicate to manage something like that."

Spencer scraped his spoon around the bottom of his bowl, collecting the last of his ice, puzzled by her look of triumph. "Not necessarily. They may have used an implement."

"A what?"

"A belt, or a ribbon. Something that could tighten around his neck to make up for the lack of strength in their hands."

He looked up to see both women sharing a horrified look. He grimaced. He had forgotten himself. They were ladies, unused to hearing about such distasteful things. "Forgive me. This is not an appropriate conversation with ladies."

Albertine waved her hand. "Psh, we don't mind all that. I was just thinking . . . It would be handy if we could view the mark on his neck. To ascertain just what kind of mark it is. If it was made by a man's hand or another type of implement. A ribbon or belt would surely leave a different kind of mark than a man's hands."

The last spoonful of ice caught in Spencer's throat and he spluttered into his hand. Surely she wasn't suggesting what he thought she was.

"If only there was a way to see his body before they buried it," she mused.

Spencer looked at Joan, who was shaking her head at Albertine. "No, no no no. Absolutely not."

"I was thinking . . ."

Spencer looked at Joan, who widened her eyes at him in horror.

Albertine finished. "We could go to the morgue and ask to see his body."

Silence.

"I don't think it works quite like that," Spencer said once he had regained some of his senses.

"Why not?" She ran her tongue along the spoon and he looked away.

"Well . . . for a start." God, why couldn't he think of a reason? All he could hear was his mother's voice—*things just don't work like that*. "Things don't work like that." He cringed.

"I could say I am a long-lost aunt and I am unable to sleep without seeing him one final time. Or Joan could be a spiritualist, committed to bringing him back from the dead? You could be his brother?"

Spencer's lip curled before he could stop it. The thought of being related to Grendel, even in his imagination, was repulsive.

"You come up with a better idea then," Albertine said peevishly, misunderstanding his derisive lip curl.

"I'm not entirely certain why we are required to see Grendel at all, to be frank."

Both Joan and Albertine took a sudden interest in the bottom of their bowls.

"Has Lady Grendel hired you to find out something?"

Joan and Albertine shared a look that set his senses firing.

"Yes. That's what has happened." Albertine lifted her chin defiantly.

"Why didn't you just say so? I would have asked her for the payment, *up front*, when we visited earlier."

Albertine smiled tightly. "No need for that. We've made a private arrangement. I have offered to find out who murdered Grendel for free."

*When?* Why hadn't she mentioned this before they had visited Lady Grendel?

"I thought the entire point of hiring me, was to ensure that you received payment for your work?"

"Do you really think me so gauche as to touch a lady up for money while she is grieving her husband?"

Spencer lowered his eyebrows. Was she smirking? Lady Grendel could hardly be referred to as grieving. She hadn't seemed bothered at all.

Had Albertine found something out when she was in the house that she hadn't shared with him? Mitchell *was* right. She was up to something.

"I think it would behoove us to lay eyes upon Grendel's body. To . . ." here she paused as if searching for a reason. ". . . ascertain if he was in fact strangled by . . . a man."

"To what end?"

She blinked at Spencer. "I beg your pardon?"

"What does this achieve? What exactly is it that Lady Grendel is looking for that Scotland Yard couldn't determine? They are on the job, and I have full confidence they will be able to find whoever murdered him."

"Highly trained they is," Joan interjected. "Those men. They know how to find things out."

"Thank you, Joan," Albertine said coldly.

"Just sayin'."

"Well . . . don't." Albertine tapped her spoon against her lip lightly. "Lady Grendel is looking for proof that . . . that . . ."

Joan interrupted. "She has her suspicions about who killed him and she thinks if she can prove it were a man, the police might take her seriously."

Albertine smiled. "Yes! That's right. Lady Grendel has her suspicions about who killed him but no one is taking her seriously. So, she's taking matters into her own hands."

Spencer narrowed his eyes and watched as Albertine studied the table.

"She informed Scotland Yard that she had reason to suspect a certain man?"

"Oh, aye, but men don't listen to women, do they?" Albertine eyed him so ferociously, as if he were personally responsible for the deaf ears of every man that he held his hands up in surrender.

"Oh, not you," Joan ran her tongue along her teeth in a manner that made him sit back in his chair, ensuring he was out of reach. "I reckon you'd be a good . . . listener, so you would."

Spencer's head spun. This was the first he had heard about these suspicions. Lady Grendel hadn't mentioned anything to him when they were in her drawing room, nor had Mitchell mentioned anything. Spencer would have been the first to hear if Lady Grendel had offered the name of a suspect. Why was Albertine so keen to see Grendel's body?

She rummaged in her bag, pulling something small from it, and began to fumble with the bangle on her wrist.

"Allow me." He reached out to assist her.

She dropped a small golden bead into his hand. "Thank you. That twists on there."

He fingered the piece of jewelry. Where had he seen this before? The image of it dropped into his mind with a suddenness that took his breath away. He had seen this exact bead in the items that had been removed from Grendel's study.

As he gazed at the ladies sitting across from him, he couldn't help but wonder what on earth was going on. But he knew one thing for certain, they weren't going to the morgue to view Grendel's body.

Not if he could help it.

# CHAPTER 13

"Devastated. I've never been so heartbroken." Albertine used the edge of her black veil to wipe at her eyes. "Truly tragic."

She pressed a fist to her mouth and sobbed.

Joan gazed at Albertine through squinted eyes, her lip lifted doubtfully. "This ain't the West End."

Albertine straightened. "Everyone is a critic, are they?"

Joan shrugged and adjusted her veil. "It don't matter to me if you get strung up for murder."

"Joan!"

"Well, I'm just saying, ain't I! This is no time to be testing out your acting chops. You're the sister of a dead man who no one liked. Get in, have a look, and get out."

"As you wish." Albertine responded through gritted teeth.

Although it pained her to admit it, Joan was right. She cast another glance over the outfit she had chosen. She was wearing the plain mourning dress she had last worn to Papa's funeral, a low-cost dress with a new black hat and veil she had purchased on their way back from Gunter's. Yet another expense she could not afford.

While they walked home, Joan and Albertine concocted their plan.

They would go to the morgue and as Grendel's out-of-town sister, Albertine would request a viewing of the body to cut a lock of his hair for her mourning brooch. While cutting his hair she could check his neck for marks that proved he had been strangled, hopefully by a man with large hands.

Spencer had seemed distracted and had left them to their shopping, promising to call back in the morning. He had left rather abruptly, which suited Albertine and Joan just fine. They talked about going to Mitchell when they had their new information, which they were certain would strike Albertine off his suspect list. Perhaps then he would leave her be and she could fulfill her promise to Algie of living the life that he had dreamed of and could live the life that she dreamt of—living in the countryside of Cornwall *without* fifteen children to care for.

She crossed her fingers and sucked in a deep breath.

Things had improved since Spencer had joined them. She no longer had to climb out the window, because Spencer had gotten rid of Wallop. In fact, she hadn't seen him since they'd had their conversation on the roadside.

"Let's get this over with," Joan said as she adjusted the black lace covering her face.

Albertine nodded as they walked from the room. It was a mere afternoon's work and then all this nonsense would be behind her.

★ ★ ★

"Grendel?"

The man ran a stubby finger along a column of names. He tapped the page once and closed it with a final sounding slap.

"Gone."

Albertine blinked. Of course he was gone, wasn't that the entire point of the morgue? "By gone, you mean . . ."

"You missed him. He's already being transported."

"But the funeral isn't until this afternoon."

The man raised a disinterested shoulder. "He got other plans?" He laughed. "Late for summink, is he?"

"Thank you so very much for your assistance." Albertine cut him off coldly.

"Yer welcome," he said with a jolly tilt to his head, still chucking at his joke.

Joan opened her mouth but Albertine clutched her arm before she spoke. She shook her head when Joan met her eyes. There was no need to cause a scene.

"I don't suppose you know how long ago they left?"

"Meybbe a couple of minutes ago. Depending on the roads, you might even beat him to the funeral."

Albertine smiled tightly at the man and dragged Joan from the room. Once they were on the street, she raised her hand to summon a hansom cab.

"Let's go find that carriage. If we can beat him to the funeral home, we could get to him before he's put in the ground."

Instead of moving with haste as Albertine had assumed she would upon hearing the new plan, Joan rolled her eyes and heaved a great sigh.

"London ain't Wednesbury. You think you can just walk into the funeral parlor and ask them to open a coffin?"

"I am a grieving sister, remember."

"Oh aye, I wonder if his family, who will all be in attendance, will remember you? Or maybe," Joan inspected her nails with an air of disinterest that positively irked Albertine. "They'll call the bobbies on you and you will be arrested."

"Joan."

"*Alber-teen.*"

They glared at each other, the stiff wind whipping their skirts around their ankles.

"It's all right for you, but I need to prove it wasn't me that murdered him. You heard Inspector Mitchell. They believe it was an attendee of the party that murdered him and as the last person to be seen with him, I'm suspect number one."

Joan tsked a sound of disbelief. "I don't think they consider you to be a suspect at all. I think it's a guilty conscience. You're worried that your sleeping potion killed him."

"I beg your pardon?"

"Think about it. They're burying him, ain't they?"

Albertine bit back on a surge of annoyance. They both knew he was being buried today. "Yes."

"Would they do that if they weren't sure how he was murdered? Whatever they know, they already know. You finding out if he were strangled or not ain't going to help you if they decide you're the one who done it."

"But I will be able to prove that I didn't! That I couldn't have strangled him!"

"Like our Sweetman said, you could've used something. A belt or a scarf."

"But if the mark looks like hands . . ."

"And if it don't?"

Albertine lifted her veil and scrubbed her hands over her face. What if it didn't? Then she was in deep, deep trouble.

"What else can I do?" she asked quietly.

"Call it a day," Joan said, not unkindly.

Albertine looked up in surprise.

"Leave London. Give up this idea about being *the Mayfair Dagger*. What you thought was going to happen, ain't. That's clear now."

"You think I should go back to Crawford and marry the farmer? Spend the rest of my life drowning in laundry and drudgery?" Albertine's voice wavered.

Her throat felt as if it were closing, and she gulped for air. Joan was all she had, her only friend, the closest thing she had to family. She had taken her unwavering support for granted, had always believed that it would be given.

"Psh, of course I don't think you should. But nor do I reckon you should stay here and get strung up for something you didn't do. But this is life of a woman, innit? You just do what you have to do to keep safe."

Albertine took a deep breath. This was the first time Joan had expressed the belief that Albertine hadn't killed Grendel.

"I didn't do it, you know."

Joan raised her eyebrows as if to say, *Not my place to say if you did or you didn't.* "Someone must think you know summink about it. Inspectors don't call by your house for no reason."

*No, they didn't.* And it hadn't been for no reason. Mitchell had said it was simply to ascertain if Albertine had seen anything that might help in their investigation.

*But.*

Despite his boyish demeanor, there was a shrewd light to Inspector Mitchell's eyes and a sharp line of questioning that told Albertine that he wasn't a man to be underestimated.

He had appeared to take her answers at face value, but the idea that she had been the last person seen with Grendel gave her a cold chill when she thought about it. Which she did near constantly. It kept her awake at night, restricted her breathing until she felt she might go mad. The idea that her options were fast narrowing to hanging for a murder she didn't commit and marrying the farmer was impossible. She would not give up now. It was not in her nature.

"We need to hail a cab and try and get to the cemetery before Grendel. Hopefully a couple of coins will aid the priest's willingness to allow us a private moment with my dearly departed brother." Albertine waved her hand frantically at a passing carriage. It clattered by without stopping.

She growled in frustration and searched alongside the other side of the road. A man leant against the brickwork of the building opposite, his hat low. Albertine gasped as the cool blue gaze of Mitchell met hers.

*Ah.* Not so willing to take her answers at face value after all.

"Joan," Albertine muttered from the side of her mouth. "Do not look but we are being watched."

Linking her arm through Joan's elbow, Albertine set off along the street at a trot.

"What's going on?" Joan asked, her voice loud with indignation.

"Shh. We are being watched," Albertine murmured from behind her hand.

"Eh? Where?" Joan's head shot from side to side.

"Don't look. Please."

They ducked into an alley and it was with considerable relief that Albertine saw the small lane led them behind a row of shops and would take them through to another street.

"I shall tell you all later but for now . . . run!" Albertine lifted her skirts and quickened her pace.

Joan huffed loudly as she kept pace, thankfully holding back any questions.

It was moments like this that Albertine appreciated Joan enormously. Other women might question why they were running, or indeed where they were going, but not Joan. Joan simply raised her skirts and got on with it.

Three months ago, when Albertine had informed her of her decision to take the kitchen dogcart and abscond to London, she had expected Joan to bid her Godspeed. Instead Joan had nodded and announced she would come along. She might believe it was best for Albertine to acquiesce, but she would never push her to do so.

The alley was dim and dank, and they dodged and weaved to avoid crates and broken crockery. They burst out onto the busy street, crowded with street hawkers and market stalls.

"There!"

Joan darted across the street, standing in the way of a cab, her hands outstretched.

The horse whined and the driver cursed at her as he pulled to a stop. Unperturbed, Joan leapt up into the cab, shooting Albertine a look that told her exactly what she thought of her tardiness.

Picking her way through discarded cabbage leaves and onion wrappers, Albertine shot a glance in the direction Mitchell would appear from if he had followed them. It was blessedly clear.

Rushing across the street with her skirts still lifted, Albertine leapt onto the cab. "Highgate Cemetery, if you please."

She adjusted her skirts around her knees; crossed her ankles, adjusted her mourning veil, and patted at the perspiration that had erupted at her hairline.

The driver clicked his tongue, whether at the horses or at the women, it wasn't clear, but either way they took off at a trot.

"Now, what was that about?" Joan demanded.

"I'm sure it is nothing more than a coincidence, but Inspector Mitchell happened to be across the street from the morgue."

Joan's eyes widened and she twisted in her seat, peering over her shoulder at the road behind them. "It don't look like he's followed us." She turned back to Albertine and raised a brow. "He's onto you."

Albertine frowned. "It does not go without notice that whenever it suits you, you refer to this as *my* problem."

"I had nothing to do with killing the fella, did I?" Joan burst out indignantly. "I did naught but enjoy the music. I didn't even get to finish my lemonade."

The driver shot a glance at the ladies and Albertine elbowed Joan, gesturing furiously to the driver with her head. She pulled at her ear to remind Joan the driver could hear them.

"I had nothing to do with the killing of the *fella* either," Albertine returned in a hushed tone. "As you well know."

Joan folded her arms across her chest. "It don't look like Mitchell feels the same."

Albertine stared at the passing streetscape and didn't respond. It didn't look that way at all. *Much to her dismay.*

The driver made a cluck of irritation and slowed down to gesture rudely to the driver of a cumbersome carriage that had pulled up on the side of the road, causing the passing traffic to slow to a crawl as they maneuvered around it. Albertine watched idly as the other driver climbed down from his cab and ambled into a corner pub. A long platform on wheels was hitched to the back of the carriage, and a large rectangular box sat atop the platform.

The cab rattled as it gained speed as they made their way along the street.

"Stop!"

Both the driver and Joan jumped at Albertine's exclamation.

"We are alighting here." She thrust some coins at the driver, and leapt from the carriage, gesturing madly to a slow-moving Joan.

Albertine shot a glance to the tavern she had witnessed the driver enter. The small windows were streaked with dirt, the lighting too dim to see inside.

"Look," Albertine gestured to the carriage. "A coffin. Grendel's coffin."

Joan looked doubtful. "It could be anyone's."

"It could but it isn't. Look," Albertine almost laughed at the surge of excitement she felt as she pointed at the Grendel crest painted on the top of the coffin. "This is our opportunity. You keep a lookout for the driver and I'll jump up and sneak a look."

"You'll do no such thing!" Joan screeched grabbing at her arm. "Ye can't do that here. For the love of crisps, you really *will* get locked up."

Albertine looked up and down the busy street. Joan was right. She couldn't really leap onto the back of a carriage and open a coffin in broad daylight.

"Get on."

Joan blinked blankly at her.

Albertine gesture with her thumb at the carriage. "Get on. We'll take the carriage around the corner, have a look in the coffin, and return it. We'll have it back by the time the driver gets out of the tavern."

There was a moment of stillness and Albertine thought Joan might refuse. They didn't have time to consider if it was wise or not. She thought of Mitchell. If he were following, he wouldn't be far. This was her only chance to see if Grendel's neck was bruised. Ideally in the shape of a large man's hands.

It was if God himself had placed the carriage in her path, and she wasn't going to miss her opportunity.

Albertine unhooked the reins from the nail on the gas lamp and clambered into the driver's seat. Joan searched along the street and back to Albertine, shaking her head once before climbing up beside her.

"For the record, I do not approve of this."

"It is recorded, Joan," Albertine said as she flicked the reins. "I can assure you."

The horses started into motion and Albertine gave out a little whoop. The street was full of slow-moving traffic, carriages stopping and starting as they unloaded and delivered their goods. If the driver was to exit the tavern, it wouldn't be hard to spot them and to jump aboard the carriage to stop them.

They needed to get off the main street. Albertine yanked on the reins and the horses turned down a laneway. The pungent smell of the Thames wafted along the narrow, dim lane.

If they could get down to the docks they could park up and Albertine would have a chance to have a look in the coffin. The river's edge was full of carriages loading and unloading goods; one carriage parked for a moment wouldn't be worth noticing. The horses continued down the laneway and they came to the docks. Men swarmed around them, packing and unpacking carriages. No one spared a glance to one more carriage, even if it was a being driven by a woman dressed in mourning clothes.

There was a large oak tree at the water's edge. Leaves littered the ground beneath it, and its canopy shaded the overhead sky. Although it was right at the edge of the sharp embankment, the thick trunk would shield them from any interested eyes.

"Right," Albertine said, with far more confidence than she felt. "I guess we get back there and have a look."

Joan arched a brow at her. "*We*? You stole the body, you can look at it. I want nothing more to do with it."

"I have merely borrowed the sleeping lordship. Once I have seen what I need to, I shall return him. You keep lookout. If you see anyone coming, give me a holler."

"And?"

"And, what?"

"And what are you planning to do if someone, like that delicious Inspector Mitchell, *is* following?" Joan jerked a thumb toward the coffin. "This is a little hard to explain."

Albertine smiled with a gusto she did not feel. "Leave that to me."

*If you say so,* Joan's raised brow said.

"I will have a quick look and have him returned by the time the driver leaves the pub to collect him."

Albertine jumped down from the driving seat and walked around to the back of the bier. Two leathers straps tied the coffin to wooden railings that ran the length of the platform. She unbuckled the first one with little difficulty and moved on to the next. The final strap was tighter, and her fingers worked uselessly at the buckle. The cold metal dug into her fingers and her fingers slipped, and the clip closed tightly around her thumb, tearing her nail.

She paused, sucking on her thumb to relieve the pain, the metallic taste of blood in her mouth.

Suddenly she felt as if she were watching herself from afar. *What madness was this?* The idea had seemed harmless enough, but faced with actually opening the coffin of a dead man, she saw how ridiculous it was. Even if Grendel's neck was marked with a handprint and the signature of the murderer, all she would have to prove it was her word. She would need a photo, and of course she couldn't arrange a death photographer.

She hadn't even been accused of anything. Perhaps Joan was right and this was more about proving to herself that she hadn't killed a man.

She ran a hand along the smooth wood of the coffin. Certainly the police would have already taken notes about suspicious marks on his body, or even photos but if they chose not to share them it was her word against theirs. It would be far too easy to charge her with his murder. If anyone had seen her enter or exit his study then she was done for. She had no money to hire a legal defense. The chances of Lady Roche confirming she had requested she retrieve letters for her were non-existent. The entire point of Albertine retrieving the letters was so Lady Roche could deny the existence of them.

But it couldn't just be coincidence that Mitchell had been standing at the front of the morgue. Why was he there at that exact time? Was Mitchell following her? Since Wallop had disappeared, she had become lax in taking circuitous routes or checking for followers. The police had allowed Grendel's body to leave the morgue. Her blood chilled. There was only one reason for Mitchell to be guarding the entrance to the morgue. *To see Albertine.*

She gazed at the wooden box, took a deep breath, and released it slowly through her nose. A wave of calm washed over her. As crazy as this all seemed, she just had to know. And if there was no man-hand-sized mark on his neck then she'd leave London immediately and start over in Cornwall.

It wasn't worth risking her life over this nonsense, despite what she had promised Algie, despite what she had hoped for. Their dreams of becoming a famous London detective duo like Holmes and Watson had been the fantasies of children—she saw that now. Her life was at stake. She wasn't so foolish as to believe that she would be able to talk her way out this.

Two small iron steps hung on the front edge of the platform and she mounted them quickly, before she could change her mind. There was very little room on the bier and she leaned over the coffin awkwardly. Digging her fingers between the lip of the lid and the thick wood, she tugged. The lid of the coffin lifted slightly but the strap at the foot of the coffin did not allow it to open fully.

Leaping down from the step, she threw a glance toward the street. There seemed to be nothing but the usual dock workers. The wind picked up, sending leaves scuttering around her feet.

"Can't you go any faster?" Joan asked.

"Many hands make light work," Albertine muttered in return.

"Oh aye, and the devil finds work for idle hands."

Albertine smiled to herself as she worked at the second buckle. Joan's mother had often admonished them with that saying when they were young girls. She highly doubted Mary had ever expected them to be repeating it to each other while one tried to pry open a stolen coffin, but life moved in mysterious ways.

Her fingers were stiff with cold and the thick leather strap too unwilling. Albertine pressed her shoulder to the wood and pulled with all her might. The buckle finally gave way and she landed on the dirt with a thump. The strap hung limply over the lid of the coffin. Her skirts swirled around her feet as the wind picked up.

"I'm fine," she called to Joan as she remounted the steps. "Thank you for your concern."

Joan lifted a hand in her direction without turning her head.

Working quickly, Albertine slid the lid to one side, holding it against the coffin. Her thumb throbbed painfully at the pressure of the heavy, padded lid against her hand.

Lifting her face to the sky she inhaled deeply to steel herself before peering into the coffin.

In death, Lord Grendel's face was drained of the ruddy coloring that a life of excess had tinted him. He was gray, his previously lively face now flaccid and droopy. He looked peaceful and calm, as if he were merely asleep.

Licking her lips to combat the fierce dryness that had overcome her mouth, Albertine touched his cravat with a tentative hand. The lid of the coffin slid in her nerve-dampened hands. The wind gusted, sending her slightly off balance. As she wobbled, the lid of the coffin caught in the wind. Her fingers grappled uselessly, too slick with sweat, and the lid too heavy. It slid off the carriage, through the damp leaf debris along the steep embankment, gaining speed until it reached the oily surface of the Thames.

Joan shifted in the seat, shooting Albertine an accusing look.

*Wonders.*

The lid stopped safely on the bank, next to a broken clay jug. But half of it floated dangerously on the water. She needed to move quickly before the lid drifted away. That would be hard to explain.

But first, she had to see Grendel's neck. She had to know. Righting herself, she struggled untying Grendel's cravat, which appeared to have been tied by a sailor highly skilled in tying complicated and elaborate knots. Yanking at the final bow, she let out a little whoop of success as a two large, oval, purple marks presented themselves. She held her thumbs against the marks—twice the size of hers. Albertine let out another, louder whoop of relief. The horses startled at the sound, and took an uneven step forward. Albertine fell forward, gripping the edges of the coffin, her face frighteningly close to Grendel's gray one.

She was right. He had been strangled, and by someone with much larger hands than hers. A wave of relief washed over her and she almost sobbed. He hadn't died from the potions— someone had strangled him. She closed her eyes and offered a prayer up to the sky.

*Thank you, thank you, thank you.*

She hadn't murdered him after all. He wasn't a good man, but she didn't want to be responsible for his death.

"Sorry, old chap," she said, straightening Grendel's cravat with a little pat.

Another gust of wind bought a smattering of cool rain-drops across her face.

"Bertie."

"Yes, Joan, I'm going to get it now."

Albertine leapt from the platform.

"Bertie . . ."

Whatever Joan was trying to say was lost in the sound of the wind roaring through the trees. Albertine clamped her hat onto her head and picked her way to the edge of the banks. A knee-high brick wall shielded the banks from view, but as Albertine tipped her head over to peer at the lid, she pressed her hand against her mouth. The stench was unbelievable. Lengths of discarded and broken wood, rotten fruit, and dead fish floated along the top of the thick, black water.

"I'm going to need help," she called to Joan over her shoulder.

There was no way she could clamber over the brick wall and retrieve the lid of the coffin wearing a dress.

Dratted dresses. *Again.*

"Joan," Albertine called again.

When Joan looked at her, she gestured to the wall. Joan's gaze shifted to the wall and back again to Albertine. They stared at each other for a moment before Joan lifted a lip and shook her head.

Albertine huffed an indignant breath and rolled her eyes. Lifting her skirts, she walked toward the wall. Another gust of wind sent her hat spiraling along the riverbank. She watched uselessly as the hat wheeled along the bank. The hat was gone. They needed to get the lid back on and have the coffin returned before the driver got out of the pub. Surely Joan wouldn't really leave her to manage this all on her own. She cast a glance back to Joan, who was watching through narrowed eyes.

Albertine smiled widely and bought the tips of her fingers together in prayer.

"Please," she mouthed.

Joan rolled her eyes and slapped the reins onto the seat next to her.

At the exact moment Joan's feet hit the ground, a crack of thunder resounded overhead. It echoed through the air like a gunshot.

Albertine jumped and the horses startled.

One reared up, letting out a noise of distress, and the other jolted forward.

Joan threw herself out of harm's way as the horses bolted. The coffin, now unsecured, began to slide. Time seemed to slow. Seconds lengthened into what felt like hours as the coffin slid from the carriage, along the damp ground, over the wall before landing in the Thames with a splash.

Albertine blinked into the frigid air.

After a moment's silence Joan appeared at her elbow. "Oh, that's you done for."

"Thank you," Albertine returned frigidly.

The coffin listed on the surface of the water. It would be impossible for two women to carry a coffin of that size out of the river and back up onto the shore. Albertine thought furiously. If she and Joan managed to get it on to the bank of the river, they might be able to use the lid as a ramp over the steep step down. They might be able to pay one of the dock workers to help them lift it back on to the cart.

"It will be all right, we will just fish him out," she said, hope in her voice.

Then a strange gurgling noise came from the river. In heartbreakingly slow motion, water began to bubble out of the foot of the coffin.

"Is that . . .?"

Albertine gazed at the coffin, watching with a frozen horror as it listed on the surface of the Thames. That gurgling sound again and then bubbles erupted as the foot of the coffin began to sink below the waterline. Albertine took one step toward it but Joan placed her hand on her arm, stilling her.

"There's no point."

The coffin rocked from side to side as it sank, inch by inch, into the thick, murky water.

Albertine stared blankly at the space where the coffin had been.

"Let's go." Joan's voice sounded as if she were a mile away. "Bertie. Let's go. Get out of here. There is nothing we can do about that now. We are just going to have to make a dash for it and hope for the best."

Albertine grasped Joan's hand and the women struggled up the bank. The sodden dirt sucked at their boots and the damp weeds pulled at their skirts. The rain had increased and now pelted at them in earnest. Raindrops dripped into Albertine's eyes, her hatless hair sticking to her face. As they trudged up the hill, Albertine's neck began to prickle.

She turned, and let out a loud shriek as she met Spencer's hooded gaze. "*Spencer.* What on earth are you doing here?"

His gaze held steady on hers, but she couldn't help feeling as if he were trying his best to not look at the water.

"Did you just . . .?" He gestured with a gloved hand toward the river.

Albertine grimaced. "Yes, it appears I did."

# CHAPTER 14

It was Mitchell that Spencer saw first.

His protégé and friend was hard to miss, his back as broad as one of the dock workers that were watching them warily from their perches aboard the boat decks and wharves. The novelty appeared to have worn off fairly quickly, but even the most weathered dock worker had shown interest in a bunch of peelers fishing a coffin from the Thames.

Spencer's stomach twisted at the thought of it. He had arranged for another bier, and a fresh coffin to return Grendel's body to the morgue once they had collected him from the river.

He had personally spoken to Lady Grendel to explain her husband would be late for his own funeral, blaming the police investigation for his delay. She had taken the news with good grace and simply ordered a footman to open another bottle of wine. He suspected it wouldn't make any difference to her if the body of her husband arrived tonight or tomorrow morning

While Grendel's position as a lord of the realm would ensure there were enough people at his funeral, Spencer doubted that any of them were there to genuinely pay their respects, and postponing his funeral would only add to the drama that surrounded his death.

"Why'd you think she did that then?" Mitchell asked as Spencer neared, his eyes not moving from the men combing the banks of the river.

Spencer paused. Mitchell hadn't turned his head toward him. Spencer was very good at ensuring people did not hear him if he didn't want them to, but Mitchell had noticed. In his mind, Mitchell was the young, green man he had taken under his wing and taught everything he knew. It seemed now, without Spencer realizing, Mitchell had learned all he had taught.

The thought pinched. Spencer had hung his hat on being indispensable to the service, had convinced himself that he would be abandoning his duty to his colleagues if he were to take on the commitment of the Erleigh estates.

What was he if he were not indispensable to the service?

*A duke.*

Spencer cleared his throat at the bile that had begun to rise at the thought. "It was an accident."

Mitchell screwed his face up and narrowed his eyes at the men unloading the coffin from the barge that had docked on the banks. "Nah. Stealing a dead body, dumping in it the Thames. I reckon there's some sort of proof on him. That ties her to the murder, like. She was clearly trying to do away with it."

Spencer thought back to the horror in her eyes when their eyes had met. No, she hadn't intended for Grendel to end up in the Thames. But the rest was inexplicable. The last conversation they'd had about it, and the one he had relayed to Mitchell, was that she intended to view his body at the morgue. Not steal and dispose of it.

"Let's walk," he gestured with a gloved hand in the direction of Scotland Yard offices. "The horses bolted at the thunder, knocking the coffin over the edge. It was an accident." He repeated the story she had breathlessly recounted to him.

Mitchell huffed a doubting breath that left Spencer in no doubt how he felt about that tale.

"I saw her at the morgue. Shifty as, like. She was there to snatch that body. Maybe to sell it to a body snatcher or hold it to ransom. The men will confirm if any of his jewelry is missing."

Spencer kept his face neutral. He would have come to the same conclusion had it been him in Mitchell's shoes.

But it wasn't.

For the first time in Spencer's life emotion was getting the better of him. He had always been able to analyze a situation and make a decision on the best course of action, based on facts. But here he was, convinced these things couldn't be true about Albertine, no matter what she did. His head swum. He, who had never doubted himself, had never once questioned his decisions in life, believed regret to be a useless emotion. Spencer looked at facts, determined the best course of action and took steps toward it relentlessly.

He made a noncommittal noise. "What did the man at the morgue have to say about it?"

How he wished he had gone in with her, to see what outlandish story she would have come with. To watch how she would have bamboozled the coroner. He bit back a smile. Utterly inappropriate for him to have gone, of course, but still he wished he had heard what had happened.

Instead, he had informed Mitchell of what she had proposed and had arranged to have Grendel's body moved early to the funeral home, in the hopes of scuppering her ridiculous plan. He still wasn't entirely clear on what she had hoped to gain by viewing his body. Lady Grendel had confirmed that she had not hired anyone to take on a private investigation. Her confusion about his line of questioning had left a pit in his stomach. Albertine had lied to him about her reason for seeing Grendel's body. Both she and Joan had been careful not to mention the police investigation in his earshot, but all of this had to have something to do with Mitchell's visit to her. He refused to think of the possible reason the visit of an inspector had triggered her to steal the body of a murdered man.

"The two of them claimed to be Grendel's sisters. Sisters!" Mitchell spluttered and his face reddened. "As if the two of them could pass as his sisters. Anyone would only have to look at Grendel once to know that there is no way he could be related, not even in a passing fashion, to a woman who looks like that."

Spencer stiffened as a burst of something hot and indefinable surged through him. "Like what?"

"Well . . . well," Mitchell tugged at his collar and kept his gaze firmly trained on the horizon. "There's no denying she's beautiful. I've never seen hair that color before. And those lips . . ." Mitchell trailed off.

Spencer tamped down hard on the electric burst of rage sprung through him. He sucked a deep breath in through his nostrils. "I thought you believed the woman capable of murder, and yet here you are senseless with wonder over the shape of her lips."

"Murder?" Mitchell's gaze shot to Spencer's, his eyes as bright as the summer's sky. "Not the countess, I'm talking about that maid of hers."

The spike of anger that had flooded Spencer dissipated just as quickly as it had arrived, bringing with it a burst of laughter. Mitchell was waxing lyrical about Joan. Was the man blind? Joan was attractive enough, to be certain, but the countess was like no other woman he had ever laid eyes upon.

"Joan?"

Mitchell's usually open and friendly face darkened at the sight of Spencer's smile. "Not right for a duke, I suppose. Not right for a Scotland Yard officer either, I shouldn't think. Too good for the likes of me by half."

Mitchell's shoulders dropped along with his words.

Spencer clapped him on the back, magnanimous now. The poor boy had it bad. He thought about the first time he had met Joan, her humor, her openness, the ferocity with which she loved and protected Albertine. He thought back to the way she had reached for Albertine as they spoke about her brother, and her hand on his arm when he had shared his story about Stephen. Anyone loved by Joan should spend their life counting their lucky stars.

"I think you could do a lot worse than Joan."

"Oh, and don't I know it! No, not for the likes of me she is," Mitchell repeated sadly, the words sounding as if he had spent hours repeating them to himself.

"What have you found on the countess then?"

What had he found out about the countess? That she was kind, soft-hearted in just the right way, funny and heart-stoppingly, breathtakingly beautiful when she smiled.

"Well?"

Mitchell was staring at him quizzically and Spencer realized he was woolgathering.

"I have found out precisely nothing."

Mitchell nodded like he'd said something profound. "Sophisticated type game, is it?"

*A game where she went to great lengths to make sure old ladies had the dogs they dreamed of.*

"No sign of anything criminal. Wallop is wrong. She's not running any type of game."

"What about this detective nonsense then?" Mitchell asked with a suspicious turn to his lip.

"She wants to be a detective. There's no scam, and she's not taking anyone's money illegally."

"The bead we found in Grendel's study?"

*That was inexplicable.*

"A common enough item, perhaps?"

Mitchell scoffed. "What about that tiara?"

"Send a man to the pawn brokers on Bond Street. I'll bet one of the Wallops pawned it. To claim the insurance—if it even existed. It was never reported?"

"Not until he came in that day. To report the countess."

"Strange, isn't it that the Baron and Baroness Wallop would not report the theft of a very costly tiara?"

"Not so much, sir," said Mitchell. Although young, he'd been on the beats a long time and there was little he hadn't seen. There was little that would surprise him about human nature.

Spencer pulled his notebook from the pocket in his jacket and flipped it open. "Baron Wallop. Banned for outstanding debts at White's. Banned for outstanding debts at Brooks's. Membership revoked due to outstanding debts at Boodle's."

"I'm sensing a theme here," Mitchell said, pulling a similarly shaped notebook from his own pocket. "Wallop currently has outstanding debts at Crockford's and Goody's. And I found the connection between the countess and him. Apparently she outed the baroness and the baron for running some kind of rig at a bridge game. The lady whose game it was blackballed them. These ladies take their cards seriously."

He pulled a face that showed Spencer just what he thought of bridge games and the ladies who partook in them. "Mind you, some people got real problems, eh?" Mitchell brayed a laugh.

Usually Spencer would happily engage in a bit of ribbing about the lives of lords and ladies, but something tingled in his brain.

He held open the door to the Scotland Office and gestured for Mitchell to enter.

"The name of the lady? Who ran the bridge game?"

Mitchell glanced down at his notebook. "Lady Dufferin."

Spencer nodded. "I'll pay her a visit and find out how she came to hire Albertine."

"Albertine now, is it?" Mitchell said, raising his eyebrows.

*Damn.*

Spencer ran a hand along his face. "That's her name. She asked me to call her by it and it would seem strange if I didn't. As we are working together, after all."

Mitchell studied Spencer for a long moment. "How is that all going?"

It was as if before Spencer's life had been a newsprint, monochrome, everything laid out in orderly boxes and columns, but now was a masterpiece of color, light, beauty. It was like he'd sat upon a spinning top, his head so full of color, noise, laughter, he barely knew himself. That in the first moments of wakefulness, where there had been a dark shadow that chased him there was now light.

"Fine," Spencer said dismissively. "I'll be back in the office as soon as I get a handle on what exactly is going on here."

They walked to Spencer's office, his lie echoing along the hallway behind him.

They sat in Spencer's room perusing paperwork—at least Spencer assumed Mitchell was, while Spencer himself was doing nothing but thinking about Albertine and why she had stolen Grendel's coffin. No matter which way he turned it, he kept coming up with the same, unwanted answer. *She was hiding something.*

A light rap sounded from the doorway and both men turned to see the head of Jenkins pop around the open door.

"Sir . . . er, sirs. I have the application you requested."

"Thank you, Jenkins." Mitchell took the papers from the young man and handed them to Spencer. "That's that then. Our application to have the countess arrested."

The blood seemed to freeze in Spencer's veins. He had expected others would demand it, of course—the scene at the edge of the Thames hadn't done her any favors. He worked to keep his expression neutral.

"We didn't discuss that."

Mitchell raised his eyebrows and straightened in his chair. "No, we didn't discuss it. But I assumed as she had dumped the body of the man she is suspected of murdering in the Thames, and was seen to do so by someone on her Majesty's payroll, and a duke, it required no further discussion."

Spencer pretended to consider the papers in his hand, but the words were all jumbled together and he couldn't read them. He had to do something, and now.

Mitchell was right, he had witnessed Albertine and the coffin but he had also seen the look in her eyes. "I don't think she intended to push the coffin into the water."

Mitchell huffed a disbelieving breath.

The words righted themselves on the page and a sentence leapt out at him. "The murder of her husband too?"

"I say we have enough to charge her with the murder of Lord Grendel, and we throw in the accusation about her husband as well. A murder charge against one's wife should be enough to bring him out of the woodwork, and if he doesn't appear, then we have the proof we are looking for."

Mitchell steepled his hands over the desk in a manner that sickened Spencer, because he recognized the gesture as of one of his own.

The gesture of a man so certain that he was on the right side, making the right decisions.

But Spencer was still his superior and he wouldn't give the call. Not yet.

Spencer cleared his throat. He was a man of facts and figures, not suppositions and theories. He couldn't tell Mitchell that he had come to know Albertine in a way that was truly to know her. Not as one would say they knew each other within the ton. No, he felt that he understood Albertine in way of close friends who had known each other for much, much longer than they had.

"I'm not convinced."

Mitchel gave a low whistle. "She's really pulled a swift one on you. Of course she has you convinced, she's a highly skilled charlatan. A thief. A damn good one, I'll give her that, but this woman cannot be trusted to tell the truth. And that maid of hers." Mitchell's face was mottled, his cheeks flushing

"Joan?"

"Aye, if she's a lady's maid, then I'm a monkey's uncle."

Mitchell's gaze bounced about the room, flitting from object to object, studiously avoiding Spencer's look.

Mitchell was right about that much. Joan wasn't a lady's maid. He thought back to the first appointment they had gone together. She'd had the hump about being required to act the part of a maid. Spencer had asked her if she wasn't and she had replied unhappily in the affirmative. But she had known Albertine's family. There was no doubt of that. The way she had offered comfort to Albertine about her brother. The silent hand of a long-trusted friend who felt her own pain about the loss and shared the loss herself in some way.

"She's from up north isn't she? You recognize the accent?"

Mitchell sucked in a breath. "Sounds like the Black Country to me."

Spencer nodded as an idea formulated in his mind.

"Where is it you're from? Wednesbury?"

Mitchell's eyebrows pulled together as he tried to determine where Spencer was heading with his line of questioning. "Aye."

"Not a big place is it, Wednesbury?"

"Not so big. Not compared to London," Mitchell replied warily.

Spencer had little to go on but her brother's name—Algernon.

"And we've nothing else on the count?" Spencer drummed his fingers on the desktop.

Mitchell shook his head.

"Nothing. No mother, no father. No heir looking to claim the title?"

*Tat-tat-tat* Spencer's fingers went, faster as his mind whirred.

Mitchell reached for a small packet of letters, held together with a clip. "This is all we have. False reports and near sightings. He paid in cash for the property in Belgravia but the property owner never met him. Dealt solely with the countess. There are copies of his written requests in there, but there is very little to go on."

Spencer flicked through the papers inside the packet sightlessly. He knew there wouldn't be anything to find in there. These papers had been picked over by England's most thorough detectives.

The count via the countess paid upfront for three months' rent. The countess claimed he was poorly, and his letter indicated he was. She said he had recovered well enough to go to the Continent, to take the waters in Switzerland and on another occasion, to take the waters in Lourdes.

Mitchell continued to flip through his papers. "Baron Wallop said he had a friend in Romania who had heard a rumor the count had been murdered."

Spencer narrowed his eyes. *Wallop again.* Everywhere he looked, there was Wallop.

"Where did Wallop befriend the count?"

Mitchell looked nonplussed. "Not sure I understand, sir?"

"He must have met the man somewhere, would he not? How has he formed such a strong friendship with the fellow that he has concerns that are not shared by the man's own family?"

Spencer could tell from the blank look on Mitchell's face that it hadn't occurred to him. He stood and dumped the papers into the wastebasket at the corner of Mitchell's desk. "That is little more than stuff and nonsense. What do I always tell you? Question the premise. Start at the root. Why is Wallop concerned about the whereabouts of the count? Not *where is the count.* You won't find him there." He gestured to the papers on the desk.

If Spencer was right, and it was a bloody rare thing that he wasn't, they wouldn't find him anywhere. The count didn't exist, and more than likely never had. But Spencer still couldn't work out why Albertine had invented him. He understood the mechanics of it finely enough. A widow was one of the few positions where women wielded any power. Albertine wouldn't have been the first woman to hide behind a man's name, and he didn't begrudge her that. The idea that she had done it simply to fleece the wealthy members of the ton didn't sit right either. It was inconceivable that someone who went to so much trouble to locate a dog for a lonely old woman would do that. She had spent hours looking for that dog, and received nothing but a tongue-lashing in return for it.

Spencer reached for his coat and shucked it on. "Do not do anything in regards to this case until my return. That is a direct order."

Mitchell nodded. Had Spencer not been so preoccupied as he left the room, he might have noticed Mitchell bend to fish the papers from the basket.

# CHAPTER 15

Joan's laughter floated into the study, followed by the deep tones of Spencer's voice. Albertine folded the paper carefully and laid it on the edge of the desk. Spencer would be thrilled when she showed him the article about John Taylor's arrest amidst accusations of running a dognapping ring. *What were the chances that he had been found out and arrested after their encounter with him?* The world worked in mysterious ways.

Her heart fluttered like a bird in a cage. She was equal parts embarrassed that Spencer had witnessed the spectacle down by the Thames and just plain excited to see him.

After they had run into each other along the Thames, he had waved down a cab and bundled her and Joan into it, promising to sort the debacle for them. She had been on tenterhooks since, jumping at every rattle and clatter outside, expecting the bobbies to appear to cart her away to jail, but . . . nothing.

As promised, Spencer had sorted it.

She had known he would. After so long relying only on herself, trusting another was a strange feeling. Like the tingling one got in their foot when sitting in one position too long.

But she had come to think of Spencer in a way she never would have dreamed possible.

He was bold, brave, as sunny as the brightest summer day, and she was yet to see him respond to any situation—no matter how peculiar—with anything but good grace.

And as if her thoughts conjured him, he appeared in her doorway.

They stared at each other in absolute silence for one long second before breaking into grins.

"Hullo. Haven't seen you since you dumped a lord in the Thames, what?"

She placed her head into her hands and groaned. "Oh now, please don't tease. I can't bear it. That was . . . that was . . ." but she couldn't think of a single word that would sum up the terror of what she had done.

"I think you'd better tell me how that happened." He placed a chair next to where she was slumped across the desk and circled his hand over her back. His touch thrilled her, and even though she knew it was supposed to be comforting she couldn't help but arch toward him, just the tiniest amount.

"I have been told I am an outstanding listener. Top of my class. Non-judgmental—unless required, in which case I'm awfully judgmental—barely interrupt, and very rarely fall asleep."

After a moment, she lifted her head from the desk. "I do have something to tell you."

He leaned back in his chair and nodded eagerly. "I'm all ears."

She sighed. If he was the man she thought he was, then he would take this all in his stride, but the chance that once he found out about her lies he wouldn't want any more to do with her still sent an icy hand along her back.

"I . . . I . . . am not a countess. Not the Countess Von Dagga. There is no Countess Von Dagga and there is no count. I am Albertine Honeycombe. I came to London to escape my cousin."

She risked a glance at him. His face was expressionless.

"When Papa died his title and the house went to my cousin, an odious man named Franklin. A disgusting bully, he was never supposed to inherit but Algie . . . Algie died and Papa got sick and hadn't time to make arrangements for me. Which left me at Franklin's mercy. Of which there was little. He informed me that the estate couldn't afford to keep me, so he brokered a deal with the farmer on the neighboring property, with a stipend involved for Franklin. I was to marry this farmer and raise his fifteen children."

Spencer's impassive expression broke into a horrified look. "Fifteen?"

"Yes. Both his previous wives died. Probably just to get some rest."

They shared a rueful smile.

"Papa was a scientist as well as an earl. A rather famous scientist actually, who discovered a compound that alleviates headaches." She paused thinking how to best sum up her unique, bold, loving Papa. "He raised me to be independent, and actively discouraged the belief that there were things I couldn't do because of my gender. Cousin Franklin does not feel the same. And neither does the law."

Spencer nodded in encouragement. "So . . ."

"So, Joan and I borrowed the kitchen dogcart and drove it to London. I took what I could and sold it along the way and figured if I looked and acted the part, then I could *be* the part. I invented both the count and countess as an entree into society."

She closed her eyes, too scared to see how his expression would change. Hurt. Betrayal. Anger. She expected to see it all.

"Clever."

Her head jerked up. She had been so certain he would be disparaging. But of course, he was a trickster himself. The night she had seen him at Lady Grendel's ball he was pretending to be part of high society and had bluffed his way in, much like her. And he had taken this job and agreed to pretend to be the count when needed.

"Society is built on appearances, lies, and deception. It isn't hard to fool most of the people of the ton because they are so very foolish." Now his tone *was* disparaging.

"I was at the ball where Lord Grendel was murdered, as you know," Albertine pointed out.

He smiled at the memory. "I remember, very well, Cleopatra."

She smiled at the memory too.

"Now as I feared . . . another man has *happened*. But there is little helping me with this one."

He smiled, remembering their conversation when she had hired him and tasked him with managing any men that might *happen*.

"This man is a member of Scotland Yard. Or the Home Office. I don't know. He's someone. And he thinks I killed Grendel."

His eyebrows lifted slightly but otherwise, he was as still and watchful as a cat outside a mousehole.

"I didn't. But that's why . . . how . . ."

"You stole the coffin."

She sighed. He was so direct. "It sounds terrible when you put it like that."

"How would you put it?"

"I *borrowed* the coffin—at least that's what I meant to do— borrow it, and put it back, cart and all. I was trying to . . . I wanted to . . . I *needed* to see how he died. Lady Grendel told me he had been strangled, and I thought if I could see the mark on his neck, I could tell Inspector Mitchell that it wasn't me and he would believe me."

Hot shame snaked through her. It sounded so utterly foolish spoken aloud. She had been a ninny.

Spencer looked at her, but she couldn't read his expression. "You were scared. I know you didn't mean for that to happen."

"That's the truth of it. I have gotten myself into water far deeper than I could have ever imagined."

The room was so silent that she could hear the horses rattling along the street below.

She couldn't help but ask her next question. "Do you think less of me?"

"Albertine, I could never think less of you. What you did, leaving your home with all your earthly possessions, to start fresh on your own terms. It's inspiring."

Her stomach flipped. "Thank you."

"For what?"

"Being so nice."

His face contorted. "Nice?"

She smiled at his obvious offense. "Yes, nice. Do you have a problem with nice?"

He grimaced. "It's just so . . . blancmange. Apples are nice. Babies are nice. A sunny day is nice. Surely you can do better than that."

Albertine pretended to consider. "Lovely then."

Spencer scoffed. "That's almost as bad. A cup of tea after a long day is lovely. Resting your chilled feet in front of a fire is lovely."

When Spencer smiled, three horizontal lines appeared at the corners of his eyes. His hazel eyes danced and she knew he wasn't serious.

What would he say if she told him being around him was like the feeling of the first sip of tea in the morning, the warmth of a fire on a frigid winter's day, sliding into clean sheets after a long day.

That wasn't quite true.

All of those things invoked a feeling of comfort, contentedness, pleasure even.

Being around Spencer was like arriving home after a long, arduous journey. He felt like a soft place to rest her head after months of frantic running. His laughter made her want to climb into his lap and curl up. That sometimes the way he stared at her while she spoke, the way he nodded while listening to her intently, made her hands shake and her heart pound like a drum.

What would he say if she told him that?

She thought she knew how he would respond in most situations. He was cool, calm, and rational. Even when their eyes had met as Lord Grendel's coffin was sinking to the bottom of the Thames, he had remained the epitome of calm.

She could almost see the cogs turning as he considered what to do.

There was no problem too big, no complaint too trivial, no coffin too sunk in the Thames for him to deal with. He took it all with logic, grace, and no objections. There were no complaints about being in the employ of a woman. He never took advantage of Joan, no matter how she threw herself at him.

He was charming good grace, sunshine no matter what the weather, and steadfast in a manner that made Albertine feel safe, in a way she hadn't since Papa had died. But she didn't know how he would respond if she told him that.

"What would you prefer then?" Her voice emerged as a croak.

She pressed her fist against the base of her neck and cleared her throat.

He rarely smiled but when he did, her lips lifted immediately in response. He didn't smile now, just eyed her, and sighed. "One would rather prefer something along the lines of strong, manly, robust. Did I mention strong?"

He puffed out his chest and gave a wink that set a cascade of butterflies free in her stomach.

She rolled her eyes at him. "Well, I like nice, lovely things. Strong, manly things sound . . . difficult."

"Difficult. I like that."

Albertine burst into laughter. "As you wish. Mr. Sweetman, I officially decree you difficult. Duke Difficult."

A peculiar strangled sound emerged from Spencer's lips. His face was devoid of any color.

"Are you feeling well? Is something the matter?"

Spencer stood from the chair abruptly and moved to the other side of the room, keeping his face averted but not before she noticed the color had come rushing back to his face. His ears were beet red.

She watched, perplexed as he stared at the blank wall above the mantel. A series of emotions played across his face until he cleared his throat. "Albertine."

"Yes, Spencer?" she replied, mocking his formal tone, but he made no attempt to speak, instead just stood silently staring at the wall.

"Albertine, I must tell you something."

His eyes searched hers. They stared at each other so long she could have counted the gold flecks around his pupils. He cleared his throat again.

"Albertine."

"Spencer."

"I . . ." A flash of pain shot across his face, as if what he were feeling was too much for him.

"What is it?"

Her heart lurched. *Had he some bad news to tell her?* She moved toward him and clasped his hand. His skin was warm and rough underneath hers and suddenly she was aware of the improperness of her action.

His gaze rested on their entwined fingers. Embarrassed, she tried to release his hand but he inhaled a shuddering breath and increased his grip. His thumb began to trace tiny circles upon hers, so lightly that she might have imagined it but strangely, it was all she could feel. Her mouth was dry, and swallowing took an effort. He took a step closer. He was so close that she could feel the heat that sprung from him. The smell of him was everywhere, lemon, leather, and that other, inexplicable scent that made her think of Crawford House.

"I rather, that is, I would like, I *do* like . . ." he trailed off.

She waited, but he didn't finish his sentence. His gaze was on her mouth and her skin began to heat as if his gaze were a match, and her lips tinder.

Although they were pressed against each other, he made no move to touch her other than her hand in his.

"You like . . .?" she croaked.

He shifted his gaze to her left shoulder. "You. I like you."

A basket of butterflies set flight in her stomach and she almost laughed with the joy his words had released.

He was still staring at her shoulder. She gently placed her palm against his face, thrilling at the touch of his stubble against her hand, and moved his head back to meet her gaze. "I like you too."

She more than liked him. He had become like the sun to her, and she, a winter bulb coming to bloom in his heat.

His hand, that one that wasn't in hers, came to rest at her nape and anything else she had thought to say disappeared like smoke.

It was clear he thinking about kissing her. Perhaps was even planning to. Oh, how she hoped he was planning to!

Her pulse thundered in her ears as his face neared.

Albertine screwed her eyes shut, opening them again when his mouth didn't make contact with hers.

Their eyes locked, his lips so close she could feel his breath against hers and she couldn't have looked away, even if she had wanted to. Which she didn't. She definitely didn't. He raised his eyebrows in question and she nodded.

Yes, she wanted him to kiss her. More than she had wanted anything in her life.

His mouth was finally on hers and it was heaven. She had no other word to describe how his soft lips felt pressed against her, the thrill that shot through her body at the touch of the tip of his tongue as it explored hers.

He released a low groan and her knees began to tremble. She clutched the lapels of his jacket to steady herself. Sliding her palm between his jacket and shirt she placed her hand on his heart, which hammered unsteadily against her hand.

The hard wall of his chest, the thud of his heart against her hand. She felt all of it as if it were her own. He pulled away and rested his head against hers. His eyes were tightly closed.

Placing his hand over hers against his heart, he squeezed once and pushed away from her.

"Spencer."

Maybe she'd done it wrong. She had enjoyed kissing him immensely, frankly it was the most enjoyable experience of her life, but his eyes were tightly shut, his breathing labored and the hand that covered hers was gripping hers so tightly that his knuckles had whitened.

"Er . . . Spencer? My hand."

His eyelids fluttered open and he realized her hand abruptly. "God. Sorry. I . . ."

She cupped his face in her palms. "Are you all right?"

Instead of answering her, he pulled her against him, encircling her with his arms. Her face fit perfectly into the dip between chest and shoulder. He smelt like lemon and leather and something indefinable that would forever remind her of him.

Suddenly hot tears prickled at her eyes. She hadn't been held in so long the mere act of resting her head against him, of resting for just a moment was enough to undo her completely.

It had been too long since she had felt safe. Since Papa had died, she had not stopped. Not stopped planning, scheming, running. Here, finally, she could stop. She could rest. Safe in the knowledge that Spencer would keep her protected.

He tensed as her tears became sobs. Taking a step back he grasped her arms and stooped to meet her eyes. His face was a study in anguish. "Albertine. Was the kiss that bad?"

She hiccupped a half-laugh half-sob. "It was strong. Manly. Robust."

"No." He placed a gentle finger on her chin and tilted her face to make eye contact again. "That kiss you can definitely call lovely. Because that *was* lovely. That was the loveliest thing that has happened to me for a long time. Perhaps ever."

His eyes shone with a light

"For me too," she said between tears as she pressed her face against his shoulder.

Home, she thought. He smells like *home.*

# CHAPTER 16

"Good afternoon, Lady Dufferin."

The lady in question gasped dramatically, as if she hadn't been handed Spencer's calling card merely moments ago.

"The Duke of Erleigh. Calling on me? I am beyond honored."

She held her hand toward him for him to kiss. He raised it to his mouth, holding it inches from his lips and made a smacking noise.

She giggled and held her hand to cheek. "To what do I owe the pleasure of this visit? I had heard rumors of an opening on the marriage market for a duchess. Word travels fast. But I must remind you, Your Grace, I am a married woman."

"Doesn't it just? Official business, I'm afraid. Lord Dufferin is safe. For now." He gave her a wink.

She flung her hand to her forehead in a swoon. Spencer closed his eyes, fighting a wave of irritation at this mindless nonsense.

"More's the pity," she said on a sigh.

A waft of sherry hit Spencer in the face. He darted a glance to the mantel clock and tried not to raise his eyebrows at the hour. Like his Gan-Gan had always said, it's never too early for sherry.

"I work for Scotland Yard."

She widened her eyes and clutched at the cameo that hung around her neck on a string of pearls. Her tongue ran slowly across her top lip and her gaze slid along his body down to his boots and back.

He met her returned gaze with a raised brow. Spencer cleared his throat, and repeated what he had said. "I work for Scotland Yard."

"Very manly of you. Keeping us safe from the riffraff. How thrilling. Tell me, where does a duke find the time to also work at Scotland Yard?"

Spencer sucked in a breath through his nose and counted to ten. Lady Dufferin was a prime example of why he preferred to avoid society.

"It's tough, I will admit. To find all the hours in the day one requires to get through one's chores *and* get to their club. But I prevail. I am actually here to speak to you about an instance where you employed the Countess Von Dagga."

Lady Dufferin slapped her hands onto her knees and widened her eyes, clearly relishing the opportunity to retell this story. "Oh, I did! I hired her to find out why the Baroness Wallop kept beating me at bridge. Insufferable bore. And that husband of hers. *Yuck.*"

They paused their conversation while the maid laid out the tea service on the small marble table between them. Once the maid had departed, Lady Dufferin walked Spencer through the thrills of her regular bridge game, its infiltration by the Wallops, and how their cheating ways were outed by Albertine.

"I knew, I just *knew* the baroness wasn't a better player than me." She looked at him with glee. "And she wasn't."

Spencer cleared his throat and fought the urge to check his timepiece.

"And how much did you pay her for these services?"

"All in all, the baroness won over twenty guineas. Stole from me, really, when one considers the circumstances. But really, there's no need for Scotland Yard to get involved."

"The detective, madam. How much did you pay her for her services?"

Lady Dufferin's smile tightened. "I'm afraid I don't understand the question."

"Lady Dufferin, she performed a service for you. At your request."

"Yes. And did a jolly good job of it." She nodded.

"You employed her. As a detective, I believe."

She nodded again. "I knew Wallop was up to something but if any time I tried to catch him in the act I couldn't. And of course, bridge is a challenging game. One must keep their mind solely on the task at hand. I couldn't for the life of me work out how he was doing it. Scoundrel. Utter scoundrel. Don't worry, they've been banned. Blackballed at Almack's and Annabel's too."

She gave him a self-satisfied smile and appeared to be waiting for him to respond.

"Very good," he said.

"They won't be doing that again, I can assure you. No need to pay me for doing your job for you, though." Her laughter was the tenor of fingers along a chalkboard.

Spencer gave her a tight smile and cleared his throat. He couldn't stand much more of this. "How did you come across the countess and her detective skills?"

"She put a little advertisement up near Almack's. I saw it and thought it was just the ticket to squash those cheating fraudsters."

Spencer pulled his notebook from his pocket and flipped it open. "So, you replied to advertisement in which the countess had advertised her services. Correct?"

Lady Dufferin nodded.

"She came and performed said services, to a high degree of quality, which resulted in your preferred result." He looked up from his notepad with a questioning brow and she nodded again.

"For free."

The smile slid slowly from Lady Dufferin's face.

"Did she ask for compensation?

The smile reappeared on her face. "I very generously offered her some vouchers for Almack's and I personally vouched for her myself. That sort of thing is very risky, you know."

Spencer gulped at his tea to hide his expression. This sort of entitled nonsense was what grated him about society. The belief that someone would put themselves at personal risk, for that is what Albertine had done for this woman, simply out of the kindness of her heart and an Almack's voucher was selfishness and stupidity of the first order.

Albertine, fearless, wonderful woman that she was, had been singled out by Wallop now because she had helped this lady. She had suffered at the hands of Wallop because she had stopped him from taking advantage of these women and all she'd received was Almack's vouchers *that* she wouldn't be able to use.

The thought of her crawling out her window to escape Wallop and his abuse made him want to hit something rather hard.

Instead, he placed his teacup into the saucer with a crack.

"My lady, if I may, I would like to offer you a word of advice. Money is what makes the world go around. We are in a position of great privilege and power. And if we do not use that privilege and power for the betterment of the world, then what is the point of it?"

Lady Dufferin shrunk away from him as if he'd raised his voice, horrified by the mention of money.

"When someone performs a task for you, you compensate them appropriately. Would you pay the milk boy, or your dressmaker with vouchers?"

"Don't be ridiculous," she returned archly. "I'd never invite someone of that class to Almack's."

He flipped his notebook closed and slipped it back into his pocket. Her eyes followed it as he slid it back into his coat pocket.

"Did you note that down?"

"Which part?"

"That I didn't . . . fiscally reward her. It's just—" She patted her elaborately styled hair. "You made that all sound rather . . . gauche. All that money talk. We have plenty of it, you know. It was merely an oversight." Her words shot out quickly. "We aren't down on it, by any stretch."

And there it was. What truly mattered to this lady. What other people thought of her. She was happy to use people to suit herself, as long as word of it didn't affect how she was perceived by the ton.

Spencer stood and gazed down at Lady Dufferin.

He was free, he realized with a jolt. No matter his title, or job. He was free because he saw these people for who they truly were. The crawling desperation that lay behind their machinations, the lies, the deceit, the treachery, the shallowness. There was no gossip or approval or whisper that could touch him.

His title ensured no one would dare give him the cut direct, but with a woman like Albertine by his side he could affect real change.

For the first time in his life, he saw some benefit to being the Duke of Erleigh.

He smiled down into the woman's wide, pleading eyes. "I tell you what, you get in touch with the detective directly and make an arrangement, and I'll keep this schtum."

She nodded.

"I trust you'll do the right thing," he said as he pressed his lips to the back of her hand again.

He could be part of this game. He could play without being part of it.

And he could win.

★　★　★

Spencer stood, hands clasp behind his back, chin tilted, feet spread. The standard Eton posture. Take the blows, let the words wash over you, think about being anywhere but here.

Lord De Vere, the head of the Home Office, gazed at him through blue eyes the color of a frigid pond in the depths of Siberia, in the middle of winter. *Scratch that*—a frigid pond had more warmth than this man.

Nicknamed Lord Devil, he was as unfeeling as any man Spencer had ever met. Every interaction he had with the man had left him wondering if someone had finally worked out a way to create an automaton that looked and sounded like a human because he was certain no human heart beat in De Vere's chest.

"And what did you find out while you were playing make-believe with Von Dagga?"

"She's no murderer."

"Just happened to find herself in London, impersonating a titled woman with the express intention of infiltrating society and taking advantage of members of the ton, did she?"

Spencer's eyelids flickered. He wouldn't show this man any emotion. Men like De Vere didn't believe in emotion. It was facts and figures only. As Spencer had once been.

"In an effort to avoid being married off to an elderly neighbor, she moved to London and began to work as a detective for the ladies of London under an assumed name, yes."

"Baron Wallop attests that he saw her leaving Grendel's study. A piece of her jewelry was found in Grendel's study."

"Wallop is a liar. And owes most of London money. Including a substantial amount to Grendel. As he does to Brownely-Watts, Lord Dalston, and the Dufferins. That man's word is worthless. The bead is . . . inexplicable."

"Indeed." De Vere's impassive face twitched as he ran his gaze along the report in his hand. The very report Spencer had put in Mitchell's trash.

Spencer was going to have a very firm word with Mitchell about that report. A. Very. Firm. Word.

"Then, there is the matter of the deceased's body. It says here that she stole and attempted to dispose of Grendel's body in the Thames? And that it was witnessed by . . ."

Spencer resisted rolling his eyes. De Vere knew exactly who it was witnessed by. "Me, sir."

"Ah, yes." He looked up from the paper and pinned Spencer to the spot with his stare. "You. The Duke of Erleigh. Head of your division at Scotland Yard and, I hear, a recent employee of this Honeycombe woman. Highly irregular."

The man had a mind like a steel trap. Nothing got past him.

"As I advised my team, she had intentions of viewing Grendel's body. She had some idea that viewing the marks on his neck left by the murderer would somehow prove who it was that had strangled him."

"She stole a body and disposed of it to avoid suspicion." De Vere corrected.

Spencer tried not to flinch. It was going to take everything he had to convince these men otherwise.

"Not intentionally. Not because she murdered him."

De Vere's eyebrow lifted a fraction.

"She did it because she *didn't* murder him and wanted to prove so."

"Hmm." A plethora of meaning was held in that one noise. None of it good.

De Vere continued. "I believe this is to be your last case with us, Your Grace."

Spencer nodded.

"I understand this was a difficult decision for you to make."

Spencer nodded again. "It was."

"Your mother paid mine a visit."

Spencer coughed. "Your mother?"

"Yes," De Vere pursed his lips. "Apparently they were under the impression that if your mother spoke to mine requesting you complete your tasks here at Scotland Yard, I would relieve you of your position."

It had been a long time since Spencer had allowed his mother's behavior to embarrass him, but right now he longed for the floor to open up and swallow him.

"I don't like being told what to do," De Vere said coldly.

Spencer wondered if De Vere had ever been told what to do. He had probably decided when he would be born and had spent his childhood giving orders to his nanny.

"Quite often, upon receiving an order, I churlishly partake in the exact opposite," he continued. "Your work with us has been exemplary. You are well respected by your peers. That's not easy. Gaining the trust of the working-class man when you have a title. But you've done it. Scotland Yard will be sore for losing you. However . . ."

Spencer braced himself for a blow.

"I believe there is something clouding your judgment in regard to this Countess Von Dagga."

Spencer shook his head. He wasn't the type of man who allowed emotions to get the better of him. Renowned for keeping a cool head under pressure, he prided himself on his ability to remain impartial.

How to tell De Vere that he had never been surer of anything in his life than Albertine's innocence? It looked bad, worse than bad if he was perfectly honest, but that didn't make her guilty of murder. It just wasn't possible.

Not his Albertine, his wonderful, unique, kind Albertine.

A thought hit Spencer with such a force that he almost fell into the spare chair across from De Vere. He'd gone and completely fallen head over heels in love with Albertine.

"A young man presented to us this morning. Claims to be the countess's *paramour*. Apparently, in the throes of passion, she admitted to him she had done away with Grendel. Poisoned and then strangled him. Murdered her husband in Czechoslovakia."

Spencer stood as abruptly as he had sat. "Absolute bollocks. Give me the opportunity to speak to this fellow, I'll get the truth from him."

"That will not be possible. Your work on this matter is completed. I'll take over from here."

Spencer felt as though he had taken a blow. He was being stood down from Albertine's case?

Before he could argue his case, the door opened and Jenkins popped his head through. "Ready, sirs?"

De Vere nodded and pushed himself back from his desk. He let the papers fall to his desk with a terrifying slap.

"Ready for what?"

De Vere remained silent but the glint in his eyes as he shrugged on his overcoat made Spencer's heart bang in his chest like a hammer.

"Jenkins?"

But Jenkins merely shot a look from Spencer to De Vere and closed the door. The *rat-tat* of his shoes on the hall would have been comical had Spencer an ounce of humor remaining.

"Ready for what, De Vere?"

But the man said nothing, just smiled that horrifying smile that was not a smile at all, but a predator licking his lips before the kill.

# CHAPTER 17

Albertine signed her name with a flourish and folded the letter into thirds. Placing it neatly into the envelope, she printed the address carefully.

*Inspector Mitchell.*

Once sealed, she pressed the envelope to her chest. Inside was a letter outlining everything. The desk break-in the night of the ball, Lady Roche's letters, how the disaster with the coffin had unfolded and finally, her real name and how she came to London to live as Countess Von Dagga.

The conversation with Spencer last night had been life altering. The kiss too, but the conversation had changed the way she saw herself. It was time to put this foolishness behind her. She was chasing a ghost. No amount of living out Algernon's dream would bring him back. She had thought that by living out her promise to him, by doing the things they had spoken about, she could keep his memory close. But he would remain in her heart, regardless of where she was and what she was doing.

She realized there was very little call for lady detectives, and even less for jobs that actually paid. It was folly, all of it. Yes, she had wanted to live out the dream her brother had wanted so badly, of them becoming detectives in London, working together, and had tried her best, but without him it was an impossible dream.

But now, while closing this door, she saw the possibility of opening another one, a better one, with Spencer.

He had met her honesty with kindness and a thoughtfulness that had become so common in her dealings with him. It was time for her to start her new life, that was true.

But she saw now that living a lie was not a new life.

The thought of Spencer bought a galloping to her chest as it normally did, a warmth that spread wide. He didn't need her help, she knew that, but she felt responsible for him all the same. The same way as Joan. Her footsteps slowed. Not quite the same way she felt about Joan. But . . . she pressed her hand to her chest. She had feelings for Spencer. Not just regular, everyday feelings.

She was in love with him.

Now he knew the truth of her, the distance that she'd needed to keep between them had crumbled. He knew everything that she'd done and he still cared for her. Because he did, that kiss proved that. And now he knew that she was not a married woman, nor a titled woman, they were free to be together.

She pulled open the front door and was delighted to come face to face with him. He was breathing hard. A damp sheen collected on his forehead, his hat in his hand. Albertine couldn't halt the smile that spread across her face.

"Just the man I wanted to see."

His expression was stricken.

"Albertine."

His hand reached for hers and her body reacted in kind, reaching for his in return. Heat sparked where their palms touched. His fingers tightened around hers briefly before releasing her completely.

It was then she noticed the dark-suited men standing on the steps behind him. Inspector Mitchell with a face like stone. Three men she had never seen before crowded around him, as if protecting him.

The smile on her face froze and she blinked in confusion.

"Countess Von Dagga. Stay where you are."

Her blood turned to ice in her veins and her gaze flew to Spencer's. She wished she hadn't. His expression was shuttered in a way she had never seen before. Albertine turned back to Mitchell with her brightest smile.

"How lovely to see you again, inspector."

Mentally, she rehearsed. She could have the door locked and be out the window and through the backyard before they would be able to break through the door. But Spencer. What would they do with Spencer? She couldn't just leave him here.

"Countess Albertine Von Dagga. I am placing you under arrest for the murder of Lord Grendel and Count Albert Von Dagga."

The inspector looked so solemn that she burst into laughter. "Is that so?"

But instead of laughing in response, the inspector gestured to the men to the side of him. They crowded upon her and grasped her wrists roughly. She yanked her hands from them but they tightened their grips. She let out a little cry of frustration.

"Spencer."

She twisted to face him, to warn him. To ask him to find Joan who had gone to the markets. But what she saw wasn't the open, cheerful face of the Spencer she had grown to know and love. There stood a stranger, his face a watercolored painting of the man she knew. Any sign of laughter had been washed out. The lines around his eyes no longer hinting toward easy laughter.

His jaw was clenched so hard that a muscle flicked in his jaw. His mouth was pinched. But it was his eyes that were the worst of it.

Bleached, washed-out, as dark as the bottom of a well.

Empty.

Albertine dug her heels into the ground and yanked her hands from the vise-like grip of the strange men. One hand pulled free, but the other man tightened his grip, jerking her toward him.

Spencer stepped forward, his hand outstretched. "Easy," he ordered.

The men lessened, but did not release their grip on her. Albertine looked at the men. Why were they taking orders from Spencer? Why was he not making any move to protect her?

"Sir?" Mitchell addressed Spencer.

*Sir?*

Spencer bit his lip and stared blankly into the distance.

"Spencer?" Her voice quivered with confusion.

*What on earth was going on?*

"See that she is well taken care of. If I hear of a single hair on her head out of place, I'll personally rip your heads from your bodies." His voice was like ice.

Thick, cold, and utterly fearful.

The men nodded. "Yes, sir."

There was a roaring in her ears, a sound that flooded her head so that she couldn't think, couldn't see. Her chest tightened so terribly she thought she might collapse. The truth of it all came upon her like a house of bricks.

"Sir? You work *with* them. You work with *them*." The agony of the realization apparent in the pitch of her rising voice.

Without meeting her gaze, Spencer bobbed his head toward the men and strode down the steps of her townhouse.

Many awful things had happened in her life. Algernon's illness, Papa's death. Growing up motherless. But this was a pain she had never felt before. Spencer had betrayed her. Her laughing, smiling, *Sweetman* was a treacherous snake. A liar.

He was just like the rest of them. The thought brought her to her knees and she was grateful for the rough hands at her elbows as her legs finally gave way. They were the only things holding her up. Hands dug into her armpits as they half lifted, half carried her toward the waiting carriage.

She let them. Any desire she may have had to fight for a better life ebbed from her with the knowledge that she had been betrayed by the man she loved.

# CHAPTER 18

The cell was cold and damp and the cold seeped from her skirts into the back of her legs. The smell was like nothing she had ever experienced. Damp straw, rats, too many bodies pressed too close together for too long. Albertine didn't know how long she had sat on this cold concrete bench—time had ceased to hold any meaning for her.

She sat, staring blankly at the floor of the cell. Her breath was a labored, grinding noise, and she found a queer kind of comfort in it. It was proof she was still alive. Because if there were a heartbeat in the cavern of her chest, she was unable to feel it. She was dead inside.

Spencer had lied to her.

He had tricked her, fooled her, humiliated her.

Not some down-on-his-luck gentleman happy to be the face of her business at all, no, he was a traitorous double agent for Scotland Yard. She had told him everything last night but he had still had her arrested. The thought was like a hot blade between her ribs and she struggled to breath, pressing her hand against her breast as if it could still the agony within.

But nothing could. Nothing ever would.

He had stood there, on her steps, watching with a cool expression. A face like a brick. He didn't so much as flinch.

"Who is he?" she had asked the officer as he secured the manacle around her wrist to the thick iron bar that ran the length of the carriage.

He had looked out the door at Spencer and back to her with a smirk. "Him? Only the Duke of Erleigh."

"No, not him." She had assumed he was referring to the other man who had grabbed at her. She gestured with her head to Spencer, who was standing at the base of the steps, watching the carriage with a dark gaze.

The officer followed her gaze. "Aye. That's the duke. You wouldn't know it. He's actually a good fella."

Albertine had felt as if she had been slapped—would have preferred a slap. It was shattering to believe everything had been a lie but there was so much evidence pointing to it. *Every word out of Spencer's mouth had been a calculated untruth designed to entrap and charge her with the murder of Lord Grendel.* And the count. The completely nonexistent count.

The idea of being charged for the murder of a man who didn't exist was almost enough to make her laugh aloud. Perhaps she would have if her heart wasn't a block of ice floating in a frozen lake, as bottomless as the ocean.

She shivered. What stupidity this had all been. And for what? She had failed. She had failed Joan, she had failed herself, and worse of all, she had failed to make good on the promise she had made her beloved brother. Instead of living a life that was true and good, she had made a hash of it all and put Joan at risk. And to top it off, she may well be hanged for her troubles.

Thick footsteps made their way toward her cell, fought their way above the din and chaos of the jail. Spencer's footsteps. Of that she was certain, she couldn't have said how, but her body tensed, all her nerve endings exploding with joy. Even now. She hated herself for it. Almost as much as she hated him.

She stared blankly at the floor and set her jaw.

"Albertine."

She didn't look up.

"Go away." She clenched her teeth so hard that something cracked.

"I need to explain."

"No, you don't." She gave a bitter laugh. "You don't at all. It is all perfectly clear, *Your Grace.*"

She did look at him then and was gratified to see him wince at her use of the correct address but was just as quickly sorry she'd looked at him. He was as beautiful as he had ever been, even in his distress. And she knew him well enough now to know that the pinched line of his mouth, the rapid beating of his lids were signs of his distress. She hardened her heart. Let him suffer.

"I guess we were both pretending to be someone we were not."

"I wasn't pretending to be . . ." He broke off, gripping the iron bars between them, his knuckles whitening. "I have never felt more myself than when I was with you, Albertine. Being with you was the first time in my life that I felt free to be me. Truly me. Please believe me."

"Believe you? Oh, that is rich. Believe a man who has lied to me from the moment we met, who although a duke, has proven himself to be nothing more than an immoral trickster. No, I will not believe another word you have to say."

He pressed his lips into a tight line and inhaled sharply through his nose. "I do not believe you murdered Grendel, nor the count."

At the mention of the count, she burst out laughing. It was a brittle, ugly sound.

"Oh, the count! Don't forget about the count! As dead as a dodo, he is. Deader than the deadest thing one could find in this stinking, rotting city. Deader than my heart. Lock me up and throw away the key. I confess! I murdered the count with my bare hands." Her voice had begun to rise, rather unsteadily. "I killed the Count Albert Von Dagga!"

Hysterical laughter burbled from her lips.

Spencer looked at her with a grave expression. He knew that the count had never existed. Perhaps he was wondering if she was, in fact, insane. She certainly felt it.

No. She shook her head. *Get a hold of yourself.* She could not allow one single drop of fear to seep through the door she kept tightly shut. All those fears. A crack would become a flood, she could not afford to fear, to feel. The only way for her was to look forward, consider, plan her next move, always pushing her feet forwards, onwards.

But when would it end?

When could she rest, allow someone else to be in charge, when would someone take care of her? Hot tears flooded her eyes and she screwed them shut. She had thought she'd found that person in Spencer.

"Albertine, please don't—"

"Don't what?" Rage bought her to her feet and she paced the tiny cell toward him. "I admit it," she yelled, "I did it. I murdered Count Von Dagga. I poisoned him. No, I stabbed him. I battered him around the head. You should take care." She jabbed a finger in Spencer's direction.

Spencer's face shifted from a sickening shade of gray to a shade of crimson. He glanced along the hallway and took a step backward. "Albertine, I know you didn't murder anyone. You are the kindest, loveliest woman I've ever met. I am going to get you out of here, trust me."

"Trust you?" She narrowed her eyes, rage swirling around in her chest, so hot it felt as if the words would burn on their way out. Her hands trembled in the effort to stop herself from battering at the bars. "You have made sure that I will never trust another person as long as I live, *Your Grace*."

Spencer pressed a hand to his chest, his face taut with pain.

"Albertine, this last month with you. I . . ." he cleared his throat and studied his shoes. "I have formed an affection for you."

An affection for her? If it were not for the absurdity of the situation, she might have laughed. As it was, it was all she could do not to cry. The man she had fallen completely and absolutely in love with had lied, betrayed her, and was now telling her he felt little more than affection toward her. Her anger was the only thing that kept her standing.

"Is this how you show your affection for a woman?"

She daren't refer to herself as a lady, they both now knew she wasn't. She flicked a hand around the tiny cell. "You accuse her of murder and have her locked up? I don't presume to be an expert on such matters, but I daresay this is not the way to go about winning a woman's heart, Your Grace."

Spencer pinched the bridge of his nose in the manner she had become so used to, only this time there was no humor, only despair. "Please stop calling me that."

"Your Grace? Is that not your title, Your Grace? Are you not the Duke of Erleigh, as well as a liar?"

He opened his eyes and stared at her a long moment. She thrust her shoulders back and gave him a hard glare in return.

Hell would freeze over before she let this man see how much he hurt her. She imagined her back a rod of iron, her face the frozen cover of a lake in winter, her heart a deep, empty cavern.

His eyes softened and she bit her lip until her mouth filled with the taste of metal. She would take no notice of the familiar flecks of gold that lined his irises, or the lines that bracketed his mouth when he lifted his lips in a humorless smile that broke her heart all over again.

"I did not lie."

Albertine widened her eyes and huffed an indignant breath. "Oh no?"

"I simply never said. Had you asked—"

"Had I asked?" She barked a bitter laugh. "Had I thought to ask a man pretending to be down on his luck—"

His head jerked back and she enjoyed a moment's satisfaction.

"I never pretended to be down on my luck," he objected.

"Well, then, a typical bloody man pretending to be a nice man. How absurd of me not to ask him if he was in truth a duke working for Scotland Yard. How very foolish of *me*."

Spencer screwed his eyes shut and rubbed the heels of his hands against them. He inhaled deeply before speaking and she could almost feel how hard he was working to hold in his emotions. The room fairly vibrated with it.

"Perhaps I should have mentioned it."

She scoffed. "No *perhaps* required. You absolutely should have."

He cast a glance at her. "I didn't. The situation simply"—he spread his hands—"got away from me."

Albertine had no response to that. The situation had fair gotten away from her too.

"I attempted to tell you, yesterday but it got away from me and then it was too late. I wished to tell you. To be honest with you."

His voice had become wooden, as if he were a bad actor reciting lines being fed to him from the darkened wing of a stage she could not see. Had he been told to say these things to her in the hopes that she would confess and tell him all? If so, then he would need a better script than this nonsense. She had already told him the truth, it was on him if he chose not to believe her. Fool her once, shame on her and all that nonsense. No, she was as sharp as a dagger, like Papa said, and it would take more than a foppish fool in the shape of a duke to get one over her.

"Why is a duke working for Scotland Yard? Don't you have tenant farmers that you need to exploit? Who will ensure they're working all the hours of the day to give you their hard-earned money while you are here chasing ghosts?"

He cleared his throat and stiffened, he seemed to become rigid, "It is a, uh, fairly recent eventuality. And one I am still adjusting to."

The brother he had told her about, the one that had died must have been the previous duke. Despite her anger at him, Albertine's heart clenched. To lose a brother was one thing, she knew the agony of that only too well, but to lose your freedom as well must have been unimaginably difficult for him. But there was no room for gentle feelings for him. He had proven himself to be a liar. A man willing to do anything to get what he wanted. Hadn't he been honest about that, though? That was a trait that had appealed to her, because she was the same.

No, they were not the same, she and he. She may have lied, but it was for self-preservation, not to trick him into caring for her, to make him think that theirs was a connection that held hope, possibility, love. He needed to leave before the pain that was pressing through her chest burst out and she fell to the floor, wailing, in front of him.

"Please leave. You are not wanted here. I would rather the company of the rats than yours," she bit out.

He stepped closer instead, an intensity in his gaze that set her already fragile nerves alight. "I will leave, but I will get you out of here. Out of this."

Albertine stepped forward too. "I do not need your help. I do not need anything from you. You may have gotten me into this mess, but I will get myself out of it."

She turned and strode the two steps it took to reach the far wall. Facing it, she began to count silently in her head until the sound of his footsteps echoed along the hall.

It wasn't until the clank of the door as he exited the level reverberated down the hall that she allowed herself to sink to the hard iron cot and cry.

# CHAPTER 19

It wasn't until the rain hit his face that Spencer realized he was standing on the street outside Albertine's house.

Albertine was going to spend the night in that awful place. He swayed and pressed a hand to the wall to steady himself. A pressure was building in his chest that made it impossible to breath. Thoughts swirled around and around in his head. He'd really made a mess of this.

"Sweetman?"

He opened his eyes to find Joan peering at him. Her hand was at his elbow and she gave it a little jog. "Ye all right, luvvie?"

His stomach clenched at her open, friendly face. How quickly that friendly face would change once she found out what he had done. Wiping a hand across his face, he let out a sigh that rattled from deep within his body. "No, Joanie, I'm afraid I'm not. And frankly, I'm not sure I will ever be."

Joan bit her lip and looked up at the sky, appearing to consider what to say next. "Come inside for a cuppa. Me ma used to say there ain't nothing that can't be fixed over a cuppa."

"This is more mess than a tea will sort, Joan, I'm afraid. Albertine has been arrested."

Joan widened her eyes, her mouth moving into a frown that would have been comical in any other circumstances.

"And I'm an inspector at Scotland Yard who has been pretending to not be a duke, pretending to be a non-existent count who was pretending to be . . ."

The words escaped him. He wasn't sure when he had stopped pretending. All he knew that here with Albertine and Joan, he had been more himself than he'd been in a long time.

Perhaps ever.

"One of us? A normal man?" Joan supplied.

"Indeed. I've been pretending to be a man."

Joan thrust her corded shopping bag at him. "Looks like you need to come inside."

★  ★  ★

"Fifteen children." Spencer sat back in the hard-backed chair.

Joan raised a brow that said *Tell me about it*, and nodded. "Fifteen children. She said no of course, but Franklin told her it was that or she would be turfed out on the street. As her next of kin, he reckoned he could marry her off to whoever he wanted. And coz Mr. Cunningham owned the farm next door, he reckoned it made sense for her to marry him. So . . ." She took a deep gulp of her tea. "We got all the money her father had left her, bundled up dresses and jewelry, nicked the kitchen's dogcart and drove it to London, rented this townhouse and she became the countess."

Spencer blinked at the rapid-fire recount of the events that confirmed what Albertine had told him last night. Not that he had ever doubted her.

"And you?"

"Ah," she winked, "I just thought it would be a bit of fun, didn't I. Figured her life was over one way or another so we might as well have a bit of a laugh before we had to settle down."

"Indeed." Spencer didn't know what else to say.

They sipped their tea in silence. Outside the light rain had turned to a deluge. It battered against the glass, and wind howled, shaking the windows in their panes. The house felt cold and empty without Albertine in it.

"Will ya go now?"

Spencer startled at Joan's words. "Go where?"

"To the jail and spring her, like. Tell them all what I just told ya. She ain't a murderer *or* a countess. Just Albertine Honeycombe from Crawford who wouldn't hurt a fly."

Spencer cleared his throat. "It doesn't quite work like that."

"Well, ain't you a duke? Just tell them it works like that."

He couldn't help but smile. "Joan, if all being a duke entailed was telling people how things were going to be, then I should actually rather enjoy it."

He rapped his fingers on the table, the engine of his mind cranking. "Irritatingly, Scotland Yard requires a pesky thing called proof before they will let her out."

Joan scoffed. "Why? They didn't have none to arrest her in the first place."

Spencer leveled a look at her and she had the grace to flush.

"That business with the coffin was all a mistake." She screwed her face up and looked at the ceiling. "I suppose there's the potion thing. But that didn't kill him, like."

"It is rather frowned upon to go around concocting potions and putting men, of any standing, to sleep, Joan."

"Ooh, you lot are an uptight bunch, aren't ya?"

He smiled. "There's no denying that."

"Who did it then?" Joan asked with frustration. "Someone killed him. It weren't Bertie. If we find him, then she's free and clear."

Spencer cleared his throat. "A fellow presented himself to Scotland Yard this morning, claiming she admitted to murdering Grendel."

Joan's mouth dropped open. "That's a lie, like!"

Spencer nodded grimly. "I agree. I expect he's been put up to it, but unless he admits, it is his word against hers."

Spencer had a few ideas how he could get the fellow to admit he was lying, but unfortunately, now he'd been stood down he wasn't able to get his hands on him.

"You'll fix, it though. I know you will."

Her belief in him was almost his undoing.

"Joan, I apologize for misleading you, it was never my intention."

She waved her hand in the air between them. "You're a good egg you are. And apart from this arrest nonsense, you've bought a sparkle back to Albertine like I never thought I'd see again. She's got a big heart—the biggest—and she'd do anything for anyone. This ain't fair."

Even just hearing her name sent a pang through him. "And she in turn, for me. It isn't fair, Joan, but I'm going to make it right."

She nodded but swallowed hard and blinked rapidly. "Will she hang?"

His blood chilled. "Hang? God, Joan. No." He pressed the heels of his hands against his eyes. This was a mess.

"That's what happens when you are found guilty of murder though, ain't it."

Her voice was small and Spencer realized that for all her bravado, she was frightened. He grasped her hand. It was as small as Albertine's but dry, warm, and work roughened, and he realized just how much Joan had given up for Albertine.

"It does. But I know Albertine didn't kill anyone and I will make it right."

Joan didn't respond, just sat looking smaller and sadder than he thought possible.

"She's lucky to have you, Joan."

"I'm lucky to have her too. She's a sister to me. Ma lived in the village and her father hired her to take care of Albertine when her mother died. He was a good man, her father. Different, like. He tried to send her away to school but gave up the third time she broke out and appeared on the doorstep."

Spencer laughed. He could well imagine it.

"She's never been good at being told what to do," Joan said wryly.

Neither had he. Which is how he'd ended up working for Scotland Yard. He'd spent his life grateful that he wasn't the heir, and he'd ended up there anyway. What he needed wasn't someone who would encourage him to perform his duty, sacrifice his own needs and desires, confine him to a box that society believed a duke's should be in, the way they should act, behave, feel, or as the case was, not feel.

Albertine would never do that.

Life with her, even as a duke, would be full of laughter, fun, lightness and, most importantly, truth. She would never tell him to hide how he felt, or that it was wrong to feel. The way she shared her feelings made everyone around her feel safe to share theirs. He thought of the dowager and the dog, of how Albertine seemed to cut through nonsense and get to the heart of people. Life with her would be everything he'd never even dreamed of, not believing that it was possible. But it was.

With her, it was.

"That's what I love about her."

Joan's eyebrow's shot into her hairline and she stared at him, wide eyed and wide mouthed for moment before bursting into laughter. "Ooh Sweetman, if you think you're going to have our Bertie for a duke's mistress you got another think coming."

Joan slapped her knees and rocked back and forward as she laughed.

"Who said anything about a mistress? I was hoping to ask Albertine to marry me."

A spike of pleasure shot through Spencer as Joan sat bolt upright in her chair, her laughter abruptly cut short. She wiped her eyes with the hem of her skirt, showing a flash of pink and green bloomers.

"Marry her?"

"I love her." And he bloody well did. Saying the words sent a flush of energy to his hands. "I love her." He repeated firmly.

He shook his head. He, who had never uttered those words or had them said to him in his life, not to his family, nor any of his lovers, was sitting across from a maid, telling her he loved her mistress.

Joan pressed her lips tight and gave him a stare hard enough to rival that of any teacher at Eton and those ever-expressive eyebrows twitched. "She is very loveable."

"She is."

"But you've made a mess of it."

"I have."

"She might not forgive you for this." She twirled her finger in the air, gesturing to the empty kitchen in a way he assumed encompassed her absence in the house.

"I will spend the rest of my life working for her forgiveness and will never, never lie to her again."

Finally, Joan smiled. "She isn't as strong as she pretends to be. She needs to be loved. I know if anyone can do it, it's you."

His stomach twisted at her support, belief in him. He didn't deserve it.

"This is my last job before I have to take up the ducal residence in Cornwall. You could come and be her lady's maid there. Or whatever it is you actually do?"

Joan pursued her lips. "Maybe. Turns out I love living in the city. You never know what's going to happen, or who you will meet. I was bored with Crawford. Same ol' faces, same ol' men."

Spencer clapped his hands together, the sound like the clap of a gun and sending a thrill through him.

*Crawford.*

"I will go to Crawford and collect this Cousin Franklin and bring him back to confirm that Albertine was never a countess, and that the count never existed." He would have a good hard word with him while he was at it. "As for Grendel . . ."

His mind was blank. He knew that man was lying. But there was little Spencer could think to do except start digging on his own to find out who could have killed Grendel. But he didn't have a lot of time.

Joan was right—there were a number of things that worked against Albertine. But if he could get her cousin here and prove that all she was guilty of was a few white lies, mostly necessary to protect herself, perhaps that would help the judge see that she wasn't capable of killing anyone. It was far less than he would hope for.

Joan gestured to the bag of groceries on the table between them. "I'll take this down to the jail and make sure she's got food to eat at least and take her a clean set of clothes."

Spencer nodded. "I'll send a note ahead and ensure you have access to her. I arranged for her to be in her own cell and have a man stationed outside her cell to ensure nothing happens."

*That nothing further happens.*

He broke off as frustration burst through him. Albertine should not be in that place. The woman he loved should not be in that place.

He had to get her out.

# CHAPTER 20

The first door that led from the jail entrance to the floor that currently housed Albertine had a damaged pin in its barrel. The key stuck while being turned left to unlock it. It didn't stick when locking, which told Albertine one of the spring-loaded pins was broken. Probably due to the damp, years of use, and lack of proper maintenance.

The key had to be turned to the left and then turned right and jiggled before it would open correctly.

Albertine had time to study the sound of that lock. She had time to consider what made it stick and how it could be repaired. She had time to imagine just how a dicky lock would hinder her chances at escape. Of course, she had thought of myriad ways of escape. From cajoling to trickery, to her current favorite fantasy—knocking the guard from his chair. The guard whose nose made an irritating whistling nose as he breathed. *Four breaths in, four whistles, one throat clear, and repeat.* All. Night. Long.

After listening to that all night, Albertine was feeling rather murderous. She was already accused of murdering two men, what was one more?

The click of the outer door. She waited four beats. *Key out, door closed, key back in, click. Inner door.*

Footsteps thumped heavily along the floor. Albertine pressed herself up on her elbows on the hard wooden slab that was considered a bed in here. One set of footsteps.

It wasn't Joan. It wasn't Spencer either.

Every hair on her body stood to attention. The footsteps moved past the cells, never slowing. There were five cells between her and the door. Although it was overcrowded and noisy, the songs and stories had kept her great company. Usually the women in the cells, some of them regulars, sang out to the guards. Calling names, asking questions but this time, they were silent.

The footsteps continued and then slowed. Albertine sat, throwing a glance at the dozing guard. He lurched from his seat, knocking it to the floor with a clatter. He nodded once and fumbled at the keys held to his belt with a large iron hook.

*This was it, then.*

A large man she had never seen before appeared in her line of sight and she swallowed hard. A cold sheen of sweat broke out along her skin. For the first time since this had all began, she was truly scared. Although this cell was damp, noisy, and dim, it had become familiar to her. Positioned directly in front of the guard's desk, she had never felt scared for her personal safety. She had created rich internal worlds for the guards, most of them more than happy to pass the time during their shifts by chatting with her.

She'd discovered that Tom wished more than anything to be a sailor and believed himself destined for a life of adventure and travel, but felt beholden to stay in London and care for his ailing mother.

Despite his noisy breathing, James was a slow and gentle-hearted man who worked days at a butchers and night as a guard here, saving every penny to start a life with his sweet-heart, a girl called Sarah.

Ian was a sour, cruel man who picked his teeth and watched the women in the cells with a predatory gaze that made Alber-tine's skin crawl. She never spoke to him, instead talking with the women in the cells around her, hearing their stories. The camaraderie, good humor, and care for one another these women showed had leveled Albertine. She had promised her-self that as soon as she got out of here, she would do whatever she could to help them. Because she was going to find a way to get out. Surely. Any minute.

She inhaled deeply, held the breath, and exhaled slowly, as if blowing out a candle. Focusing on the problems of the peo-ple around her had enabled her to avoid thinking about her own. There was nothing a calm mind couldn't fix, Papa had used to say. Whenever she had encountered a seemingly insurmountable problem she would lie on her bed and allow her mind to wander, thinking of weird and wild ideas that could solve the issue. During the free exploration the solution would often appear to her, as if dropped like a pebble into a pond.

But not this time.

This time her mind had remained resolutely, blackly closed. No wild and wonderful idea had appeared. Nor even an insipid, uninspired one.

She was locked up and now this cruel-faced man was tak-ing her to her fate.

The keys on his ring rattled as he twisted it roughly in the lock. He yanked the door open and jerked his head to indicate she was to follow him. She ran her damp hands along her skirt and stood.

"I don't think I've had the pleasure of an introduction." Her voice was bright and cheerful and only those who knew her well would be able to hear the tremor in it. "I'm Albertine."

The man stared at her blackly. "I know who you are. Out."

Butterflies erupted in her stomach. Although imprisoned, she had been protected and rather well looked after here. Joan had visited daily bringing a basket of food, change of clothes, and any comforts Albertine had asked for. It had lulled Albertine into a false sense of security. This had not really been prison and she had a feeling she was about to find out just how hard prison was. Her hands began to tremble. Hopefully they would just fit the noose and get it over with quickly.

"Lovely. I could do with a little walk. Where are we off to?"

The large man didn't move to make way for her so she was forced to brush against his large belly. He smelled like metal, salt, and something undefinable. Something rotten.

He slammed the door behind her. Yanking at her hands roughly, he slammed thick iron cuffs onto her wrists. His breath was loud and wet in her ear as he screwed the cuffs smaller and tighter. Hot tears pricked behind her eyes. She closed her eyes and forced herself to take a deep calming breath. She could do this. This wasn't the worst thing that had ever happened to her. *Algie. Papa. Franklin. Spencer.*

No, this was merely a blip. She, Albertine Honeycombe, might not be Countess Von Dagga but she *was* the Mayfair Dagger, as sharp as a dagger. The cuff pinched the delicate skin on her wrist, sending a blade of agony along her arm. Her eyes flew open to find the large man watching her with a delighted, searching look.

She blinked and smiled widely. There was no way she would give this man what he wanted.

"I don't suppose they go any tighter, do they? Wouldn't want to slip out, would I?"

He grunted in response and tugged at the cuff. Her shoulder pinched painfully.

She smiled again.

"Toodle pip, James. Best of luck with Sarah."

James touched his forehead awkwardly. "Er, yes, thanks and best of luck yourself."

"Luck? Don't you worry about me, James, I'm the luckiest woman you'll ever meet."

James's gaze flicked to the man tightening her cuffs and pressed his lips together. He nodded once and moved back to his desk, avoiding her gaze by busying himself with some papers.

The man gave a yank and she was flying, her feet lifting off the ground as he dragged her along the hallway to the external door.

"Goodbye, Clare, see you soon, Malerie. Look me up when you get out. Looks like I'm being released."

The women in the crowded cell next to her swarmed to the bars, their hands reaching out to squeeze and pat at her as she walked by.

The guard slapped them away with a threatening growl but it didn't stop them.

"Goodbye, my lady."

"We'll miss you."

"Don't forget to find my Johnny and tell him I love him, will ya."

This time the tears didn't just prickle at her eyes but rolled down her cheeks. Such cheerful kindness from these women who had nothing. Their hopeful belief that she was being released was touching. It was unlikely that she would see any of these women again, but that hadn't stopped them from looking out for her, sharing what they could, even if it was just a friendly pat. Their stories of abuse and exploitation had been painful for Albertine. It had reminded her that really, they were all in the same boat.

She had been furious when her cousin had informed her she was to marry Mr. Cunningham, and that she had no choice in the matter. Furious, and also scared. What marriage entailed she barely knew, but she knew that Cunningham, with his dirty hands and rough way of speaking, was not a man she could spend the rest of her life tending to. It had seemed better to take her chances and rely on her wits here in London than spend her days toiling with his fifteen children, farm work, and whatever duties would be required of her as a wife.

Now she prayed Franklin would appear and demand she return and marry the man. She would gladly marry him. Would thank the Lord on her knees every day of her life if she could marry him, work the farm, and raise his children.

And Spencer.

She hadn't thought of *him* the whole time she had been in here. Which wasn't strictly true. Thoughts of Spencer tore through her like a gale. She thought of not thinking of him nearly every second of the day. Where was he? What was he doing? And in the darkest hours of the cold mornings, why wasn't he here. Fighting for her. With her.

His betrayal burned, like she'd swallowed poison. It had started in her chest, but soon enough the agony of it, of falling in love, of believing that finally she had found a soft place to land, of the look on his face when she'd opened the door to him, had spread to the rest of her body. First it had burned, but slowly it turned everything numb until she felt nothing.

She supposed he thought her a murderess like the rest of them. Although he had promised he wouldn't leave her and believed she hadn't done it, she hadn't seen him since his declaration of *affection*. Her heart twanged painfully. He hadn't even been able to tell her he'd cared for her—instead giving her that silly little wooden speech about affections. And to think she had believed herself in love with the man.

Ridiculous.

It shouldn't be hard to prove the count had never existed but proving she hadn't killed Grendel was another thing entirely.

She had nothing. No money to pay for a lawyer even if she did have a chance at defense.

No, not nothing, she corrected herself.

She had herself, which was all she'd ever really had anyway.

# CHAPTER 21

Spencer bit down on a wave of frustration as his carriage finally pulled up in front of the Old Bailey. The front of the building was blocked by a throng of well-dressed people milling about on the roadside. The courthouse was teeming with people, which wasn't unusual. What was unusual was the quality of the outfits people wore. Feathered hats and beaded parasols were plumped and adjusted as a stream of overdressed ladies from the ton milled about the entrance to the courthouse.

All onlookers and interlopers here to gawk at Albertine, he assumed. The papers had caught on to the case and had printed sensationalist headlines twice a day. Running headlines like *Countess Von Murderess* and *You Can Countess On Her For Murder.*

Spencer growled with impatience. He needed to get to the judge before the hearing commenced.

He had hoped to have arrived hours before now but one of his horses had lost a shoe and swapping the horses had added hours on to the return journey. Precious hours he desperately needed.

The carriage door opened and Spencer leapt out, watching impatiently as the other man in the carriage checked the seat and patted at his pockets.

"Come on. This way." He gestured to the imposing entrance where a young man, little more than a boy really, was frantically trying to control the crowd.

Spencer didn't quite pull at the arm of his companion, but the hand he placed on his arm was a touch firmer than it needed to be.

"I say," the man said in a whiny tone that had become far more familiar to Spencer in the last twenty-four hours than he would have liked. "Won't we have time for a cup of tea at least? I'm parched."

Spencer tightened his grip and all but pulled the man up the worn stone steps. He didn't so much as glance at him until they reached the top. There he finally turned his gaze on his companion. A pigeon-faced man with a receding hairline that reminded Spencer of his old headmaster at Eton. Petulant blue eyes stared back at him. How this cretin could be even remotely related to Albertine was beyond Spencer. But, by all accounts he was, and the fact was, Spencer needed him to be.

Albertine's freedom depended upon it.

Spencer bared his teeth at him, finding it impossible to summon a genuine smile. "How about we find ourselves a nice quiet spot in here and as soon as you've spoken to the judge, I will find you a cup of tea. I'll make it myself if I have to."

Franklin Honeycombe's thin lips pressed together in what Spencer assumed to be a smile, presumably at the thought of a duke making him a cup of tea. Spencer didn't care, as long as he told the judge who he was and who Albertine was . . . is, Spencer corrected himself. *Albertine Honeycombe.* Not a countess, and not a murderer.

Just his Albertine.

And hopefully, if things went his way, the future Duchess of Erleigh.

That is, if she ever spoke to him again.

Spencer had arranged for both Joan and Jenkins to check in on Albertine daily and report back to him. He had been gratified to hear that she had been faring as well as could be expected. In a cell that housed only her, rather than the many that usually crowded the small dank cells of prisons, but Joan had increasingly shown great concern about her friend. She had grown thin and wan, Joan had informed him—choosing to dish out almost all of Joan's food deliveries to the women in the adjoining cells rather than consume it herself. Spencer couldn't help but smile as he recalled Joan telling him the men tasked with managing Albertine's cell now greeted Joan with welcome relief, as they grew weary of Albertine's incessant questioning.

"You can't come back here," the young man guarding the entrance to the judge's chambers said to Spencer as they approached.

"We need to speak to Judge Kettle. Immediately."

The young man gave Spencer a dead-eyed stare. "Can't."

Spencer's fingers tingled with the urge to smack the young man and sucked in a breath through his nose. "I think you'll find I can. And will."

Grasping Franklin's sleeve, he towed the man past the guard.

The young man reached for Spencer's arm, wrenching at his sleeve roughly. "Aintcha got ears? I said you can't."

Spencer froze, turned, and leveled a frigid stare on the young man's hand on his arm. There was a moment of absolute stillness. Spencer flicked his arm sharply, causing the boy's hand to release the fabric of his jacket.

The young man was saved by Spencer's name being called from the hallway. The *tin-tin* of shoes rapping quickly along the tiled floor drew all eyes toward it.

Spencer met the light blue gaze of his old friend.

"Mitchell."

"Sir."

They stared at each other a moment.

Things hadn't been the same between them since Mitchell had arrested Albertine against Spencer's wishes. He understood why he had of course, but it didn't change how he felt.

"I'm here to speak to Kettle."

"Aye. He's in his chambers." Mitchell rocked back and forth on his heels.

"Ya can't just walk in here." The young man was back.

"I know you don't think she did it, like, but that fella said she told him. I had to tell De Vere."

Spencer nodded. He probably would've done the same but it didn't change the anger and frustration he felt.

"That fellow has been paid by Wallop to lie to us, with the express aim of having her arrested. One must question why he would go to such lengths. I have been accused of lacking judgment in regard to this case, but I am about to prove it isn't me that is wrong."

Mitchell looked anguished, but Spencer had no time or energy for anything other than ensuring Albertine was safe.

"Let's go." He gestured with his head toward Franklin and then to the long hall that stretched in front of them.

He was getting Albertine out of here.

★ ★ ★

Spencer rapped his knuckles against the oak door twice and paused until he heard the throaty tones of Sir Rupert Kettle.

"Enter."

Kettle had been a friend of his father's and was a pompous, stiff-shirted man—the very worst of what Spencer saw in the House of Lords. It would pain him to ask this man for a favor, but ask he would. For Albertine he would do anything.

Spencer checked that Franklin was still beside him and pushed the heavy door open.

Kettle sat behind an elephantine desk, its thick squat legs sprouting heavy wooden curls. The room was awash with blue cigar smoke and the stench of damp wool and unwashed hair.

Kettle peered at Spencer through the dim lighting.

"I know you from somewhere." Kettle hacked a thick sounding cough.

Spencer schooled his face. "Erleigh."

He braced against what he knew would follow.

The judge peered along his nose at Spencer with narrowed eyes. "Ah. The latest duke, are you?" Without waiting for Spencer to confirm he carried on. "Good man your father was. Knew him at Eton. Ruddy good at rugby."

Spencer pressed his lips together, fighting against the surge of irritation. As if being good at rugby was all it took to made you a good man.

He nodded. "I'm here on business. The Countess Von Dagga case."

"Working? A duke?" He puffed on the cigar, his cheeks inflating and deflating comically.

Although, Spencer was having a hard time finding anything remotely funny about the man.

"I work for Scotland Yard and—"

"Desmelda."

Spencer blinked into the smoky room. "Beg pardon?"

"Your mother. Desmelda, isn't it?"

Spencer nodded curtly. "Your honor. I have been investigating the countess for some time and this man here—" He snatched at Franklin's sleeve and yanked him forward into the blue smoked room. "Will prove that she is not what, or who, she says she is."

They still hadn't been offered a seat. The judge waved his hand and leaned back in his chair, his stomach straining against his shirt buttons. "Want me to throw the proverbial at her, do you? Easy enough done, Your Grace."

"Actually—"

Franklin stepped forward but Spencer pulled him back with a warning shake of his head. "You are not to speak until I tell you so."

Franklin pouted and huffed.

"This man here is her cousin and he will testify that she is in fact, Albertine Honeycombe from Crawford. She is not, and never has been the Countess Von Dagga."

Judge nodded slowly as he exhaled a long plume of smoke. "I see. Impersonating a countess. That's worth five years in prison. Got to teach these people a lesson. One must be born into this life. We can't have any old riffraff claiming to be one of us, ruining our reputations."

Spencer tried again. "Your honor, she was never Countess Von Dagga because there *is* no Countess Von Dagga."

Judge stared at him blankly. Spencer fought the urge to groan. He needed a stiff drink. Or two.

"There is also no Count Von Dagga." He spoke slowly to allow the buffoon to grasp what he was saying.

The silence stretched on. The man clearly hadn't read the briefing at all. Spencer released a long slow breath and fought the urge to massage his temples. He had ridden for hours, hadn't bathed, and had been forced to spend thirty-five hours in the company of this buffoon Franklin. What remained of his patience was swiftly departing.

"She is accused of murdering Count Von Dagga."

The judge raised his large bushy eyebrows in shock. "A husband killer, eh? Probably one of them suffragettes, as they are calling themselves. We can't have it. We just can't have it." The judge banged his fist upon the desk. "That's another five years. I'll make it ten. Killing your husband is one thing, but when the man is a count, well that's another thing altogether. Although, Von Dagga . . . sounds foreign." He looked at Spencer suspiciously as if he were responsible for the man's ethnicity. "Was he foreign?"

This time Spencer did sigh. England was in serious trouble if this was the quality of man making decisions for the people. "He was, in fact, not foreign because the man did not exist. He was completely fictional. Imaginary. Invented. Made up."

The judge pulled a face as if he smelled something truly awful. "Well, how did she murder him then?"

"Your honor, if I may." Franklin stepped forward with a pompous little flourish made Spencer grit his teeth.

"Albertine is my cousin. An Englishwoman. She grew up in a rather lovely house called Crawford on the outskirts of Wednesbury. Her father passed on." Franklin crossed himself piously. "And it has befallen to me to care for both Albertine and Crawford House. Which I am happy to do, of course."

Good God. The man was speaking as if he had a plum wedged in each cheek. Which Spencer would happily do for him if he didn't stop talking. Or at least get to the point.

"She was always a rather difficult child. Flighty. Imaginative. Had fancies. Her father was a scientist, and as her mother had passed on, he doted on her."

"Dead? Murdered was she? By this Albertine?" The judge scribbled something on the pad on his desk.

"Murdered, your honor? No, I believe it was childbirth."

The judge scrubbed at the pad. "Continue."

"Yes," Spencer growled. "Continue."

"As I was saying, the father doted on her and allowed her to to participate in his scientific whims and fancies and she took it too far. Became unmanageable. Unmarriable."

Spencer fisted his hands and took a step toward Franklin. "Get to the point," he muttered murderously in the man's ear.

Franklin blinked rapidly and continued. "I arranged a marriage for Albertine. A good match. A good man, with a parcel of land and children who needed caring for after his wife passed."

The judge looked up sharply. "Was *she* murdered?"

Franklin grimaced apologetically. "Afraid not. Childbirth again."

The judge slumped and waved his hand to tell Franklin to continue.

"When I informed Albertine of the contract, she stole my dog cart and kitchen hand and absconded. Never to be seen again. Until this man, the, uh, the Duke of Erleigh, arrived on the doorstep of Crawford House demanding to know her details."

Franklin pressed his hands together at his chest in prayer.

"Until he appeared, I had feared her dead." Franklin's attempt at a caring tone rang falsely into the room. The only thing Franklin cared about was the two pounds a month the father of the fifteen children had agreed to pay him to marry Albertine.

The judge scribbled on his paper. "Theft. Impersonating a countess. Breach of contract. Seems like I have enough here for two decades of jail, at least."

This was not going the way Spencer intended. He opened his mouth when a knock at the door interrupted.

"Your honor, the court is ready for you."

The judge heaved himself from the chair and stood like a child, arms outstretched while the clerk placed his thick black robes over his tweed suit.

"Your honor, we didn't come here seeking further charges on Miss Honeycombe—"

The judge adjusted his wig and brushed past Spencer stepping out into the hallway.

"I have a duty to the Queen to see people like this removed from our streets and punished for their sins. Good day, Your Grace."

This had not gone at all the way he had expected it to.

He felt sick to the stomach at the thought that he had just made things worse for Albertine. He had been so certain of his ability to swoop in and fix everything. He hadn't even considered that he wouldn't be able to right this.

"I don't suppose you could rustle up that cup of tea now, could you?"

Spencer snarled at Franklin. "Your cousin is at the risk of hanging and you are worried about a cup of tea?"

Spencer had reached the end of his patience with this selfish git. He had reached the end of his patience with this entire situation. He was going to go out into that courtroom and get

Albertine out even if it meant he was going to have to carry her out over his shoulder.

★ ★ ★

Her face was blank. Shadowless and aloof as if nothing was amiss, as if she found herself in a courtroom accused of murder every day.

But everything was amiss.

She looked tired, the skin on her face pulled taut as if she had been tasked with holding an enormous load. She had always carried a weight, he realized. His brave, bold, and wondrous woman had always shouldered the weight of whatever responsibility had been given to her, whether it was caring for her injured brother or the death of her father. And when it had become clear that no provision had been left for her she had shouldered it all. Not only shouldered, borne it like it was nothing but a feather.

He felt unsteady, as if he had been at sea for months. The floor lurched beneath him and his blood galloped unsteadily through his veins, he could feel it thump at his neck, at his heart. He resisted the urge to place his hand over his heart to steady the ache that had taken up residence there since he had last seen her.

Her eyes drifted slowly along the faces of the people sitting in the public viewing gallery.

*I'm here.* He willed her silently to meet his gaze, staring hard at her face. *I am here, my love.*

Her gaze shifted with agonizing slowness, searching each person's face in the courtroom, one by one until it finally settled upon his.

And then something incredible happened.

Her deep, brown eyes met his and she smiled.

Not the practiced smile of the Countess Von Dagga, nor the benign, polite smile she wore in public. No, this was the wondrous, earth-shifting smile of Albertine Honeycombe. The smile started as a gentle curve to her lips but her whole face, her whole body was consumed by it.

He felt that smile somewhere deep in his chest and he couldn't help back but smile back.

She smiled as if she were seeing the only person in the entire world she wanted to see. She smiled as if they were alone, laughing together in the garden of Gunter's, or talking in her study, instead of in a courtroom in front of hundreds of onlookers.

He saw the very moment she remembered where she was and why. The smile slid from her face. First her face froze, the corners of her lips dropped, her eyebrows pulled together. Her mouth tightened into a thin line and her eyes became as blank as an empty page.

His heart hammered as if it would break.

Her body lurched as the bailiff jerked her arm to hurry her along. It was then Spencer saw her hands were encased in irons. A wave of rage at the way she was being manhandled burned through him. Didn't the fool know who he had in his hands? How precious she was? How unlike anyone else in the whole kingdom she was?

He charged through the crowd, oblivious to the muted tsks of displeasure and cries of 'I say!' He was oblivious to everything.

Except her.

After what felt like an eternity, he reached the front of the courtroom but a dark-suited man held his arm out. "You can't come back here."

"I think you will find that I can, and will and am about to do so." He summoned every ounce of his willpower to keep his voice calm and controlled. He wanted to tear every man that stood between he and Albertine apart limb by limb.

Raising his nose, he narrowed his gaze at the bailiff.

The other man's eye's darted from Spencer's frigid stare to the people hovering behind him. A knock to Spencer's back and the sound of shouting increased as a scuffle broke out behind them.

"I am in the employment of Scotland Yard *and* am the Duke of Erleigh," Spencer announced.

For once this proclamation didn't cause a cool sweat to break out along his hairline and he hadn't needed to swallow against a dry mouth.

He was the Duke of Erleigh and he needed to get to his Duchess.

# CHAPTER 22

"And then I dissolved a handmade sleeping draught in his drink."

The courtroom inhaled one loud collective breath.

"He was alive and breathing when I left. The sleeping draught didn't kill him." Albertine's voice was steady.

A collective gasp sucked the air from the room before the courtroom erupted into a cacophony of noise.

Albertine had been nervous when she'd been bought into the dock. The courtroom was so crowded that it was standing room only, and even then, judging by the jostling, there wasn't much standing room left. But the crowd was vocal and energetic and the energy was similar to a show on the West End. Albertine had almost begun to enjoy herself, forgetting it was actually a courtroom where she might be sentenced to hang.

The judge banged his gavel on to the sound block. "Quiet. Quiet."

He peered down at Albertine from his raised platform. "You poisoned him, you say."

Albertine sniffed. The sawdust they had laid on the floor was playing havoc with her sinuses. It didn't hurt that it made her sound contrite. "I didn't poison him. Just sent him to sleep."

The judge lowered his spectacles on to his nose. "It says here he was strangled."

Albertine blinked. "Yes, he was strangled. By a man. The marks on his neck were twice the size of my thumbs. It couldn't have been me."

The judge peered over the spectacles. "Who told you that?"

Albertine gazed to the ceiling. "That is a little trickier to explain. I did, however, see the marks on his neck with my very own eyes."

The judge gazed down at his papers and made a noise. "When you stole his body from the morgue and dumped him in the river?"

*Rude.* She had *borrowed* the body and the coffin *fell* into the river. But before she could point that out, a voice called out into the room, "Wait!"

Joan's small dark head bobbed amongst the crowd. Albertine smiled as her eyes met Joan's bright blue gaze.

"Sorry," Joan mouthed.

Albertine's eyebrows furrowed—what on earth did Joan have to apologize for?

A second later, when the ruddy, bovine visage of Franklin appeared it all became clear. Her stomach twisted.

"This woman is no countess. This is my cousin, Albertine Honeycombe. From Crawford House, Wednesbury."

The judge peered at Franklin. "What say you, sir?"

"I am Franklin Randall, tenth Earl of Suffoldshire and this is my cousin. She is not and never has been a countess."

"The count doesn't exist like, we made him up," Joan yelled. "To escape this one." She jerked her thumb at Franklin. "He wanted her to marry the neighbor but he's got fifteen younguns."

The judge nodded. "That is rather a lot of children. What say you, Countess, er, Miss Honeycombe?"

Albertine swallowed against the small bubble of hope that had begun to grow in her chest. "It's true. I made it all up. The count never existed. He was a figment of my imagination. No one murdered him."

"Well, now. What's this about the murder of Lord Grendel, then?" The judge scowled at Mitchell over his glasses.

Mitchell gulped and threw a look toward Spencer, who was standing behind him looking murderous. He leaned his hands on the large desk that sat between Albertine and the crowd.

Another voice spoke. "I have something to say about that."

The swarming crowd parted and Lady Cobham appeared, fake Fancy in her arms. Fancy yapped once at the sight of Albertine and shook his head. The red ribbons tied to his ears flapped and Albertine smiled.

"Hello, darling," Albertine called out.

"Beg pardon?" the judge asked archly.

"I was speaking to the dog." Albertine smiled at Lady Cobham, who raised her nose and pointed a gnarled finger at the judge.

"Rupert, you stupid boy. Release this girl immediately. She has killed no one. She was with me all evening the night Grendel was murdered."

The judge banged his gavel again. "You can't come in and speak to me like that, Aunt Petunia," he hissed. "I am working."

"I don't care. You always were a stupid boy and you're stupid now. Let this girl go."

"She just admitted to drugging a lord," he spluttered.

"That may be the case, but as you just said, he was strangled. And she was with me all evening. How dare you drag this poor young woman over the coals like a common criminal, instead of concerning yourself with who actually *did* kill the man. You ought to be ashamed of yourself."

Lady Cobham met Albertine's surprised gaze and gave her a tiny wink before banging her cane on the chair in front of her. The man sat in it turned around, shooting her a punitive glance. She glared at him until he turned back to the front.

The judge's cheeks flushed crimson and he glanced down to the papers on the table in front of him.

"I say. I am a judge and you can't come in here and talk to me like that." But his voice was low and Albertine doubted Lady Cobham could hear it.

"Excuse me," a feminine voice sang out into the courtroom. "I say, excuse me. I have some information that is pertinent in this case."

A flash of red fluttered through the crowd and suddenly Lady Grendel was standing at the center of the viewing gallery. Her posture was rod straight, her hair loose around her shoulders. She looked younger, lighter somehow, as if a great weight had been lifted from her shoulders.

The crowd oohed and ahhed, nudging each other at the sight of her.

"Order," the judge yelled. "For goodness sake. Does no one respect the rules of this court? Or me?"

"I am Lady Grendel. I saw a man leaving my husband's study the night of his murder."

Albertine stared at Lady Grendel through narrowed eyes.

"Why didn't you provide Scotland Yard with this information?" the judge scolded.

Lady Grendel leveled an icy look at the judge. "They didn't ask me."

The judge heaved a sigh. "Is it lunchtime yet? No? Well, if asked to, could you describe this man?"

"I very well could."

The judge lowered his glasses and peered at Lady Grendel over the top of them. His bushy eyebrows hung like disapproving caterpillars.

"And *would* you describe him, should the police provide you with a man that could perform a sketch?"

"I can do better than that." Lady Grendel lifted a corner of her mouth in a smirk that was equal measures self-satisfied and really rather wicked.

The band that had wound itself tightly around Albertine's chest since the moment she had read the headline about Grendel's death began to loosen. She leaned forward, the manacles around her wrist biting at her skin.

"I can show you him, as he is right here in this very room."

The crowd erupted into a flurry of noise. Heads whipped from side to side as members of the audience shot each other accusing looks. Lady Grendel met Albertine's gaze. Lady Grendel nodded once before turning back to the judge, with wide and innocent eyes.

"And will you put us out of our misery and point this man out?" the judge asked, his tone making clear that he was losing patience with the entire debacle.

"I will indeed."

Lady Grendel lifted an elegant hand. The entire courtroom held its breath. Chins lifted, and necks craned to be the first to see where her hand was gesturing.

She extended a finger and a short balding man Albertine had never seen before clutched at his chest. His face reddened with indignation and the woman next to him hit him on the arm with her folded fan. He shook his head and a burst of movement behind the man had all faces turning upward toward the gallery.

The crowd parted and Wallop stood as still as a statue amongst the rabble.

He lifted a lip in disdain and shook his head. "Good luck trying to pin this one on me."

The rustle of silk and linen was loud as gunfire as the room all turned back to Lady Grendel. She smiled, lowering her outstretched finger and began examining her nail with a disaffected air. Had the matter not been quite so urgent, Albertine would have been impressed at how she commanded the room. There must be close to a hundred people jammed into the hearing room, yet it was as silent as the bottom of the ocean.

The magistrate breathed out loudly through his nose. "This is highly irregular, Madam. Baron Wallop, what say you?"

"I was with my wife, all evening at our fashionable townhouse in Mayfair. She worked on her embroidery in front of the fire, while I caught up on correspondence."

Another lady stood, her face semi-hidden by a large fashionable hat. Lady Roche smiled when Albertine's shocked gaze met hers. "No, you weren't. Unless you were in the back of The Twelve Cocks Tavern with your wife and her paramour. They were seen by two of my footmen. And the barmaid."

The crowd erupted into a sea of commotion, people began to catcall and whistle and someone stomped his feet in a cheerful rhythm on the wooden floor.

The judge banged his gavel against its block.

Wallop's usually ruddy face was beetroot red. "Footmen?" he scoffed. "A tavern wench? Their word against a lord's?"

"No." A voice boomed from the back of the room.

Spencer appeared as the crowd parted around him.

While as stylish as ever, he looked slightly rumpled, a dark shadow of stubble around his jaw, his trousers creased, and the lines around his eyes more pronounced.

"It is a duke's word against a liar, a cheat and now it seems, murderer. Who happens to also be a baron. You, Wallop, paid that young man to lie and say he saw Albertine with Grendel before he died, and that is a crime. You harassed this innocent young woman to the point where she needed to hide to evade you after she exposed you and your wife as card cheats. Which is also a crime."

The crowd began to jeer and jostle at Wallop. He glared at Spencer for a moment and then shifted his hateful gaze to Albertine.

"*You*," he spat. "You just couldn't keep your mouth shut. You cost me. We aren't welcome in any gambling hells because of you. I owe men money and your big mouth made me lose the chance to make that money back. You don't know these men. You don't know what they're capable of."

His face reddened further and vein pulsed in his forehead. His eyes bulged in a rather frightful manner. Albertine fought a shiver, grateful they were in a room full of people.

"*It's you I should've killed.*" As soon as the words were uttered Wallop shook himself, as if he had just woken from a spell. He pulled at his collar, and offered an awkward, muttered laugh. "I should think the murderer, that is, whoever that may be, would say that about you. You are an irritant. The murderer should have killed you."

The courtroom was deathly silent again, but this time the energy was of horrified shock, not expectant excitement.

"Baron Wallop," Spencer's voice rung through the room like a bell, true and clear. "I charge you with the murder of Lord Grendel. With harassment. With perverting the course of justice."

Wallop's gaze darted around the room, taking in the crowded room, chairs, all full, people standing in the walkway. Although he stood no chance of escape, Albertine could see he was considering his options.

After all, she had just spent the last week doing the same thing.

Wallop took a step backward, a conceited smile on his face. "All right, so what if I did it. I watched her go in to Grendel's study. I was about to go in there after her, help her understand what she had done to me. But Grendel went in before I could. I sat and waited but only she came out. Grendel owed me money, was refusing to pay up. I was going to be roughed up by the men I owed money to but he didn't care. I went in and found him passed out in a chair and I took my opportunity."

He continued to step backwards slowly as he spoke, pushing the people behind him out of his way. His eyes had taken on a glassy sheen and his fixed smile was a terrifying grimace that made Albertine think of a crocodile she had seen in one of Papa's nature books.

"I put my hands around his neck and squeezed the life out of him. He deserved it. These men that are after me, they aren't playing around. But Grendel wouldn't give me what I was owed. Was enjoying lording it over me. Enjoying my desperation, my dilemma."

He barked out a horrific laugh, like the rasp of stone on flint. "So I killed him and I stole what I could out of his desk. It was enough to keep those men off my back but not for long."

"Wallop." Spencer's voice was a firm warning as he began to push his way toward him. "Stay where you are."

Wallop let out that laugh again. "I don't think so. You think you're so smart, but I almost had you, didn't I? Well, I won't be going easy."

He threw one last lingering, hateful glance toward Albertine before abruptly charging toward the large stained-glass window overlooking the street below.

He ran toward it like a bull, lowering his shoulder and hitting the glass full speed. The crowd screamed as the glass exploded, sending colorful shards into the air. For a breathtaking moment the splinters seemed to hover above the crowd, sending prisms of colored light into the room.

The crowd, shocked into silence, held its breath as Wallop did not disappear through the window as expected, instead landing heavily against thick iron bars enclosing the windows from the outside. The communal breath was expelled in a huff of astonished noise as Wallop threw himself against the bars again and again, hoping to weaken them in some way. It was clear that the iron had been made with this express situation in mind—the bars did not budge, even a little.

Wallop looked around wildly. His face was a terrifying mask. Albertine fancied she could see the exact moment that he realized he was in a pickle.

Spencer raised a hand and even though she hated the man and never wanted to lay eyes on him again, Albertine couldn't help the little thrill that ran through her at his mastery of the situation.

"Griffin, Walker," he ordered. "On him. Bailiff—do not let him anywhere near her."

Wallop's gaze darted madly around the room, seeking an escape route. His gaze met Albertine's. His eyes were dark with hatred and anger but Albertine would be not cowed by him. If this last week had taught her anything it was that she was brave beyond her wildest imagination. She had thought that she was here merely following Algie's dream, blindly repeating her papa's words—*as sharp as a dagger*—but now she saw that she was as brave and yes, as sharp, as both her brother and Papa. Not only would they have been proud of her, but she was proud of herself.

She raised her nose in the air and smiled.

Wallop narrowed his eyes and let out a guttural sound unlike anything she had heard. He shoved the people standing between them out of the way and kicked a chair.

"I'll kill you before I go," he roared.

There was a blur of motion as Spencer vaulted over the hip-height barrier separating the spectators from the lawyers. A large oak desk stood between him and Wallop. Because bailiffs had moved to protect the judge across the room at the beginning of the kerfuffle, nothing stood between her and Wallop, now charging toward her like a bull toward a red flag. The irons around Albertine's hands had been attached to a bar that ran the length of the desk. There was nowhere for her to go. She took a breath and braced herself for impact.

Instead of ducking her head, she focused her gaze on Spencer. If she was going to go, she wanted his face to be the last thing she saw.

With one swift glance, Spencer took in Wallop and the mammoth desk, assessing and calculating, and in what appeared to be one movement shrugged off his jacket and threw himself across the wide expanse of the prosecution's desk, sliding across the highly shined top. Landing lightly, he whipped his tangled length of jacket at Wallop's feet, furling it around his legs. A painfully loud thump reverberated throughout the courtroom as the tangle of fabric bought Wallop's knees down onto the stone floor. Spencer then flew through the air at Wallop, connecting with a thud and pinning him to the ground.

Wallop kicked and bucked underneath Spencer, and the room exploded with activity and color as police officers swarmed the grappling men. Two men grabbed one of Wallop's arms and another two lay atop his kicking legs. It was only when Spencer was certain they had him under control that he got off.

"Here, sir, let me help you up."

Spencer shrugged off the officer's outstretched hands. "I can take care of myself. Make sure he is locked up. I won't have him anywhere near Miss Honeycombe."

At her name he looked up and met her incredulous gaze.

His gaze ran over her, quick and impersonal, as if to reassure himself she was all right. He lifted a brow in enquiry and she nodded.

The courtroom was in chaos. Women had fainted and were being carried from the courtroom. Men stood, blood dripping from some of their faces, cut by the flying glass. Police officers barred the doors; women tending to cuts called for doctors.

Albertine searched the chaotic crowd for Joan. Someone who looked quite like her was being cradled in Mitchell's arms, his body facing the crowd in protection. Albertine narrowed her eyes as the small figure ducked her head under Mitchell's arm to meet her gaze. Joan winked at her from under Mitch-ell's armpit.

"Are you all right?"

Albertine kept her gaze trained on the courtroom. Spencer was so close that she could smell his unique scent, tea and lemon. If she looked at him now, she knew everything she had been holding in so tightly would come bubbling to the surface and who knows where that would lead them. Nowhere good, she was certain. It had been a moment of weakness, a reflex, smiling at him earlier. It had felt like a lifetime since she had seen him and her disloyal body had betrayed her by responding the way it had.

He had looked so beautiful, storming through the crowd like that. His brow furrowed the way it did, nearly always. He was so stern looking, so reserved, but their eyes had met and he had visibly softened. The creases in his eyes had appeared and he'd smiled. It was that rare momentous action that had undone her. It had been so long since she had seen that smile that she had simply returned it without thinking.

Before the weight of all his betrayal had come crashing back down.

"Oh, absolutely. Just another day in the life of the Countess Von Dagga," she replied blithely.

There was a tremor in her voice she hoped desperately he hadn't heard. She gripped the iron bar tightly to steady herself.

"One imagines that this all means one is no longer accused of murder?" She could hardly bring herself to say the words.

As horrifying and shocking as this had all been, it had felt as if she was watching from afar. Or as if she had left her body and was floating above the courtroom. As soon as Lady

Grendel had stood she had held her breath, allowing it sink low and deep into her body and it felt as if she had not released it since.

All she could think was, *Thank god, thank god, thank god.*

Even the sight of Franklin hadn't dampened her hope. He would expect her to go back to Crawford House with him now, she presumed, to ensure that the marriage and his monthly stipend would go ahead. And she would go. That had been part of the mental bargain she had made as she left the jail. *Gallows or marriage.* It turned out she would choose marriage any day.

"As Wallop has confessed to the murder of Grendel and the court knows that there was no Count Von Dagga to murder, all charges will be dropped. I told you I would get you out of here, and I meant it."

For a fleeting moment she wondered how he could be so sure, but then she remembered he was probably in charge of every police officer in London. Him. A duke. She still couldn't believe it.

"Did you just *I told you so* me?" she returned lightly.

He made an amused sound and she blinked into the court-room to stem the tears that threatened. Even now, they got along so well. But his betrayal stung, tearing at her skin like stinging ivy. Memories washed over her like waves, running through Hyde Park together, the moment they had shared with her shoe, laughing together, that kiss, sharing their pain about their brothers.

She screwed her eyes closed. That hurt the most. That she had opened herself to someone, had allowed herself to get close to someone only to find that all of it, all of it, was lies. He probably had a rich titled lady ready to marry at a moment's notice.

Had they laughed about her, his betrothed and him? Did they sit together in front of a roaring fire in some grand town-house while servants served them tea and scones and laugh about the pathetic woman he was fooling?

And how foolish she had been. How prideful, how deluded.

Franklin was right, Papa had filled her head full of stuff and nonsense. She was impulsive, willful, foolish. And even though she had fancied herself worldly and brave, when it came down to it, her knowledge was the things of books and stories. She hadn't been able to escape her fate. She would have to marry the farmer and settle into life with him. There was no other choice. She had been fooling herself that there ever had been, just like she had been fooling herself that a man like Spencer would have ever been actually interested in her.

Her nose tingled unpleasantly and her lip began to tremble. She pulled at the iron encasing her wrists, allowing the pain to distract her. Spencer glanced down and misinterpreted her movements.

"I'm so sorry, that must be hurting." His gaze met the gaze of a nearby bailiff. "You," he pointed, "come and remove these irons immediately."

The bailiff looked around the courtroom. "I can't, sir, not until I get official word from the judge."

Wallop and most of the injured people had been removed. What was left now was mostly officials, interviewing people. Lady Cobham was gesturing angrily to a blank-faced man and fake Fancy was lifting his leg on the poor man's shoes. Lady Roche was making a statement to a tall man in a police uni-form, and Joan . . . Albertine scanned the room. Joan and Mitchell's embrace had changed. He was now being dragged along behind her by the hand, heading toward Albertine and Spencer at great speed.

Joan threw her arms around Albertine, clutching at her so tightly that it seemed that Albertine could barely breathe.

"Oh, Bertie, you're free. Ya off the hook. I knew Sweetman would do it. Mitchell here is going to release you now, ain't ya?"

Joan released Albertine long enough to shoot Mitchell a badgering glance. He reddened and shuffled his feet, avoiding both Albertine and Spencer's gaze.

"Miss . . . er Miss . . ."

"Honeycombe, it's Albertine Honeycombe. Like I've been tellin' ya for the last week," Joan admonished.

Albertine hid a smile. If he hadn't arrested her and almost had her hung for murder, she might have felt sorry for Mitchell.

"Miss Honeycombe. I wish to inform you that all previously laid charges against you have been cleared and I . . . I wish to apologize for any inconvenience this incident may have caused you." His tone was stiff and formal but it was impossible to miss the note of true regret behind it.

Something about Mitchell had always made Albertine feel warm toward him. Whether it was his Black Country accent or something else, she had always felt he was a genuinely lovely person. She watched as his miserable gaze met Spencer's hard one.

"No hard feelings, Mitchell. I am sure you were just doing your job," she said, sweetly. She could afford to be magnanimous now she knew she wasn't going to hang.

He looked at her finally then, his cheeks pinking. "I am sorry, miss. But you have to admit. It was all a bit odd."

She smiled a true smile then. "Yes, you're quite right. It all was rather unusual, wasn't it?"

And it had been. Unusual. Fun and exciting.

Hopefully those memories would keep her warm on the long dreadful nights on the farmhouse that stretched out in front of her now. As if her thoughts had summoned him, Franklin appeared in the throng of people that had descended on Albertine.

The bailiff released the cuffs on her wrists, markedly gentler than they had been put on. At the final click she rubbed her wrists, not out of pain but sheer pleasure.

She was free.

She met Franklin's gaze and abruptly made a decision. She would not marry the farmer. Come what may, she would *not* be forced to live a life that was not one of her own choosing.

Spencer, with a rather murderous expression, watched her rub her wrists. She glanced away. She should think of him as Duke Erleigh now, rather than Spencer. Her stomach flipped painfully as memories of how she and Joan had worried about his financial situation. Wonders, the man could probably buy the entire ice cream shop, and she had worried that buying Joan more than one scoop might be beyond him. And how she had scraped together enough money to make payment to him for his first week as her employee. Her cheeks heated. He must have been laughing at her the whole time, amused by her gaucheness, her naivety.

"Franklin." Joan's voice was like a thunderclap in the courtroom. "You tell Albertine here what we just discussed."

Franklin yanked at his necktie and screwed his nose. "Well now, I don't recall, er, exactly agreeing to anything."

Joan stepped between Albertine and Franklin, raising herself up to her full height, which still didn't see her to

Albertine's shoulders. Affection for Joan flooded through Albertine and she reached for her hand. Joan might be slight, but, she realized now, it was she that was the bravest person Albertine had ever known.

"Aye, you just told me that you'd no longer try to force Albertine to marry Cunningham. Or anyone."

Franklin pulled a face and glanced about at the much taller men that were now staring at him with avid interest.

"I . . . er . . . the farmer has found another woman so Albertine will not be required to marry him. But the estate cannot afford to bear the costs of . . . of . . ." Franklin trailed off as Spencer stepped toward him.

Albertine placed a quelling hand against Spencer's arm. "How perfectly lovely for Cunningham. But you have no need to concern yourself with me. I do not require any monetary support from you.

Albertine thought of the cottage in Cornwall. If she could make this utterly ridiculous situation work for her, she most certainly could make a simple living for herself in Cornwall.

"I have a position elsewhere but I do wish to secure your word that you will not arrange any future marriages for me."

Franklin looked from Albertine to Spencer. What he saw in Spencer's eyes made him blink furiously like he had when they were children and he was confronted with a lie, of which there had been many.

"You have my word. No more marriages." He pulled at his necktie. "I say, I was promised a cup of tea. I'm parched." He looked hopefully around the crowd.

"Come on then." Joan offered her elbow, to Albertine. "I don't know about you but I've had enough of this place. Let's go."

Albertine smiled at Joan and tucked her elbow into hers. She couldn't bear to meet Spencer's gaze, which she could feel like the heat from a fire when one stood too close. "Yes, let us go then."

Together she and Joan made their way toward the door. Overcome with a wave of affection she patted Joan's hand. "Thank God for you."

Joan paused and looked up at her. "Thank God for this lot. I was certain you was done for." Her dimples exploded out of her smile. "And you know I couldn't be doing with finding a job as an *actual* maid. I'm not cut out for this nonsense."

Albertine burst into laughter, the first since she had stood on the stoop of her house and looked into Spencer's eyes. "Happy to oblige."

The laughter stayed in her heart as they walked toward the exit. They would be all right, she and Joan.

They'd be more than all right. They would be grand.

# CHAPTER 23

Spencer watched as Albertine walked from the courtroom. This was not the way he had imagined things going. He had imagined he would storm into the chambers and demand her release. Dreaming of her gratitude at his efforts had sustained him through the dark nights.

But here she was.

She had saved herself simply by having been herself.

Through her kindness to others, she had forged friendships and loyalty that had filled the courtroom and secured her release. She was truly remarkable.

He couldn't let her leave. Not without telling her everything that lay in his heart. Even if she never wanted to speak to him again, he had to tell her. He would spend the rest of his life in tormented regret if he didn't.

Pushing through the crowd, he called her name.

He was jostled from side to side as the crowd swarmed around her, people hoping for a moment of her attention. He reached for her hand as he neared, pulling him around to face him. The feel of her soft, warm hand turned his stomach to a pit of snakes.

He couldn't live without this woman.

She pulled her hand from his and raised her gaze from his collar to meet his eyes.

They stared at each silently, her large brown eyes clear and candid. Her dress was stained around the neckline and crumpled. Large twirls of hair tufted around her head. The sun streaming through the broken window lit them so they glowed like a halo; a streak of dirt ran from the corner of her eye to along her cheek, as if she had been crying. His hands began to tremble with the effort not to reach out and run his thumb along the mark, to erase the tear tracks.

*To undo it all.*

"Well, Spencer Sweetman. This is where we part ways." She held a hand out for him to shake.

He pressed his lips together at the hot pain that swirled through his chest at the thought of this being the last time he saw her.

She cocked her head and gazed at him silently considering. "It was fun, wasn't it."

It truly had been. For the first time since Stephen had passed, perhaps even before that, he had experienced fun. Not the enjoyment of performing his tasks well, cracking a case, or running a tight operation. Just pure fun. For fun's sake.

He thought back to their race through Hyde Park, the day of the dog swap, the way she and Joan had leveled and lifted each other in equal parts, and the way they had so openly welcomed him into their twosome, accepting him for himself.

Not his title, his position, his standing in society. They wanted him, as Spencer.

He couldn't imagine his life without her now. Anything without her would be colorless, empty.

"Albertine. Not only are you the loveliest, nicest woman I have ever met. You are also the strongest." He cleared his throat against the lump that had lodged itself at the back of it.

She shifted her gaze to his collar, her face blank.

"I deeply regret my foolishness. I should have spoken with you and if I had . . . things would have been different. Please know that."

She nodded but didn't raise her eyes from his lapel.

He reached for her hand and was gratified when she didn't pull away. "I wouldn't blame you if you never wanted to speak to me again. I can barely look at myself in the mirror. I am deeply ashamed."

"Miss Honeycombe?" A man with a small notepad and a pencil was hovering behind Albertine. "Just a few questions, if I may?"

"Shhh," Joan hissed at him. "We're trying to listen here. He's got summink to say."

Spencer smiled at Joan, who had managed to position herself at Albertine's right elbow without either of them noticing. Then, as if a cloud lifted, Spencer noticed that they were surrounded by nearly everyone in the courtroom.

Every single person that had watched the hearing with avid interest now watched them.

He swallowed hard. "Should we, perhaps go somewhere? I should like to speak to you about this, somewhere quieter. More private."

It was the wrong thing to say. He lost her, he could see it. It was as if he had slapped her. But why? She straightened.

His hand was freezing cold as she pulled hers from their embrace.

"I appreciate the offer but we are leaving London rather promptly." She turned to leave but the crowd was too thick.

"Albertine. The only one I let down more than you, is me. Will you give me the opportunity to make amends?" Spencer looked around at the sea of faces surrounding them, pushing and jostling to get a better view of the near murderess and the duke who had, they believed, almost had her hung.

Albertine and Joan began to press their way through the crowd of people toward the exit.

He knew he had to make a grand gesture here. There was no second chance. Once she left this courtroom, she would be lost to him. It was now or never. He sucked in a breath and called her name.

Her back stiffened but she didn't turn around.

He tugged his trousers up at the crease and knelt, placing a knee on the cold dirty floor of the courtroom.

"Albertine Honeycombe." His deep voice carried over the general murmurs of the onlookers. "They say you can't love and be wise, but with you by my side I don't need to be wise. I will have the wisest, bravest woman I know beside me."

The crowd became silent, as it had when Lady Grendel had stood and made her announcement.

Good God, he was making a scene and had never wanted to more in his life.

"Perhaps you can do what my mother despaired of anyone ever achieving, making me see sense. If I had to surrender you, I couldn't bear it. It's impossible to imagine. These mistakes are mine. Believe me, I regret. I regret so many things but meeting you, spending time with you, falling in love with you is not on that list."

The crowd let out a collective sigh and Spencer fought the urge to hide his face in his hands. This would be the talk of London for as long as both he and she lived. But it made no difference to him. He didn't care an iota what these people thought of him.

All he cared about was Albertine.

He pushed on.

"I cherish everything about you from the dimple in your left cheek to the ticklish bottom of your feet. Please do tell me if you think you might feel the same?"

She turned then, two spots of color high on her cheeks.

"You are experiencing an affection?" She remained stone faced but her voice was light.

He smiled and nodded. "Indeed, I am. Also, perhaps a heart attack. I'm having some pains." He clutched his chest with both hands.

She raised an arch brow. "Humble pie giving you indigestion?"

"I will eat humble pie every day for the rest of my life if you agree to spend it with me."

She pressed a hand to her chest in a copycat gesture to his but didn't say a word. She blinked rapidly, her eyes glassy.

"Will you please agree to marry me so I can get off this dashed floor?"

If his hands weren't pressed so tightly to his chest, the entire courtroom could see how badly they shook. How very, very badly he needed her to agree to marry him.

Her eyes widened as if she only now realized he was still crouched on the floor below her.

"I can't marry you. You're a duke."

He shook his head but changed it to a nod at the last moment. "I am. I can't help that. I don't want to be, but I am.

I don't want to do it without you. We could achieve amazing things together."

A sigh sung out across the crowd as the women swooned over his words. Albertine threw an exaggerated exasperated look at the women around them. "It seems you have plenty of willing participants here, who likely know you better than I."

Spencer shook his head. "No one knows me better than you, Albertine. No one."

He gestured to the crowd. "Do you think she should marry me?"

The crowd roared in the affirmative.

He and Albertine stared at each other, and they both laughed as the crowd burst out into cheers and whistles. Seeing her smile was as if the clouds had parted and the sun begun to shine again, after a long cold winter.

"Marry you?" she mouthed, her hands still clutched to her chest.

He nodded. "Absolutely."

She shook her head, but that smile, that perfect smile remained. "You're crazier than I thought."

He nodded again. "Absolutely."

The crowd fell away again and there was nothing but her luminous brown eyes.

"I'm not cut out to be a duke's wife," she said sadly. "Me? A duchess? I couldn't wear a big dress, and stand in front of thousands of people."

He gestured to the crowd of people staring at them in the courtroom. "Too shy?"

That beloved dimple appeared. "I suffer from nerves."

They smiled at each other.

"You can marry me any way you want. You want the whole of society there, you may. If you wish to have a priest marry us on the grounds of Crawford, you may. It's yours. Whatever you want."

Finally, she took a halting step toward him. "All I want is you. My lovely, kind, sweet man." She reached for his hand and pulled him to his feet.

"And all I want is you, Albertine. I can't do much about being a duke, but with you by my side we could take anything on. All I ask is that you refrain from pushing any more coffins into the Thames. Or, come to think of it, into any body of water."

She smiled again, a smile that made his hands tremble. "No guarantees, Your Grace, but for you, I will try my best."

"Your best is all I can ask for. All I want."

And it was all he wanted—if he spent the rest of his life being surprised and delighted by Albertine, he knew he would live an enormously happy life.

# CHAPTER 24

Albertine felt as if she were floating an inch from the ground as she and Spencer made their way hand in hand from the courtroom. He gestured with his head to the man closest to the door, who scrambled to open it for them. A thrill of electricity shot through her at this new side of Spencer. She had always found him reliable and strong and utterly, utterly capable, but this powerful side of him was new to her.

He had shared his gentle side with her and now, watching him with the men in the courtroom, she realized that side of him was one that was locked away, reserved for her only. Had they met in different circumstances, perhaps he would never have let his guard down enough for her to truly get to know the man underneath the titles, both detective and duke.

And almost certainly she would never have let her own guard down the way she had while they had worked together. Although she wanted to curl up in a dark corner when she thought about the way she had assumed him down on his luck and paid what to him was surely a pittance.

She would miss London though. Although she had found it dirty and crowded when they had first arrived, she knew she would miss the people she had come to know. The twins who ambled in matching clothes around the park in the square across from her townhouse, the old lady who fed the pigeons, the grocer two blocks away, the women whom she had come to know and care for. Fancy.

There had been a thrill to this detective work. As bad at it as she had been.

"Your Grace." A man appeared from the shadows of the hallway. Spencer paused mid-step as if considering whether or not to stop.

He stopped.

"De Vere." Spencer shook the tall man's outstretched hand. He was a tall, thin, hard-looking man. There was something cold about him. He turned ice blue eyes to Albertine and lifted a sardonic eyebrow. "The woman of the hour. A close call, Miss Honeycombe."

Albertine couldn't tell if he sounded disappointed or pleased for her.

"Indeed."

"You drugged the man before he was murdered."

Albertine's stomach twisted. Was she about to be charged for that now?

He continued in a low voice. "To retrieve something of importance for someone. That he had stolen."

Spencer's head swung toward her. She kept her gaze trained on the man. How on earth could he know that, unless . . .?

"From someone very dear to me. They were impressed. As was I."

Albertine sucked in a breath as the penny dropped. This was Lady Roche's lover.

But why would a man as powerful as De Vere simply not attend to Grendel and demand the letters back? Perhaps confronting Grendel would have been an admission of guilt De Vere couldn't afford. But to leave Lady Roche to deal with the fallout of the blackmail of these letters, and without a penny to pay for it, seemed heartless to Albertine.

Some of her emotion must've shown on her face as De Vere lowered his eyebrow.

"Thank you for attending to the matter in such a timely fashion. I would have attended to the matter myself should I have been in the country. However, I was only informed"—his strangely expressionless face tightened—"of the fact, just now. Thank you. I believe I owe you a debt and it is one I can assure you that I will repay. Should you ever need anything, please get in touch."

He held a card out between them but pressed a small folded piece of paper into the hand farthest from Spencer. He had angled himself in such a manner that all Spencer would be able to see was the thick cream card he held between them.

They held each other's gaze for a moment. Albertine tucked the folded paper into her palm and reached for the card, hiding the small paper underneath it.

"I don't say things I don't mean. So please, do get in touch." He nodded at Spencer. "Your Grace."

"Good day."

Spencer and Albertine watched De Vere stride along the hall. Men scrambled to avoid him, pressing themselves against the wall to avoid making contact with him.

"Who on earth was that?"

Spencer squeezed her hand. "That was Lord De Vere, the head of Home Office. What he does exactly is anyone's guess. I just know it is highly classified."

Albertine shrugged and squeezed Spencer's hand back. "So, what now?"

"Right now, we get you home and bathed and into a clean change of clothing."

Albertine closed her eyes in pleasure at the mere thought of bathing. How she must smell!

They released each other's hand and Spencer stepped on light feet down the steps of the courthouse. As he spoke to another colleague, Albertine unfolded the paper in her palm.

*Fancy a job?*

Smiling, she refolded the paper and tucked it into her bodice. Spencer turned, catching her smile, and responding with a questioning lift to his brow. She winked and tucked her arm through his.

She was willing to take on the biggest job of her life, as the Duchess of Erleigh.

Still . . . she would keep the note with De Vere's details.

One never knew when one might, in fact, fancy a job.

# ACKNOWLEDGMENTS

Sara J. Henry—the gods smiled upon me when they put my manuscript into your hands.

A simple thank you in English doesn't begin to cover it, so: *muchas gracias, merci mille fois, molte grazie, danke sehr, bedankt, muito obrigada, mange tak.* You're the best.

Tamra Baumann and Louise Bergin—thank you for your brainstorming and early words of encouragement for this manuscript. Your belief in me really gave me the oomph needed to get this story started.

The historical superstars—Nancy Cunningham, Sarah Fiddelears, Clare Griffin. The best teammates a girl could want.

Malerie Walker for the daily LOLs and memes—couldn't do life without ya!

Lisa Ireland, without you this book simply would not exist. Period. Thank you.

Everyone who has cheered me on from the sidelines: writers, readers, booksellers, book bloggers, none-of-the-above who picked up my books and encouraged me along the way, especially my number one fan who tells me every word I've ever written is the best he's ever read.

Thank you.